'Cracking thriller and a great female protagonist'
C.J. Tudor

'Dark, gripping, unexpected. Insanely good – like,
Dark Places good'
Elle Croft

'A humdinger of a thriller debut . . . a maze of lies,
deceit and danger'
Evening Standard

'Brilliantly plotted, tense and atmospheric. You will
doubt and suspect everyone'
Rachael Blok

'Grips you from the first line through to the nail-biting
conclusion. Psychological suspense at its best'
Victoria Selman

'An absolutely gripping thriller founded on the horror
of familiar abuse and a great, flawed, female PI'
Dame Jenni Murray

'Mackay builds tension to a fever pitch and throws in
more twists than a corkscrew'
Publishers Weekly

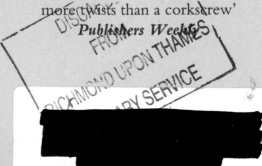

Niki Mackay studied Performing Arts at the BRIT School, and it turned out that she wasn't very good at acting but quite liked writing scripts. She holds a BA (Hons) in English Literature and Drama and won a full scholarship for her MA in Journalism. She has two published novels, *I Witness* and *The Lies We Tell* – both featuring PI Madison Attallee – and two standalone thrillers, *Found Her* and *The Girls Inside*, written under NJ Mackay. She is also the co-host of the podcast #CrimeGirlGang

NIKI MACKAY

LOADED

ORION

First published in Great Britain in 2021 by Orion Fiction,
an imprint of The Orion Publishing Group Ltd.,
Carmelite House, 50 Victoria Embankment
London EC4Y 0DZ

An Hachette UK Company

1 3 5 7 9 10 8 6 4 2

A CIP catalogue record for this book
is available from the British Library.

ISBN (Paperback) 978 1 4091 9526 9

Typeset by Input Data Services Ltd, Somerset

Printed and bound in Great Britain by Clays Ltd, Elcograf S.p.A.

www.orionbooks.co.uk

In memoriam – Elizabeth Figg, Gwynneth Rees,
Hannah Tailford, Irene Lockwood,
Helene Barthelemy, Mary Fleming, Frances Brown,
Bridget 'Bridie' O'Hara.

Acknowledgements

And a Note on the 'Hammersmith Nude Murders'

As well as writing novels I am also one third of a true crime podcast team – Crime Girl Gang. We take various unsolved cases, discuss them and solve them as we would if we were writing a novel: 'fictional solves' if you will. We've covered some fascinating cases, and if you are interested in true crime as we are, do check it out: crimegirlgang.com. My co-hosts (Elle Croft & Victoria Selman) are also crime writers and we have been lucky enough to have some brilliant guests, too.

One of the most interesting cases we covered was the 'Hammersmith Nude Murders'. Eight women were killed in London between 1959 and 1965. At least six of the murders were linked, though some argue they all were (in my fictional re-telling I have included all eight). No one was ever caught. Stranger still, to me, was the fact that I, a true crime junkie, had never heard of this case.

After we finished the podcast episodes, I delved deeper into it. There are several books about the case. I found Robin Jarossi's *The Hunt for the 60s Ripper*, David Seabrook's *Jack of Jumps*, and John Du Rose's *Murder was My Business* particularly useful. There are also a couple of documentaries. However, the case is still little known, and still unsolved, yet the 'Hammersmith Nude Murderer' or 'Jack the Stripper' – as the killer was dubbed by the press – killed more women, more recently, than 'Jack the Ripper'.

As I started reading about the case lots of things struck me, not least the difficult lives the victims had lived. It was a hard time for women who had children out of wedlock, a hard time if you were poor, and an undeniably dangerous and fragile life for prostitutes working London's streets.

The victims all left behind children, partners and friends, they had lives they were cruelly taken from them well before their time, and in the worst way imaginable. Irene Lockwood had a tattoo which led to her identification. 'In memory John', a detail that stuck out for me. She loved someone enough to have their name permanently marked on her body. She missed him. People would miss her.

All of the women were petite in stature and all had been sex workers. They all had children or unplanned pregnancies. More than one victim had been pregnant at the time of her death. They all had sexually transmitted diseases and they were all murdered brutally by someone who has never paid for the crimes.

This book, *Loaded*, is a fictional retelling. It is inspired by these events and by these women's lives, but it is not factual. I am a novelist, not a detective. I hope that I have captured some of the social and economic circumstances of the time. My main character Faith is much luckier than the women who ended up dead at the hands of a killer. I like to think she is indicative of the positive changes brought about for women as the twentieth century progressed, not least the advent of birth control.

My detective, Jimmy Rose, gives a nod to the real detective who doggedly worked the case – John Du Rose – but the name is where the similarities begin and end.

I'd like to thank my Crime Girl Gang co-hosts, Elle Croft and Victoria Selman, for working through this case with me and for their unwavering support and friendship. Thanks to my agent Hattie Grünewald and the team at The Blair Partnership who take care of me so well. Thank you to Lucy Frederick, my editor, and the whole team at Orion Crime.

Thank you to Colin Free (thefreeview.co.uk) for his recommendations of films from the 60s to set the scene, and to Shan Newman for lending me books about Biba and talking to me about London and fashions in the 1960s.

I found this book incredibly difficult to write, more so than any of my other novels, and mere weeks before I was due to deliver the manuscript, it was in poor shape. Thank you to my husband Andrew who witnessed my meltdown, read through, confirmed it was 'a bit of a mess' (less politely), and spent days reading it and helping me to knock it into better shape. If ever there was a team effort, this book was it.

Thank you to 'Criminal Minds' whose endless writing, llama and badger related chatter sees me through all the ups-and-downs of this strange writing life – jellyfish to you all. Thanks to all my friends who offer me such great support and to my sons Elliot and Eddie who keep me right-sized.

Part One

'Women have served all these centuries as looking glasses possessing the magic and delicious power of reflecting the figure of man at twice its natural size.'

– Virginia Woolf, *A Room of One's Own* (1929)

'It is vain to expect virtue from women till they are in some degree independent of men.'

– Mary Wollstonecraft, *A Vindication of the Rights of Woman* (1792)

Prologue

June 1959

Dukes Meadows, Chiswick

Now he's wishing that he hadn't offered her a lift at all. She's barely paused for air since she got into the car. It saves him from saying much, but he does think women should keep their peace. He thinks about another woman he knows who does this. Non-stop chit-chat.

That's who she'd reminded him of in the first place, the woman in the car. Probably why he'd taken pity on her. No, not pity, he'd offered help. Though driving her here is hardly helping exactly, it is what she wants. She's that type. He pulls up into a small enclosure. It's still warm, even though it must be close to midnight, and he has the windows down. He parks, killing the headlights, and an interior light comes on, revealing her staring intently at him, scarlet red lips pulled back in a too-bright smile.

He knows that smile. He's been around one variation or another of it his entire life. It's a smile that looks on the outside like it says, 'welcome' or 'come here', but actually it's a sales technique. Like a window-front full of jarred sweets to a five-year-old, that smile lures you in. It makes the brain scramble and forget the limitations of the wallet.

It is a smile that causes momentary lapses. Ones that cost an awful lot. Some that cost more than others, certainly more than money.

She leans over and her hand is on his thigh. He feels his breath start to quicken and looks away. The light in the car – set on a timer – dims. She is so close now that he can feel her breath on his cheek. He can't pull away because there's nowhere to go. She is tiny and lithe and expertly touches him. Stroking, sighing, whispering as she goes. Words he stops hearing as a roaring, faint but growing, starts up inside his head. She takes his hands, places them inside her opened top. Bare flesh on bare flesh. He grabs at the material, forcing it fully open, and she pulls back, a chuckle of sorts but annoyed, he thinks.

'Here, you've torn me dress.' And that gives him pause, just for a moment, until she adds, 'You'd better pay to replace it. We'll square up after.'

Square up.

After.

Her handbag is at her feet and his eyes fall onto it. It's bright white, showing even in the dim night-time glow of the moon. Not an understated bag. Nothing about her is understated, except for her diminutive size. She's kneeling up on the seat and bending forward, spilling out of her now-wide-open dress.

Even raised on her knees, her head is only a little above his. There is a thump as a stiletto falls from her foot onto the floor.

She's back to the little whisperings now, sweet nothings, his hands are on her once more and she is making mewling noises. Purring like a little kitten. For a second, he can almost believe it but then . . .

Square up.

4

After.

After the transaction. After she does business with him.

He'd driven her here. Offered her a lift. To save her walking. He hadn't asked for anything in return. She had offered what he considered to be a thank you — as he'd expected she might. Yet here she was still peddling him for money. No like for like. No gratitude.

No shame.

He smacks her then and she screams. Loudly.

He puts his hands out, pressing them against her mouth. Pressing with all his might to shut her up. And she keeps going for a yell, keeps wriggling, struggling, but he gets the better of her. Makes her shut up. Makes her stop moving. Makes her his for nothing.

No squaring up.

No after.

When he is done, he sits back. She's not moving. He lets go of her and she flops to the side. Both shoes are at her feet now, next to the too-bright bag and her knickers. She looks even smaller. Diminished, he thinks. She is diminished. She looks so young, her eyes wide open, unblinking, looking into his.

He feels unreal. Like he is in his body but not. His brain jumps into action and he ignores his racing heart, his sweaty palms, a scream swelling up inside of him, wrestling to get out. He presses his lips shut, forces himself to tidy his clothes, to straighten up. He steps out quietly, walks to the passenger side, opens the door and lifts her up.

He carries her as one might a sleeping child, head lolling over one arm, the other cupping her legs where the knees bend. Her feet brush lightly against his thigh as he goes.

He walks as far as the river and he is glad it's quiet tonight. Not always the way. Not even often the way. Though no one here at this time would be looking at what others were up to. He lays her down – as hidden as he can manage, which isn't that hidden at all, but it will do. It will have to do.

The whole time he is careful. Careful not to look at her face, careful not to think too much, careful to do what he must, and then go.

He resists the urge to run back to the car, walking slowly, making as little noise as possible. When he gets in, turns on his lights and starts the engine, the bag in the passenger-seat footwell almost seems to glow.

He turns the key in the ignition and places shaking hands on the steering wheel. He focuses on the road, just the road ahead, and he makes his way home.

He knows that after this night nothing will ever be the same again.

Chapter One

April 1947

Sunningdale Avenue, Acton

In the daytime, his voice was booming and loud. That was how he had gained the nickname 'Bass'. But in the middle of the night, squeezing himself into the little girl's bed, his usually gravelly roar was a quiet whisper. And yet it was no less frightening to her. She was frozen, her heart hammering, aware of the thin cotton of her nightdress and the lack of protection it provided against his big hands. Hands which had reached out and walloped her more than once, leaving livid red marks and sometimes bruises too.

But that night his hands felt almost gentle, sliding up her skinny legs. She felt each bump of his calloused palms moving slowly across her thighs. Her stomach lurched. She wondered if she might be sick. Then, if she should run. But she was too frightened to move. Too frozen in that awful moment. Holding her breath, and trying to hold her mind, which span with hundreds of thoughts. Not least memories of the terrible sounds she often heard coming from her mother, Shirley's, bedroom when Bass was in there. They had been drunk that evening. Drunk when the little girl had had enough and taken herself off to bed. She could smell it then too, on his rancid breath, coming in thick, hot waves across her small face.

She made a sound like a whimper. His hand reached further up and up her leg. His thick, massive body pressed to hers. She could feel his skin against her skin. She thought *terrible things are going to happen* and then her voice found itself. A scream escaped from her body, and she was moving, or at least trying, pinned as she was between him and the wall, her body flailing like a fish out of water gasping for air.

His hand, no longer soft, clamped across her mouth. He threw himself over her, sending all of the air out of her body in a quick and painful *whoompf*. She couldn't move, couldn't breathe, could not make a sound. She shut her eyes, her body tense and expectant.

Then suddenly there was air – space – and she gulped in large lungfuls of it. Freeing herself from the cover entwined around her legs like an awful restraint.

She had shouted again then. Hollered. Bass was next to her bed, Rae standing behind him.

Her brother, half the man's size, had somehow pulled him off. She was saying his name, reaching out her arms for him, but he had one hand on Bass's wide forehead, and she watched as the other swiped swiftly across his throat. It wasn't until she saw dark liquid pouring from his neck, felt the slump of the man as her brother released him and walked calmly from the room that Faith realised Rae had been holding the large carving knife from their kitchen. The one that Shirley used to cut meat on good

8

days when she felt like cooking and they all laughed and ate together.

She was soaking wet. Blood leaking onto her sheets, the covers. Bass's head flopped forward and terrible sounds came from him. She thought, *now he is the fish gasping for air.*

She'd felt a wave of nausea, wriggled to the end of the bed and slid her little body out, wiping her hands along her nightdress as she went. The room was never dark, always illuminated by the street lamps outside, but it was an eerie glow. The wet stains looked black, and so did Bass's eyes – turned on her now as he gurgled and muttered a word which may have been *please* but came out phlegm-ridden and rank. She looked away from him, standing on shaky legs, taking a deep breath and willing her mind to calm down.

Her other brother, Frankie, stood in the doorway, looking from her to Bass. She said, 'Go tell Mrs Malone to get someone.'

Frankie stared at her, eyes wide and glassy. He was two years her senior, but he tended to panic. She said it again, amazed at how calm and reasonable she sounded. She reached out and put her hand on his arm, which finally did the trick and he raced off, banging noisily down the stairs.

She followed the dark trail of footsteps to their mother's room. Shirley was comatose, not an unusual event. She often got into stupors so thick and deep that nothing could wake her.

Even then, with Rae bent forwards, his hands pressed

across her throat, she didn't stir. A gurgling sound came from Shirley's mouth, but her eyes stayed firmly shut.

She flipped the light on, and Rae turned to face her, letting go of Shirley, who sagged like a rag doll. His eyes were blank, a look she'd seen on him more than once; one that would scare her on anyone else. She had never thought of that look as being *him*. Her big brother who was funny and loving and would do anything for her.

She looked at him then and thought about what he'd been doing to their mother. What had happened and what might have happened next if she hadn't turned the light on.

The little girl — Faith Diamond — said softly, 'Rae.' And the boy burst into tears, stepping away from his mother's bed and going to his little sister, who held out her arms.

And that was where Cal Doyle found the pair of them when he came to take Rae Diamond to the police station in the dead of night.

Thanks to Mrs Malone's big mouth, half the street was standing outside, watching the spectacle of a fourteen-year-old boy being taken away in handcuffs, covered head to toe in blood. Next came Bass, carted off in an ambulance, alive but barely.

Shirley Diamond and her little brood had always been a good source of gossip for the residents of Sunningdale Avenue. This would be a story retold for many years to come.

Chapter Two

June 1959 – 12 years later

Sunningdale Avenue

The first time I saw Jimmy Rose was on a cold afternoon in 1959. I was twenty-three years old and one of my jobs was to answer the door when the bell went, which was far too often back then.

When Rae got out of Borstal, harder, rougher and with a cold core that would never thaw, he was taken on by Marshall Vella. Marshall ran a shitty club and a once-thriving vice ring that had dwindled under his management. But it still pulled in cash and that made him lord and master around Acton. Marshall was impressed, as it turned out, with Rae's propensity for violence at such a young age. He offered Rae a job when he was just sixteen.

I hated Marshall with a simmering intensity that I kept to myself. He used our little house on Sunningdale Avenue as his London residence.

It was his fault that the door was always going. His fault that Rae had grown up to be a fucking lunatic, and his fault that my mum and Frankie were permanently miserable. As far as I was concerned, Marshall Vella was the root cause of all our problems. The only saving grace was that because of him, my brothers earned, and earned well.

That day, I opened the door to Cal Doyle – the man who'd arrested Rae – and behind him, a young one I'd not seen before, good-looking with bright blue eyes and a firm jaw.

Jimmy Rose.

I avoided looking at him and told Cal to bugger off.

'No one's in trouble, Faith.'

I stood my ground, arms folded under my chest. Letting police over the threshold wouldn't go down well. Even though Marshall and my brothers weren't in, they'd find out somehow. Marshall knew everything. His little snitches were posted here, there and everywhere, reporting back.

Cal said, 'Faith, is your mum in?'

And that was when my heart had started to beat a little faster.

No news was good news when you had the boys in blue on your doorstep, but there were plenty of things worse than being in trouble.

I said, 'My brothers?' Every worst-case scenario ran through my mind at once.

Violence was the shadow we'd all come up under. That and the horror of sex bought and sold. As I'd grown older, grown up from a childhood I'd never really had, I appreciated what my mother had done, what she'd needed to do to survive. She wasn't perfect, but she kept a roof over our heads and, for the most part, kept me and my brothers together, too. Which is more than a lot of other women in Shirley's position had managed. But violence made me fearful and safety was always an issue.

Cal shook his head and I sighed with relief. My almost constant fear was that one of them would get seriously hurt or, worse, turn up dead. It was clear he wasn't going to tell me anything else, so I took them in to Shirley, who was sitting at the kitchen table, hands round a cup of tea, fag dangling from her lips.

She gave Cal a faint smile, his face softening when he saw my mother. I was reminded of the effect beautiful women had on the opposite sex. I knew it because I experienced it, but that beauty had never done my mum any good; I wouldn't be relying on it to do me any favours either.

She said to Cal, 'Marshall will go mad if he knows you're here.'

'He says no one's in trouble and the boys are fine,' I told her.

She frowned, 'What is it then?'

I shrugged. I was head and shoulders above her by then and often with Shirley I felt more like the adult. I said, 'I'll put the kettle on.'

Everyone sat around our kitchen table. I made tea, putting steaming mugs in front of our two unwelcome visitors, and sat next to my mum, listening as Cal told her that they'd found Liza Plum, dead on the banks of the river.

Shirley's face went white and I knew the news must have hurt. Liza was one of Marshall's girls and Shirley had a way with them all, she was well liked and respected. A lot of them came to her when they had something that might need smoothing over with Marshall, and Shirley always did her best.

I asked, 'How?'

Cal said he couldn't give details, but they suspected foul play.

Murder.

A dead Tom was par for the course and, honestly, I didn't give that girl much thought then, beyond that my mother was upset but would certainly get over it.

Little did I know that Liza's death would be the first of many and that those killings would mar me forever, and change everything.

Chapter Three

January 1961

Sunningdale Avenue

I was woken by a loud bang – the front door slamming – and raucous laughter. My bedside clock told me it was 3 a.m. I thought about feigning sleep, but there was no point. Eventually Rae would come up and find me. He had a place of his own by then and yet still always seemed to be here, treating Sunningdale Avenue as his own, just like Marshall.

The problem with my brother was that when he was around, everyone had to know about it. Ever since Marshall's son had left London at the start of 1960, he'd started treating Rae like he was his own, and the two of them had become inseparable. Frankie tagged along, hidden in Rae's shadow, like he'd always been, and as much as I felt sorry for myself and Shirley, who had to put up with Marshall and Rae's antics, I really sympathised with Frankie. He'd been a soft kid and he just wasn't cut out for the life he found himself leading. Unfortunately for Frankie, Rae saw him simply as an extension of himself. A little mini-me to cart around. He certainly never once thought to ask his little brother what he wanted to be doing with his life.

At least me and my mum weren't involved in the awful benders, though we never knew whether we'd have peace and quiet or bedlam from one night to the next. Things were pretty shit for our neighbours too, and as much as I disliked Mrs Malone in particular, her life was almost as disrupted by Rae and Frankie's comings and goings as ours were. Not that anyone would have dared complain about anything that Marshall Vella was involved with.

Rae yelled, 'Faith, you in?'

I sighed, sliding out of bed, pulling yesterday's dress over my head and beginning to descend the stairs.

'Where else would I be in the middle of the night, eh?'

Rae was grinning and swaying. Frankie was in an awkward-looking heap at the bottom of our rickety staircase. He never could hold his booze. He was always trying to keep up, not lose face and impress his big brother. Or maybe it just made the day-to-day bearable.

Rae gave him a jab with his shoe, 'Help me get him onto the settee.' The words came out in one long slur.

We lugged Frankie between us. His fair hair, just like Mum's, felt unbelievably soft on my hands. Rae dropped his feet unceremoniously, but I took a minute to try to arrange him comfortably. He was snoring gently by the time I left the room.

In the kitchen, Marshall was ferreting through the top cupboards, looking for the bottle he kept up there. I put the kettle on, staying out of his way, and filled a mug with coffee granules for Rae.

They'd been away from Sunningdale Avenue all week – a blessed but fleeting reprieve. All good things came to an end, of course, and that night was a stark reminder not to get too comfortable.

Marshall had a place in London that was his own. He had a house in the country that he shared with his wife. Rae had his own flat . . . but they always turned up like bad, unwanted pennies.

When I had been a little girl, I used to allow my head to slip into fantasy mode. I'd see other kids my age and wonder at their lives, where they might end up. I had even let myself consider a career when I was still at school and teachers filled my head with ideas – 'a smart girl like you could go far'. But far for Diamonds wasn't the same as for anyone else. My family would always need me. Rae would always find things for me to do. Admin, filing, making phone calls. The books for Vella's. I'd stopped thinking of the sort of life I might have wanted because it didn't matter. Just like it didn't matter that Frankie was a soft soul living a hardman's existence. This was the hand we'd been dealt.

I watched Marshall grip the bottle and thump Rae in a fatherly way on the shoulder as he left the kitchen. Then I heard him pulling his considerable girth up the stairs.

Chapter Four

Sunningdale Avenue

Shirley heard the door go and resisted the urge to scream in frustration, tear her own skin off and jump out the bloody window. Instead, by the time Marshall got up the stairs, she'd changed from her flannel nightie into red undies, brushed her teeth and slicked on some lipstick. She felt like sobbing for a hundred years, but she was smiling by the time the door swung open and he staggered towards her.

He didn't say anything. This was something she'd noticed a lot over the years about many of the men who'd passed through her bed. There were two types: the ones you couldn't shut up and the ones who deemed you barely worthy of a nod of acknowledgement.

Marshall had been coming round and using her body for over a decade. Shirley had thought she'd struck gold. One punter instead of many had to be better, right? But, actually, there was freedom when she could choose, freedom when money earned had been, at least in part, on her terms. Marshall was Rae Senior in a different body.

Rae Senior had been a pig too. A vicious man who'd put her on the game and then left her high and dry with three mouths to feed. Shirley could acknowledge her faults and missteps along the way, but the day she'd got rid of Rae Senior and been given her little council house on Sunningdale Avenue she had vowed that she'd never miss a rent payment, no matter what it took. And she never had.

Which wasn't to say she hadn't messed up. She seemed to lurch from one disaster to another most of the time. When the kids were little, she drank too much, too often. It was her way of coping, but it had cost her dearly. Ended up with her eldest in Borstal. A short sharp shock that made her take stock, sobered her up.

She thought about all of this while Marshall was at her — he was never gentle or soft — but she made the appropriate noises, moving herself where she knew he wanted, putting on the act that was expected of her. There was pain of course, always pain with him, but Shirley had learned years ago to distance her body from her mind and by the time he was done, huffing, puffing and seconds away from passing out, she told herself it wasn't too bad. Could definitely have been worse.

Once he was snoring, she went to the bathroom and washed quickly. She could hear Rae downstairs and knew her daughter would be trying to get a coffee into him. Trying to make him wear himself out and go to bed. Shirley went into her daughter's bedroom, tucked herself up under the covers and lit a cigarette.

Things started to quieten down and Faith came in with a sigh. Shirley passed her the fags and Faith lit one, slipping her dress off and crawling into bed next to her mum. She had inches on Shirley and took up more than half the bed. Shirley loved the bones of Faith and, more than anything, admired her daughter. There was something about her, a steely resilience that brooked no stupidity.

'Had kind of hoped we'd seen the back of them,' Shirley said.

Faith sighed, 'This is Rae's home.'

And Shirley didn't respond, didn't point out he had his own place, or mention any of the other issues he brought through their door. She'd never had an easy relationship with her eldest son. Not when he'd exploded into her life, almost ripping her tiny body in two. Not when he screamed his head off night after night or refused to sit still for more than a second through his toddler years. She loved him like she loved all of her children – that was Shirley's most redeeming feature, though her love was often haphazard and unreliable – but Rae had always given her shit.

She often thought that boy had got the worst of her and the worst of his father, all packaged up in a handsome and charming exterior.

Nonetheless, Faith adored him. Wouldn't hear a bad word spoken about him, and considering what he'd saved her from, Shirley could see why.

Faith put her cigarette out and turned off the light.

Shirley asked, 'Frankie in?'

Faith mumbled, 'He's on the settee,' and eventually Shirley drifted into a fitful sleep, warm next to her baby girl, ignoring the aches from Marshall's latest visit.

Chapter Five

West London

She smiles her silly smile and he responds in kind. The laughter silken and almost convincing. She is high, he suspects. Her pupils are wide and dilated. The piercing blue of her eyes all but submerged behind them. She is speaking fast and he lets her go on, nodding in the appropriate places at the right time, but not listening to the words. Not really. His head is humming with its own kind of sound. A roaring in his ears as blood pumps rapidly around his body. Marching in time to his pulse. His heart. The race of excitement.

They reach her place and it is nothing but a tiny room, a hovel really. He can see that she's made an effort, though no amount of scrubbing could make this place homely or even habitable. He admits to himself that the sordid surroundings don't detract from his plans. Somehow, they only add to the experience.

He takes the notes from his pocket, adding two extra, and sees her eyes widen at that, pleased.

The effort she puts in lets him know she's looking for a repeat. Silly mare probably has pound signs ringing through her tiny brain. But he won't be back. He shouldn't even be here now. Wishes he didn't want to be here. Wishes he didn't think about it.

He fills her mouth and realises she is making an uncomfortable sound. He should stop. He should definitely stop, and he does. Eventually. Just in time.

She laughs then, a nervous sound, but she's still trying. Still going. Still seeing those pound signs.

Towards the end, he slips his hand around her throat, applying the gentlest of pressure. His other hand follows and there is that sound again, and her arms are moving wildly, hands gripping at arms bigger than hers. Stronger. She is grasping, pulling them down. Which almost makes him laugh. But he doesn't. He pulls back. He stops. Just in time, again.

He thinks back to a time when he hadn't. In equal measures made happy and revolted by the memory. Of himself. By what he has done. By what he knows he might do again. But not tonight.

She's no longer all smiles as she moves away from him, forcing only a grimace. A curving up of her wide painted lips, that doesn't reach her stupid, saucer-like eyes. She looks frightened . . . and something else. Wounded. He's a good mind to take a fist to her face. Wipe that silly expression away. He feels his hands clench in preparation. He doesn't though, because he has choices, and he has self-control.

He pulls on his clothes, reaches back into his pocket and pulls out a few more notes. Leaving them on the bed. Not meeting her eye and stepping back out into the dank and mouldy hallway, down a rickety flight of stairs out onto the tattered streets. Full of a pent-up, simmering rage.

Chapter Six

February 1961

Heron Trading Estate

Jimmy loved London as much as it frustrated him. It took him a while to get used to it when he'd arrived young at twenty-three, angry and desperately alone. He'd only known the English countryside and initially he thought the city might prove too much, might overwhelm him, though he was determined to succeed there nonetheless. To follow in his father's footsteps, as though to make up for his absence. James Rose had been a policeman, a good one, and had died a war hero. These had been his streets, West London his patch. Jimmy worried he might not be able to handle it, might not live up to the man he barely remembered, but who felt like a legend of gargantuan proportions.

He'd been surprised to find himself quite at home here and spent a lot of time in his early days just exploring, imagining his dad doing the same as a young man, thinking all the time, *I must tell Mum that* and then remembering he couldn't do that now.

In his head, he kept track of all the things he'd have told her, a sort of internal conversation that brought him comfort. His impressions of the city. Each postcode with its own people, language and ways. He'd discovered all the little pockets like separate towns or villages nestled within their own bits: North, South, East and West. He'd become a part of it; he understood its people and their problems, which were legion. He thought that some days the air in London just pulsed with tension. He walked the same route, day and night.

Cal Doyle had taken him under his wing, shown him the ropes. He'd once worked with James, and his interest in Jimmy had begun as a favour to the former colleague he respected and missed and had grown into something better and deeper as he got to know the lad, quiet but sharp and astute with it.

Jimmy's route took him past boarded-up shops, burned-out cars. The city was still pitted with the scars of the war that had ravaged its streets only twenty years before. The men who'd fought to protect both the place and its inhabitants wandered stricken, unwashed, unfed. The lost men who couldn't even claim a cramped home of their own, or perhaps, Jimmy thought, didn't want to. They littered the doorways, the parks and the streets. Heroes, now beggars. A national disgrace no one was entirely sure how to fix.

So many things that need fixing. So many things wrong. If Jimmy thought about it too long, it became more than he could manage. After his mother, Lilly, had died, life itself had become more than he could manage . . . He'd been engaged, then. To Cynthia. A perfectly nice girl, whom his mother had never taken a shine to, never deemed good enough for her son. Jimmy hadn't thought about it a great deal until after his mother passed and he'd realised Cynthia wasn't what he was looking for. Wasn't what he wanted.

His mother was a kind but fierce woman. Cynthia was soft and spoiled and, whilst he was grieving, hadn't known what to do, had crumbled under Jimmy's grief, expecting him to look after her even then. He didn't want that. If ever he married, he wanted it to be to an equal and he finally understood what his mother had been saying — not unkindly — all along. She often told him over the years about her and big James Rose, the love of her life. Her face changed when she talked about his dad and when once Jimmy asked if she wished she'd married someone else — considering how it all went down — she'd been firm in her response. Unshakable. 'No, Jimmy. Love like that is worth having, even if it's only for a few years, or months even. Hold out for that, Jim. The happiness I found with James will last me a lifetime.'

Jimmy had rolled his eyes, but after she'd gone and Cynthia's shrill voice irritated him with her endless requests and trivial thoughts, he understood what she meant.

He'd broken the engagement off, sold his mother's little house and put himself into police college here. Even though he didn't have Cynthia, he'd instead fallen in love with London, and despite its problems, he'd made it home.

He took things day by day or, more often, night by

night. The crimes, the disputes, the petty grievances were dealt with one at a time. He did his best to leave the bigger picture to the politicians, but he couldn't help thinking. Couldn't help seeing. He liked to believe that he was part of the solution, part of the hopeful whispers they were all starting to feel now. The sixties had put the scent of change in the air and brought out all sorts of possibilities, and he wanted to be part of that.

But sometimes it got to him, and that night he was tired. Weary even. His mind full of longing for his mother, his little village where he'd played catch during the war, safely cocooned, attended the tiny school, played with the same set of children. Planned to marry Cynthia ever since he'd been old enough to know what girls were.

That night, he walked next to Cal Doyle, a plain-clothes detective and Jimmy Rose's boss. They broke up a few fights. Moved on girls not even attempting discretion and who sighed and eye-rolled at the intrusion. They looked as shattered as Jimmy felt and they had an even longer night ahead than he did.

When he saw a man walking quickly up ahead, something quivered in his brain. The man looked out of place. It wasn't just his fast pace, though Jimmy didn't like that much, either. The man's clothes made an attempt at flash, but they were mismatched and too much. Real wealth knew that the point was to look effortless and this man was almost a parody of 'monied'. His clothes were too big for his slight frame, most likely stolen in haste. Jimmy couldn't say what it was exactly, but he had the feeling something was amiss, looking at the skinny man in the too-big overcoat and the ostentatious top hat.

Cal followed his gaze. 'Something you don't like, lad?'

Jimmy shrugged, nervous of getting it wrong. 'It might be nothing.'

Cal said, 'Or it might not. Trust your gut, son, it'll be the best weapon you have in the war against the scroats.'

They increased their pace as they headed towards the man. Neither Jimmy nor Cal were in uniform, but a villain always knows a copper with the same sort of instincts they know him. He made a U-turn.

Cal grinned at Jimmy, 'Looks like we've finally got something to do, eh, son?'

He told his young charge to circle back as he headed towards the now-retreating figure.

Jimmy did, his senses alive, his blood pumping. He was young, fit, and now he was full of adrenaline. The tiredness creeping up on him less than five minutes ago had dissipated. He was on the chase. He took small back streets and alleys before he headed out onto the main road, where he saw the man running past. So close he could hear his ragged breath. He couldn't see Cal, but it didn't matter. He let the man move ahead, keeping himself hidden. The game of cat and mouse becoming more fun for Jimmy by the second. This was why he was here. Why he didn't really miss home. This was what he was supposed to be doing, just as his dad had done before him.

Sure enough, the man began to slow down. He was checking over his shoulder as he went and Jimmy stayed far behind him for a while. Taking it slowly, staying out of sight. Biding his time. He followed the man onto the Heron Trading Estate and, at some point, Cal caught up with Jimmy, out of breath and red-faced, no longer young and fit.

Jimmy put a finger to his lips and signalled that he was in pursuit. Cal nodded and hung back. Once the man stepped out onto the estate, he sped up and Jimmy, just seconds behind him, saw him opening a lock-up and called out just as the man stepped inside, 'Stop. Police.'

The man froze, a deer caught in headlights. Slowly he turned around, blinking under the beam of Jimmy's torch. And then he ran.

Cal was seconds behind Jimmy and the two men took chase, both aware of the open lock-up and the need to be quick, to find out what was in there. Luckily, the chase didn't last long after the skinny man caught his foot on a stone and tumbled forward, sprawled on the hard pavement.

They cuffed him and walked him back to the lock-up, where Cal let out a low whistle when they finally saw what was inside.

Chapter Seven

Vella's, Acton

I stood in the toilet of Vella's nightclub, reapplying an errant fake eyelash. The ladies' stank of body odour, urine and vomit. The place was an absolute dive and there were many places I'd rather have been on a Saturday. But I'd gone to support Shirley, who Marshall had dragged out in 'something nice', meaning a too-short, too-tight mini-dress.

I went back out into the main bar and saw my mum sitting on a bar stool so tall her feet didn't touch the floor. Marshall was next to her, his meaty paw resting possessively on her shoulder, sausage-like fingers just above her left breast. The image made me shudder and Shirley looked equally unimpressed.

Marshall somehow believed that these night outs were some kind of treat for Shirley. They weren't. They were an enforced chore and Shirley dreaded them. Times were better for Mum when Marshall got himself a new bird – which he did, frequently – or went home to his wife, which, on the other hand, became less and less often. But he always came back to Mum. More out of convenience than any fondness, I thought, though Rae said Marshall 'adored' Mum. He'd often say she was lucky . . . I'd grown sick of trying to explain to him how that would never be true.

Rae talked all the time about how Marshall 'kept Shirley out of trouble'. I had no words to explain that, actually; once Rae went to Borstal, Shirley had got her shit together by herself. I knew she'd still taken punters because the rent was paid and there was food in the cupboards. But she hadn't brought anyone home and she hadn't got drunk. It had been the happiest two years of my life, but whenever the thought crossed my mind that my happiness coincided with Rae being gone, I pushed it furiously away.

Rae had saved me. From something awful, I had no doubt. He wasn't a saint, but I couldn't think of him as a bad person. He loved me, I knew that. And I loved him too, even if he always brought chaos in his wake.

I breathed in the scents of the club. Beer, cigarette smoke, stale sweat. Vella's had been a working man's club once upon a time. Now it was frequented by plastic wannabee gangsters, though the men in there would argue their own importance till they were blue in the face — and prostitutes . . . It was essentially a brothel, housing the last remnants of the Vella girls.

Marshall and his brothers, Wesley and Arthur, arrived in London from Malta in the 1930s and set up the most lucrative prostitution ring London had ever seen. Arthur and Wesley were subsequently convicted on charges of procuring women and illegal possession of firearms.

Both fled the UK, with Arthur never to be seen again and Wesley, who made the mistake of returning, convicted for entering England illegally and deported upon his release from prison.

That left Marshall, who Scotland Yard never managed to pin anything on, and who, it turned out, lacked the Midas touch of his older siblings. What had once been a thriving vice empire was now a dwindling collection of a few sad brothels which Marshall ran cruelly and inefficiently.

Cruel and inefficient were good words to sum Marshall up altogether. Vella's was proof of that. The place was a grotty little joint and often made so little money it was hardly worth keeping it open. The Vella girls were no longer the highest-paid brasses in London. Other people had taken over the West End and Soho and Marshall hadn't batted an eye.

Something that I knew Rae resented. My brother was just itching to make a big name for himself on the scene. He wanted money, yes, but he also wanted power. Marshall's lack of ambition frustrated him.

Still, Marshall made enough. More than most, and the man was a legend in his own lunchtime and wouldn't be told otherwise.

I also had to acknowledge that the little my family had at that time was because of him. I didn't like it, but having Marshall involved in our lives was preferable to starving.

I watched my brothers that night. Rae swanning about the place like he owned it, with a kind word for those that mattered. Winks for the girls who looked at him wide-eyed. Frankie a step behind, as light as Rae was dark. Tall men in black suits with thin ties. They looked like film stars.

Rae stopped to talk to a small, blonde girl. Frankie had told me that Rae had taken on a Tom he'd grown sweet on, moved her into his little flat and everything. Roxy McCann. I hoped she could handle herself. When Rae wanted something, he was relentless, and it looked to me like he very much wanted her.

I went over to my mum. Marshall nodded at me – the closest I ever got to acknowledgement from him. He'd started letting me do the books for his club at Rae's suggestion. I was clever. I hadn't hung around in school after sixteen, hadn't seen the point, but numbers made sense to me, words came easy, and I had a quick, logical brain.

I'd done a good job so far, which may have won me brownie points with Marshall if I'd been male. As it was, he had an intense disdain for members of the female sex.

My mum was laughing at some joke he'd made and I smiled faintly, feeling nothing but sympathy for her.

She said, 'Marshall's taking me up west, love, you going to be all right?'

I nodded, 'Course I am, Mum.' I hugged her and watched them walk out of the club. A few heads turned to look at Shirley, still a beauty at forty-two. For all the good it had done her.

I ordered a vodka – a quick drink before heading home.

33

I was about to leave when a large man sat down too close to me. I hadn't seen him before, and he was definitely the worse for wear. He stared at me and said, 'Do I know you?' but the words came as one, long and slippery.

I swallowed a sigh. Reminded myself not to be rude – you never knew who these people were. This man might have been an important associate of my brother's or Marshall's.

I smiled tightly. 'Faith.'

'Lovely name, darlin'.'

I nodded and turned back to the bar, about to say goodbye to Devlin – a man who was always kind and respectful to me and Shirley. I think he'd had his eye on my mum until Marshall had come along.

But the man leaned in, too close, waving a note at Devlin. 'What you drinking?'

'It's all right,' I said, 'I'm leaving, and if I wanted a drink, I'd buy my own.'

He frowned at that. 'Girls that look like you shouldn't have to pay for their drinks though, eh.'

My smile became thinner. 'I said, I've got it.'

Devlin had started looking nervous. He said in a warning tone, 'Bill.'

But Bill glared and snapped, 'I'm talking to this little lady.'

No longer smiling, I said, 'Yeah, well, I don't want to talk to you. Thanks for the offer, but I said I'm fine.'

And then the idiot made a big mistake. He reached over, grabbing with his meaty hands and putting his arms around my waist. I dropped my handbag. Made a lunge for it before it clattered to the floor, but not before Rae and Frankie had clocked what was happening and started making their way over.

Then all hell broke loose.

I tried to wriggle out of the idiot's clutches and Devlin jumped over the bar, dreadlocked hair swinging around his waist. Both of us trying in our own way, I suspect, to mitigate the carnage that was about to take place.

But we were too late. Frankie grabbed me from behind, plonking me down away from the scene. Before I had a chance to tell him in no uncertain terms that I could handle it, there was an almighty crash.

I turned to see Bill, still with a daft, inebriated expression on his face, but now with added blood running down his forehead in thin, jagged lines. He staggered forward to reveal Rae standing behind him, smashed bottle in hand.

I opened my mouth to try to talk some sense into him, but he'd already lifted the man by his armpits, gesturing to Frankie to grab his feet.

The crowd parted as my brothers carried the unfortunate fool out onto the street. I saw Roxy, pale-faced, her hand pressed to her lips, and moved her out of the way, shaking my head once as she took a step towards Rae. Now wasn't the time for her to get in his way.

I followed them outside, taking in the trail of blood leading down the lit staircase to street level. Gingerly, I tried to avoid stepping in it.

It was freezing outside, but I barely felt it as I took in the scene before me. Frankie and Rae doing the poor sod over.

Sighing in familiar aggravation, I waded in, pounding my fists on Frankie's back. When he turned around, I hissed, 'I said I was fucking dealing with it.'

'But he grabbed you,' he said, frowning.

Rae had also stopped by then and was looking at me in confusion. The man at their feet was a bloody, pulpy mess and I was trying to avoid looking at him.

I said to them both, 'Well, he won't do it again, will he? That's enough.'

Rae kept staring. He had that glazed look that I tried not to let give me the creeps. Totally blank. Like a mask. He was there but not really.

Devlin burst out of the door, Roxy following closely behind. She looked at Rae, at the man on the floor, then at me. I shook my head at her again and, wisely, she stayed put.

Devlin looked at me and asked, 'You all right?'

I said, 'These two are well out of order.'

Rae looked at me aghast, then at Devlin and said, 'Well, pardon us for trying to keep our little sister safe, eh.'

Devlin didn't say anything. This sort of shit was a nightly occurrence for him, in one form or another. He was a nice man. It was such a shame Marshall had muscled his way in on Mum, asking Devlin what she could 'possibly want with a coloured anyway?' The last thing I wanted to do was cause him any trouble. Or

Roxy, who was visibly shaking. I assumed her life came with its fair share of horrors too.

I said to Devlin, 'You go in. I'm all right.'

And he waited one beat, met my eyes and left.

People were staring across the street and I suspected someone would have phoned the police by now.

'You should probably get out of here,' I said to Rae.

He shrugged, 'I'm sure no one saw anything.' And his face broke into an arrogant grin.

Frankie had the decency to at least look a little sheepish.

I told them, 'Well, I'm going.'

Rae shrugged, 'All right, sis.' The quivering human wreck at his feet all but forgotten. He put an arm around Frankie's shoulders and grabbed Roxy around the waist, so quickly it made her jump, leading them proprietorially back inside.

I walked across the road and said to one of the onlookers, 'Someone should call an ambulance.'

The man looked at me wide-eyed and the woman next to him said, 'They're savages.'

I bristled a bit at that.

They were my brothers, after all.

Chapter Eight

Acton

The skinny man in the too-big suit, Robert Pincasi, was high as a kite on purple hearts, and drunk to boot. Neither of which was an arrestable offence, but also not a clever move for a pickpocket not wanting to get caught and not really ideal for interrogating him either. Cal and Jimmy decided to wait until the next day to question him. It was Jimmy's day off, but he didn't mind coming in. The lock-up on the Heron Trading Estate housed a wide array of goods, which Jimmy and Cal were pretty certain would all prove to be stolen and indicated more than one person was involved.

The man, Pincasi, had been stealing from various bars, nightclubs and cars all night and had amassed an impressive array of wallets and purses to add to the treasure chest of theft. Luckily for Jimmy, and unluckily for Pincasi, he had yet to empty the cash and do away with the evidence, so they literally had him red-handed. Either that or the suspect was the brains of the century, which so far didn't seem to be the case. It was an easy arrest that would hopefully make for an easy court case.

They'd have him on pickpocketing at the very least. The harder part would be tracing the lock-up and any known associates.

Jimmy was finishing up the paperwork and about to leave when Cal came in, puffing on a cigar and holding one out to Jimmy, who took it and felt a moment of pure satisfaction. He had arrived here broken, on a swell of grief, not sure whether breaking it off with Cynthia had even been the right thing. He had a life planned out there, he'd still have joined the force, but the life of a village policeman was nothing like the life of a metropolitan officer. For the first weeks and months after he'd left, he thought and thought about it. Did he make the right or wrong decision?

But they had grown into each other: Jimmy and the city. He belonged. It became a part of him and he a part of it. He had been swallowed by its charm and beauty, ugliness and dark underbelly. Fascinated endlessly by its contradictions. Whatever else you might feel in London, it was hard to be bored.

Cal said, 'Right, we still have the small hours left where the beer flows and the women are easy. We're going out, my son.'

Jimmy grinned – there was no point disagreeing with Cal on these things, and besides, it had been a good night's work all in all.

Cal said, 'You've earned a beer, lad, and it's on me.'

That sounded even better.

★

They went to The White Hart, one of the few venues around with a late licence, though by no means the only place open. It attracted all sorts, but most of the drinkers were off the clock, whatever their line of work, and looking to relax away from the busy docks and the West End.

Inside it was loud, the jukebox was on; people were dancing, dressed in all their finery. There were prostitutes, men in drag pouring over from Soho after performances, and plenty of small-time gangsters. But there was an unspoken rule that The White Hart was neutral ground. Police drank in there but didn't bother the other punters, as long as they didn't take the piss.

They wormed their way through the eclectic crowd and when Cal handed him a beer, Jimmy lit a cigarette and started to relax. He chatted to people at the bar and a blonde woman slid onto the stool next to him. He bought her a drink. She talked and giggled and sort of danced in her seat. He'd wondered if when he got to London he might fall in love. Find someone more suitable than Cynthia. But what Jimmy had found instead was that women came in all shapes and sizes and not all of them were looking to get married and settle down like the girls at home had been. Jimmy had had a lot of fun, and nothing else. Not that he was complaining. His mother was religious, devoutly so, as was James, and they had assumed Jimmy would find one girl, settle down, have children, and observe a spiritual practice as they had done. But Jimmy didn't believe in a God that had taken his parents away from him so prematurely.

He liked women and female company, and they liked him too. Unlike many of his colleagues, he was not housed in the dorms meant for single police officers. He'd been left a small legacy by his mother and had put it on a flat. Just as well, as a lot of those officers remained in lodgings until they married, and Jimmy couldn't see himself doing that any time soon.

The now-drunk woman who sat next to him wasn't sparking his interest, though. The fatigue of earlier was kicking back in as the adrenaline from the chase and arrest dissipated. He smiled, made his excuses and stood. He figured Cal would be too drunk to care or notice what he was doing and he used the opportunity to step outside, thinking he'd slip off home and say he lost him.

He was just out onto the street, taking in great gulping lungfuls of fresh air, when he saw her.

A tall girl with long dark hair, loose and swishing around her waist. Jimmy thought she had the longest legs he'd ever seen and when she turned around, hitching a shiny handbag up and over her shoulder, he saw her face and recognised at once who she was.

She squinted, then recognition dawned and she grinned, 'Hello, Officer.'

Chapter Nine

Acton

Walking away from Vella's, anger boiled in my blood. The bloke at the bar was an idiot, but he didn't deserve that beating. I could have managed. I was perfectly capable of taking care of myself. The pantomime displays of dominance from my brothers were starting to wear thin.

Baby sister.

The only girl.

But the pair of them could be knuckle-headed idiots. More often than not, I had to do the thinking for them. I wasn't a possession they needed to mind.

As I walked through London, the heat in my blood keeping the cold at bay, I let the anger wash over me. Because of my sex, they thought I was somehow breakable. But when I looked around, it was the women who were tough, with their children and their unruly men and their limited choices. Showing up day after day, even when the odds were stacked against them. The men didn't understand that, they thought only fists and feet spoke volumes. But I had a feeling it wouldn't always be that way. Times were changing and I was not going to be any man's plaything.

I stopped for a moment outside The White Hart, twisting away from the now chilly wind and hitching my bag up over my shoulder. Then I turned to see a familiar-looking man staring at me. Tall, with hair almost as dark as mine and the bluest eyes I thought I'd ever seen. His gaze was intense, but unlike meat-hands at the bar, this man made me feel something different altogether.

The sounds of cars slowly going past and people chatting outside the busy club melted into the background. It was cold and I wasn't dressed for it, but the shivering stopped and my blood seemed to warm up.

Then I realised where I recognised him from.

'Hello, Officer.'

He grinned, 'Detective, now.'

What sweeter revenge on my brothers than a night with one of the boys in blue? A detective, no less.

Smiling, I looped my arm through his and led him off into the night.

Chapter Ten

Rae Diamond's flat, Acton

When Rae decided to start seeing Roxy, she was over the moon, but the more time she spent with him, the more frightened she became.

He was good-looking, powerful and always had money in his pocket. She was one of Marshall's girls so wasn't naive enough to think this might lead to marriage and a white picket fence, but she'd not been prepared for his mood, which could turn without rhyme or reason.

He'd moved her into his place and stopped her working as soon as he could. Marshall always took the majority of what she earned, and her ponce of a mother swooped in for the rest, but Roxy normally managed to salvage a small cut. Now, with no work to go to, she had nothing to show for her days, though Rae still bunged her mum a few quid.

Roxy poured tea for Rae and Frankie, lacing it liberally with whisky. She carried the mugs through, not quite full because her hands were shaking, and last time she'd spilled it, Rae had cuffed her hard around the head. He was busy talking business, and as soon as she handed the brothers their drinks, earning her a warm smile form Frankie and a grunt from Rae, she was dismissed. She curled up on the little armchair in the corner of the living room and looked of the window, trying to remember the last time she'd been allowed outside during daylight.

Frankie smiled at Roxy and she looked at him through wide, fearful eyes. He felt a wave of sympathy for her, but it passed quickly once Rae started speaking and Frankie found he had more important shit to worry about.

Frankie was frightened. A feeling he often got around his older brother and one that was so familiar, he didn't even recognise it as anything different half the time. Being Rae Diamond's little brother meant living in a constant state of anxiety.

Rae was drunk, ridiculously so. He'd just downed the tea Roxy had brought him, which Frankie discovered was laced heavily with whisky.

Rae had moved to the kitchen and grabbed the bottle and he was now swigging directly from it. Even the air felt infused with danger.

Frankie put his tea on the windowsill, leaving it untouched. He understood that a clear head in these situations was vital if one were to survive, which Frankie wasn't supremely confident they all would.

Frankie's brain was desperately trying to make sense of all that had led to this moment. He was fifteen the day Marshall had come knocking at their door. Rae was fresh out of Borstal, Shirley had been trying her best, keeping her work away from home, sorry at what had happened to Rae. Frightened of what could have been, had Rae not stepped in.

Frankie couldn't say it to Rae, but the two years preceding Marshall were the calmest he could remember. Then this man exploded into the Diamonds' lives. Took Rae onto his firm and trained him up like a loaded weapon. Rae enjoyed the work. Frankie knew that from watching him. Frankie just did what needed to be done. Glad there was money coming in that Shirley hadn't had to earn, though her arrangement with Marshall was little better than what she'd had before.

Rae's flat was a nice, smart place, not far from Sunningdale Avenue, and young Roxy kept it sparkling clean. Frankie had been surprised when Rae had made her his girlfriend and moved her in. He loved the Toms, Rae went for them with unparalleled lust, but he had never set one up as his girl before. He had quite strong views on what they did for a living. This one was a real stunner, mind, and placid too, though everyone became placid around Rae eventually.

She was curled up in the armchair in the corner of the living room looking out of the window. Frankie recognised that tactic. Stay small, stay out of the way, stay unnoticed. The thing was, with a man like Rae, that only worked for so long.

Especially for the women he decided upon. If someone took his fancy, Rae made sure he got them, and until he tired of them, they were as good as his. Rae saw whatever he wanted as fair game, including people, never mind the consequences.

Just like he'd done with the bloody racketeering ring he'd been running with Robert Pincasi behind Marshall Vella's back.

Like a fucking madman.

Frankie had told him several times over the past few months that he ought to consider what he was doing. Maybe stop, or at the very least talk it over with Faith – the only person Rae even vaguely listened to. But he hadn't, and Frankie had been debating whether to go to his sister himself.

Well, now it was too late. There'd be hell to pay.

Rae was almost incoherent, pleading with Frankie to see his point, muttering things like, 'My perspective' and 'Marshall keeps everything for his fucking self' in between a long rant about how he, Rae, had to do all the *hard* work – he had to administer the kickings, collect money from pimps . . . He said this with a look of deranged outrage on his face. It could have been comical, except it was not. It was not funny at all.

He slumped next to his brother at that point, his face mournful, and said, 'You understand, Frankie, don't you?'

And Frankie nodded, because anything else was bloody futile.

He didn't understand, though. The stupidity of it or the audacity. Marshall Vella was a fucking lunatic. He loved Rae as much as a man like Marshall could love anything. He considered Rae to be the son he'd never had. Everyone knew there was little love lost between Marshall and his actual kid. But Rae was the golden boy.

Rae could do no wrong. Literally anyone else in Rae's situation would have been grateful, satisfied.

Not Frankie's big brother, though. Rae took any half-decent thing and tore it to shreds. You only had to look at the skinny young woman in the armchair to know that. She'd been a bright, vibrant girl just a few months ago. Frankie had noticed her well before Rae did; it had been his staring at her that had brought her to Rae's attention. Despite what must have been a hard life, 'cause all the Vella girls got a bum deal, something about Roxy McCain had sparkled.

Not anymore though. Still beautiful, but her eyes were dark-ringed, and if Frankie wasn't mistaken, which sadly he didn't think he was, the ends of a fat lip were just settling. She was pale-faced and scared. The fucking Rae Diamond effect in full force.

And then there was this stinking pile of shit that, at best, would see them all out of a job, at worst may see one of them dead.

Rae's ill-advised little venture out into independent racketeering had, of course, been found out, just like Frankie had quietly suggested it might be. Robert Pincasi was in the nick and it seemed that Rae was either so stupid or so fucking arrogant – and Frankie suspected the latter – that he'd rented that lock-up in his own bloody name.

It'd be funny, if there wasn't a strong possibility that Marshall was going to kill him. A job he'd normally have outsourced to Rae, of course. That almost made Frankie smile, but his brother shifting with a grunt next to him brought him back to reality.

48

He sighed, stood to get away from him, to stop himself kicking the idiot full in the face. Rae smelled like a brewery, a sweaty, stale brewery. Smells that Frankie hated, associated with childhood and sad mornings crawling into bed with comatose Shirley when she smelled much the same, and he'd put up with it, just to be close to her.

Truth was, Frankie didn't really like booze, or violence, or drama, and yet he had little choice but to be dragged into all three every day of his life.

He said, 'Look, I'll nip to Mum's, go and get Faith, yeah?'

Rae looked at him through glassy, tearful eyes. Tears only for himself, though. He wasn't thinking about anyone else. He never did.

The girl stood then too, looking as scared as Frankie felt. She said to Rae, 'I'd better be going.' Adding, 'To me mum's, is all.'

At which, Rae stood up, made a lunge and grabbed her, pulling her face close to his. She flinched and Frankie took her arm, pulling her back. Rae glared from one to the other.

'No need for you to be blabbing this all over the place though, eh.'

She nodded, 'Course not.'

Frankie could see tears in her eyes and he moved himself forwards between her and his brother, smiling, cajoling. 'I'm sure she's safe as houses, Rae, or she wouldn't be here, eh?'

Rae looked at them both again and Frankie tried to weigh up whether he was going to kick off or not. But he collapsed on the settee, bottle in hand, saying, 'Sorry, Rox. You're right, Frankie, she's a good girl.' Giving her his million-watt grin and promising to 'See you later.'

The girl smiled weakly but nodded and said, 'Great, look forward to it.'

Once out on the street and safely out of earshot of Rae, Frankie asked her, 'You all right?'

And she looked at him in surprise, plastering that fake smile on her face again.

He waved a hand at her, 'You don't have to do that, love. I know he's a horrible fucker. You go home and don't worry about this shit, all right?'

She nodded. Paused, like she was about to speak, but no words came and she turned and walked off, never stopping to look back.

Frankie rushed to Sunningdale Avenue, an anxious churning in the pit of his stomach chasing him all the way.

Chapter Eleven

Acton

Waking up at Detective Rose's neat little flat was an odd moment for me. I left him snoring and snuck out in the early hours, figuring there was no need to make a song and dance of it all. It had been a fun night, one of the best I'd ever had, and there had been a satisfaction in doing something that would appal both my brothers and Marshall. But, for obvious reasons, there would be no repeat performance.

You might think growing up how I did, exposed to all I'd seen, I might have gone off men, but, actually, the opposite was true. I liked male company well enough. What I did know was that I'd never be ruled by one of the fuckers. I didn't want marriage, or kids, or any of those things. I wanted to be able to make my own choices. At that time, a lot of them were made for me, by Rae, or Marshall. But I wouldn't be controlled by my own body and my own soft heart, as my mother had been.

Yes, I liked the company of men, but I was careful too. A lot of the blokes I hooked up with were too scared of my brothers to utter a word, so I cautiously led the life that everyone saw, and occasionally I did what I wanted on the down-low.

I got into Sunningdale Avenue while it was still dark, feeling relaxed, and stayed up at the kitchen table, looking over the books for Vella's, marvelling, not for the first or last time, at the amount of wastage. At some point, I knew I was beaten and went to bed, climbing under the covers fully clothed, just as the sun was coming up.

Next thing I knew, I was woken up by hammering on the front door once again, and with the tentacles of a hangover starting to take root, I really didn't appreciate it.

I answered with a scowl, ready to tear strips off whoever it was.

Then I saw Frankie, pale-faced, and I knew something big had gone down.

Shirley came down the stairs, clutching her dressing gown around her and looking far worse than I felt.

With a hand pressed to her forehead, she said, 'Rae?'

Frankie nodded.

I was still in my crumpled dress from the night before and with a sigh, I said, 'Let me get my bag, yeah?'

Shirley muttered, 'I'll get dressed.'

Frankie looked at me and then her and said, 'Mum, you'd be better off staying here.'

The tone of his voice sent a cold wave across my stomach. 'Frankie, what's happened?'

He bit his lower lip, telling me he was frightened. He ran a hand through his fair hair and kind of crumpled as he stood. 'I wanted to say something, Faith. Knew I should and now . . . Fuck.'

'Frankie.' My voice was firm but controlled. Even if I was about to get the right hump, which I suspected I was, I sensed action was needed. 'Frank . . .' Gentler now and with a hand on his arm. I waited for him to look up and meet my eyes. 'What's he done?'

'He's been running something. Of his own.'

My brain whirred, 'Behind Marshall's back?'

He nodded. I looked from him to Shirley. Incredulous. 'That slippery fucker.'

My mum sank down onto the bottom step, hands clutched to her stomach. She of all people knew exactly what Marshall was capable of. What kind of man he could be.

I tore my eyes away from her, unable to take in her worry on top of my own, and said to Frankie, 'You've just come from his?'

He nodded.

'Marshall knows what's been going on?'

Another nod.

Shirley said, 'He got a call here not long after we were in.'

I paused. 'Did he tell you what it was about?'

She shook her head, 'No, but he was . . .'

'He was what, Mum?'

There were tears in her eyes by then. 'He was that sort of quiet angry he gets. You know?'

I did know. Which was very bad. Marshall was an idiot, not in control of his emotions at the best of times.

He had only two modes: blind, unstoppable rage, or a sort of simmering benevolence that masked the lit bomb burning underneath. Both were pretty terrifying.

But there had been just a few times when I'd seen him cross enough to become thoughtful. He wasn't a thoughtful man. Not naturally, which was how he'd managed to turn a successful, albeit morally dubious, business and run it into the ground. But when he went quiet, it never boded well.

A man on his firm some years before had attempted to take the crown from Marshall and that man had paid with his life. To this day, the whereabouts of Babyface's (AKA Clemont Barrington Abra) remains were unknown, and no one had ever been charged with his murder, either.

I felt a bead of sweat break out on my top lip and swiped a hand across my mouth.

Shit.

Shirley was standing, pulling her coat on over her nightdress, slipping her feet into her shoes, picking up her bag again. The held-back tears were running freely down her face. 'I need to get to Rae.'

I grabbed her arm. 'No, Mum.'

'He's my son, Faith.'

'And he's pissed off a fucking psycho, who is likely also on his way there right now.'

Her voice was a whisper when she said, 'Faith, he'll kill him.'

She stared at me. Her beautiful blue eyes wide and damp. I squeezed her hand in mine. I didn't do her the disservice of disagreeing, but I told her, 'Stay here. I'll be in contact as soon as I can.'

She held my gaze and so many things passed between us in that look. My eyes begging her to trust me.

'Please, Mum.'

Marshall took Rae's behaviour out on Shirley all the time and I had no reason to believe that this time would be any different. Her getting in the way would just make things harder for me. And Frankie. And, ultimately, Rae.

Shirley heard the panic in my voice. Saw each of her own worries and concerns mirrored back at her, and nodded.

Chapter Twelve

Sunningdale Avenue

The door shut behind her two younger children and Shirley sat, shoes and coat on, handbag clutched to her body like a small baby. The same way she'd once held all of them.

She remembered coming home from the hospital with Rae. The best and the worst day of her life. Everyone had gone on and on about what a big baby he was, but he looked small to her. She couldn't believe anything could be so little and so helpless.

She and Rae Senior had been in a halfway house then. A cramped, dirty room in a building full of them. Her body had been sore and broken from the birth. She'd been so young and so frightened, but she'd vowed to herself that she'd look after this child, sure that once she was old enough, they'd marry, make a proper family.

Rae Senior had come in drunk and she'd gestured to the sleeping baby, proud, pleased, scared, overwhelmed. Rae hadn't even looked in the crib at his son. He'd pushed Shirley down on the bed. Grabbed her hair and said she still looked like shit.

Shirley hadn't known how to respond. She'd seen flashes of his temper before then, put it down to stress, not fully understanding anything because, at fourteen, she was still a child, running away from a father with ready fists and unable to recognise that she'd swapped one mad fucker for another. Rae Senior was a man then, at nearly thirty, and he proved his dominance that night.

Shirley still thought of it as the worst night of her entire life. He did things to her that left marks she still had to this day, but the worst of it had been listening to her infant son cry, awful bellowing howls of hunger, and not being allowed to tend to him.

Eventually, when Rae Senior was done, he'd stood, said she needed to earn her keep from now on, now that she'd given them another mouth to feed – *trapped him*, he'd said. Then he'd gone out and she'd half crawled, half dragged herself to the crib, picked up baby Rae, who was red in the face by then, clamping him to her sore, full and bruised breast.

Shirley thought of her own mother, a woman she'd hated for years for standing idly by whilst her father ruined all of their lives, and for the first time ever, she'd felt a glimmer of understanding. The horror on her mother's face when she'd told her she was pregnant.

Shirley had been defiant and even proud. Had scoffed at her mother's concerns, convinced she would have a better life than her. But as she'd sat there that night, broken, battered, her first experience of motherhood nursing her son in a cold, dark, damp room that smelled of the assault the boy's father had inflicted upon her, she understood what her mother had been scared of. And that now it was she who was trapped. She'd cried then, the tears splattering onto the baby's head like terrible rain.

And as she sat all those years later, on the bottom step of her little house on Sunningdale Avenue, she watched yet more tears splash down onto her lap, thinking she never had been able to protect him.

Rae.

Had never been able to save him from anyone else, and certainly couldn't save him from himself, either. Despite her best intentions. She prayed quietly that he'd live through this day.

Chapter Thirteen

Rae Diamond's flat

We got to Rae's flat just in time to see Marshall leaving, flanked either side by Sam and Will. Heavies. Men who had been with Marshall years before Rae came on the scene. Men he'd usurped and enjoyed reminding of the fact. Men who were covered in what I guessed was my brother's blood.

A horrible sound slipped from me, then. Somewhere between a gasp and a whimper. I clamped my lips closed, braced myself, and Marshall stepped into my path. I felt Frankie take a step forwards, closer to me, and I waved a hand at him to stay back.

Marshall looked at me and I held his gaze, forcing myself to breathe evenly. His face was florid and red. He'd got to the point that year where he was so overweight that you could barely see his eyes. They were just dark angry slits in the middle of a blotchy pudding.

He was a greedy man, an excessive man. A man with no self-control. That thought shook me. All the things that he might have inflicted on Rae clamouring to the forefront of my mind. My knees wobbled for a second and I willed them to stay straight. Keep me up.

He said, 'I gave that little fucker everything.' As he spoke, spit flew from his sausage lips onto my face. I had to physically resist the urge to wipe it away.

It took all I had to stay there, looking that awful man square in the face, when all I wanted to do was push past him. Into the flats, up the stairs, to Rae.

I said, 'He's out of order.' Because he was. As much as I was hoping he was alive – and, God knows, the thought of him being gone would floor me like nothing else ever had – Rae was in the wrong here.

Marshall said, 'Did you know?' Still looking at me, still so close his breath came at me in hot putrid waves.

I shook my head, glad in a way that I could answer honestly, though I was adept at bending the truth when I needed to.

'And your mother?'

I shook my head again, while he glared at me. I was aware of Sam and Will either side of him. The stains on their clothes. The clunking bag on Will's shoulder, which I realised was Rae's. A bag of terrible tricks that my brother usually carried on his way to jobs, often with a smile on his face. Yet another facet of his personality that I'd diligently ignored. Now thrust at me in a way I could no longer escape. In that bag were tools that would have broken him. Perhaps taken his life. The irony wasn't lost on me, but it was humourless.

Marshall said, 'She bred a bevy of cunts. You're one. He's one.' He pointed at Frankie. 'And that fucker in there is the biggest cunt of the lot of you.'

I didn't say anything. I couldn't bring myself to agree, but I wasn't stupid enough to disagree, either. And he'd talked about Rae in the present tense, which allowed me a glimmer of hope.

Marshall ran a hand over his wide, balding head. 'I treated him better than I treated my own son.'

I nodded. It was the truth.

Everyone knew Marshall and his son, Vincent, had had issues over the years. Just as Marshall had with his wife, Nora. Vincent should have been Marshall's number two. He was Marshall's only child, after all. But Rae held that position. Not in any real sense though, not with any equality, and it had always been precarious, because blood is blood after all, and Rae had known that if push came to shove, he was dispensable.

I knew Rae well enough to know that it would be that line of thought that had landed him in this mess. Bitterness, resentment, grandiosity and a keen sense of entitlement. All the things Marshall found charming in her brother had led to his betrayal.

There was no honour among men like them. Not really.

Marshall stood for what felt like hours but must have only been seconds. Keeping me there, knowing my instinct would be to push past. Run to Rae. He'd known me most of my life. Since I was a child. He was asserting his power, as he always did.

Eventually he snapped at his two mammoth sidekicks, 'Let's go.'

And I leaped into action, Frankie holding the door, and the pair of us racing up the stairs.

Chapter Fourteen

Acton

Cal laughed his head off when they found out who the lock-up belonged to, even further amused to discover it wasn't anything to do with Marshall Vella.

Jimmy hadn't been quite so amused. He had woken up that morning with the smell of her perfume still on his sheets. The first girl who'd really piqued his interest. Sod's law. He was sorry she had left, but understood why. And whilst he hadn't been expecting a long-term thing, he realised while Cal was speaking that he'd been hoping for at least a repeat performance. Hardly likely now. Since he was about to arrest her brother.

With a wide grin on his face, Cal kept saying to Jimmy, 'There'll be hell to pay.'

Jimmy knew he was right and also knew he'd have to keep schtum about last night. There were no hard and fast rules, of course, and they bent things to suit them when they needed to. But there were some lines you didn't cross, boundaries you observed. He'd like to have blamed it on the booze, but he'd only had a few pints.

Truth was, any man would be hard-pushed to resist

Faith Diamond. She wasn't just a looker, she was extraordinary. He'd thought the same after poor Liza's murder, when they'd stood in the Diamonds' kitchen and Faith's hard face had avoided looking at him. But, last night, seeing her smile for the first time, she'd gone from hot as you like to off the fucking scale. And hadn't disappointed in bed, either.

Unless he was very much mistaken, she'd enjoyed herself too. Very different to Cynthia, not that she'd ever let him take her to bed, but even kissing her was pretty unexciting.

He'd been amazed at the girls he'd met in London. The whole scene down here was a revelation and vastly different to how it was out in the sticks, where religious rules were, for the large part, still fervently observed. Jimmy always thought of the city as being years ahead, time-wise. London gave him a glimmer of hope at how it would be soon. There was change on its way, that was for sure.

He was pulled back to the moment by Cal's cackling.

Marshall Vella and Rae Diamond were the root cause of a lot of the problems that Jimmy and Cal faced on a day-to-day basis. Jimmy knew Cal had arrested Rae Diamond when he was a minor, had been part of the team that sent him down for grievous bodily harm when he'd been just fourteen. He also knew that Cal had felt sorry for Rae then, but that pity had since dissipated.

Jimmy had been at a fair few scenes of carnage caused by Rae and his younger brother, Frankie, and fully understood Cal's dislike of the man. Though Cal always said the boys' mother wasn't a bad sort, and they knew the day Marshall Vella came knocking had changed the course of Rae's life for the worse.

Certainly, Rae was a loaded weapon, as far as Marshall was concerned. He did most of Marshall's dirty work, but he also took a great deal of pleasure in it. Everyone also knew that Marshall had taken up with Rae's mother in some sort of fucked-up parody of a happy family.

Whatever the situation, and despite the likelihood of another night with Faith Diamond growing smaller by the second, Jimmy was delighted to finally have something on Rae at least.

Rae had certainly shot himself in both feet setting up a little side line with Pincasi.

The mood in the car as Cal and Jimmy headed over to make the arrest, trailed by two uniforms, was pretty upbeat.

But as they pulled up outside Rae's block of flats and saw the ambulance parked haphazardly by the door, Jimmy found himself hoping that Marshall hadn't served justice before they even had a chance.

The ambulance was pulling away as they got out of the car, and Cal swore under his breath.

Frankie Diamond paced by the door, lighting a cigarette with a shaking hand. Cal and Jimmy went over. He greeted them with a sneer.

Cal asked, 'Is he alive?'

Frankie finally lit the fag and inhaled deeply. He had blood splatters all over his white shirt.

Jimmy snapped, 'Frankie.' Desperate to make this arrest and fed up of the theatrics.

But as Frankie finally looked at him directly, Jimmy got the unsettling feeling that the man was actually pretty shook up.

He softened his voice and said again, 'Frankie?'

Frankie muttered, 'Just about. They're taking him and my sister to Ealing Hospital.' Then, 'I'm going to get my mum.' And he walked away.

'Right, let's go,' Cal said tersely.

The drive was tense.

'Was it me or was Frankie Diamond all shaken up?' Jimmy said.

Cal sighed, 'Poor bugger.'

Jimmy replied, 'You've always liked him.'

Cal nodded, smiling, 'I've said before, lad, the Diamonds on the whole aren't a bad lot. I was called out many times to Shirley's old place when Rae Senior had done her over.'

'Rae and Frankie's dad?'

Cal shrugged, 'Definitely Rae's, but he'd put Shirley on the game before Frankie arrived, so no one can be sure about him.'

'He doesn't look like Rae,' Jimmy said.

Cal nodded, 'No. Faith does a bit, but they've definitely got different dads.'

Jimmy swallowed at the mention of her name. He wasn't relishing the thought of seeing her at the hospital. Though he was sure she wouldn't say anything.

She wouldn't want anyone to know about last night any more than he did.

Jimmy was feeling anxious and excited in equal parts, he decided. Adrenaline was a large part of his job. Policing London wasn't for the faint-hearted, but once you got used to the general skulduggery and the everyday depravity of prostitutes, petty thieves and fights, it could also be mundane at times. Long periods of boredom punctuated by things like this. Even the murders became commonplace. Usually a domestic, or accidental.

The one that had given him the proper heebie-jeebies had been poor Liza on the banks of Dukes Meadows. His first murder case, and where he'd met Cal, who had headed the investigation that led nowhere. Every death since had just reminded him of the futility of life and, in particular, poverty, where spats over a few shillings could flare up into fatal stabbings, or sad girls beaten by pimps might quietly drink themselves to death, not to be found until someone noticed the smell.

Much of that on his patch was caused by Marshall Vella. And Rae bloody Diamond.

So, it was with a glimmer of satisfaction that Jimmy saw him now, in a hospital bed, various tubes coming out of his arms, and his face a swollen mess. But he was alive and compos mentis enough to look pissed off at Jimmy and Cal's arrival.

The smile stuck on Jimmy's face, though, as Cal said, 'Hello, Faith.'

His heart did that little jump thing as he turned his eyes onto her.

She was still wearing the same dress he'd taken off her the night before, but it was covered in streaks of blood, and she'd lost the shine of just a few hours ago.

He looked at her, trying to convey . . . just what, he didn't know. Empathy, he supposed.

He needn't have bothered, though. Her furious face looked right through him and Cal as she snapped, 'Couldn't have fucking waited?'

And Cal shook his head, 'Sorry, love.'

She said, 'I'm not your love.' And stalked past them both and out of the room.

Part Two

'Hell is empty and all the devils are here.'

– William Shakespeare, *The Tempest* (1611)

Chapter Fifteen

September 1963

Sunningdale Avenue

Sometimes kings went down slowly, without even knowing it was happening. Their kingdoms crumbling round them whilst they blithely carried on, oblivious. Unwilling, or unable, to see what was happening right in front of their eyes. Sometimes hand-picked princes fell from grace. They were, perhaps, left in hospital beds, bruised and battered. Worse still, maybe the police came and made arrangements for them to be taken away.

The second time my brother was locked up was different to the first. Those years of my childhood where my ache for him to return was so strong it was almost a physical pain. When he got sent down for possession of stolen goods with intent to sell, I felt differently. I wasn't happy exactly at his misfortune, but what became apparent quickly was that knowing where he was and what he was doing was in many ways preferable to lying awake half the night wondering if he'd come in, if he'd bring Marshall and what trouble he may lay at our feet then.

Jimmy Rose and Cal Doyle undertook their duties with relish, of course. They'd had Rae in over the years on various misdemeanours. Nothing that caused him any real agony. But those few charges they had managed to make stick, coupled with irrefutable proof of an organised racketeering ring and Marshall's complete unwillingness to offer any support, meant they had him good and proper.

On the one hand, you couldn't blame them for being pleased, of course. On the other, Rae was my brother. My saviour. I loved him with a fierce loyalty that pushed away any common sense. Anything I thought about Rae, any dark intrusive thoughts, I forced out of my mind. Something I'd later regret, but at that time, the denial was still strong, and he was still my hero. The boy who'd saved a frightened little girl in the middle of the night.

I turned my anger on Jimmy Rose and, as a result, largely ignored him over the next few years.

Times were tough to start with, certainly financially, though Rae had always been good at spending a vast portion of what he earned before it got to us anyway. Some changes were for the best, though. Marshall left us alone. Frankie seemed, if not at ease, less harassed, and me . . . well, I learned that I wasn't just clever, I also had vision, and I finally started to let myself dream bigger dreams. Because it looked like maybe the world would be ready for queens soon, too.

Chapter Sixteen

HM Prison Wormwood Scrubs, White City

Frankie could have done without it. He wished that Marshall had asked anyone but him to drive. He had no idea how this – in his opinion, ill-fated – meeting was going to go down, and if he'd been given a choice, which as usual he hadn't been, he'd have given the whole thing a wide berth.

His mum had become a nervous wreck and had gone into overdrive in the house. Faith was calm, cool and collected, but that was his sister's response to everything these days. She'd always kept her feelings well hidden, but he knew, deep down, she must be rattled.

Despite the extraordinary mess Rae had caused, his incarceration hadn't gone too badly, especially for her. Vincent Vella had been brought back for good by Marshall. Vella's was in his name, anyway, as a way of avoiding too much trouble and scrutiny. Vincent had kept Faith on at the club, doing the books to start with. Unlike his dad, who considered women to be too lowly for a second thought, Vincent utilised whatever he had at his disposal.

When he'd arrived back in London and been given the dubious honour of overseeing Vella's and Marshall's other flagging concerns, he'd sussed that Faith knew more about the financial workings of that place than any of them. By the time Marshall realised Vincent had taken a shine to the girl he considered uppity and annoying, she'd proven her worth and helped Vincent increase profits. Marshall could hardly argue, but it didn't mean he liked it.

Frankie pretty much did the lion's share of what he deemed to be Vella's skivvy work now, though Vincent threw him some better work from time to time. Frankie was sure this was a directive that came from Faith, but he took it anyway. A lot of the time, Marshall was too wrapped up to bother with Frankie, which suited him just fine, he preferred it to today when he'd been summoned.

Today would be a big day. Frankie hadn't slept much the night before and his stomach was like a churning ball of acid as he waited. Rae was getting out. Back into the big wide world, having served almost thirty-two months. Frankie had been in to see him, of course, as had Shirley and Faith. But Marshall had blanked him, like the disappointing errant child he considered him to be.

Until that day when the fat fucker was sitting in the back of the Rolls Frankie was being forced to drive, puffing on a cigar and waiting for his fallen boy wonder to appear outside the gates of one of Her Majesty's finest establishments.

74

And here he came now, full of swagger and his boyish grin. When he caught sight of Frankie, he sped up, running towards the car, his smile faltering when he saw Marshall, then dropping altogether. Head down in an almost comical expression of shame.

Marshall waved at Frankie, who jumped up, climbing out and opening Marshall's door.

The big man, almost as wide as Rae was tall, stood staring at Rae, who eventually looked up and met Marshall's eye.

A moment passed. Unspoken things were communicated between the two men and Frankie looked away, feeling almost as if he was intruding on a lovers' intimate moment. The pair of them together had always caused him discomfort and today proved nothing had changed in their absence from each other.

He braced himself for violence, knowing if Marshall took a swing, he wouldn't step in and likely Rae wouldn't retaliate either. But, instead, Marshall reached out for Rae and took him in his pudgy arms. Rae clasped back and there they stood, Frankie watching in disbelief.

Marshall stepped back, looked Rae up and down and said, 'Prison life seems to suit you.'

Rae grinned, 'I adjust to whatever comes my way, Marshall.'

Marshall rolled his eyes, but he was smiling. 'Bet you could use a good night out, though?'

'Now you're talking.'

They climbed into the back, Rae touching Frankie's shoulder and nodding at his little brother.

Marshall said, 'Take us up west, young Frankie, we've booze to drink and girls to ruin.'

Chapter Seventeen

Mortlake

It's been a long night. A long few months. A long life, he thinks sometimes, though hopefully with many years left to live yet.

The city in the small dark hours is still very much alive and buzzing, and he finds himself driving – aimlessly at first, but then with purpose and direction. Before long, he is covering familiar territory. Eyes peeled.

There are women everywhere. Girls, some of them, and these are the ones that catch his eye. Tiny little things dressed, of course, with no respect for the biting cold. Hard girls with skin bared out to prove it. The girls who walk the street. Rough and desperate. He isn't going to stop. He isn't going to do anything.

And then he sees her.

A little figure amongst the rest. From the back, she could be a teenager. When he pulls up alongside her, though, she gives him the smile.

That smile.

They exchange a few words. The usual ones. She knows him after all, as he does her, by face, and now by name too.

He tells her to get in and she does.

He is only going to take her for a drive. That's all. It is cold tonight; even in the car, his breath comes out fogged, as does hers. He keeps the window open, but still the scent of her perfume grasps at him. Cloying, cheap and sweet.

She says, 'Here, we should pull over soon.'

And he takes her to the same place he had the last one. The one who would be the only one. But now here he is again.

She leans in and does a sort of fake shiver. She whispers, 'Warm me up then.'

And at first he does. Then she is doing that thing, that giggling thing, with the oohhs and aahhs.

He tells her, 'You can shut up.'

And she purrs, 'Whatever you want.'

For a price.

Whatever he wants.

At a cost.

He doesn't get why men find this so thrilling. It isn't love. It is a purchase. And yet.

He wants her.

He can see the appeal.

He feels it himself.

He can see how this happens.

How a man might fall.

He is cross then.

He levels a smack at her face and she yelps, 'I don't do rough.'

He says, 'I thought it was whatever I wanted?'

She bristles.

The cheek of it.

The nerve of her.

78

She says, 'I've got little'uns, they don't need to see me bruised.'

And that enrages him. Why would she have children? Why do they always?

He snarls, 'They are better knowing what you are.'

She stares at him, seems to sense that perhaps this isn't quite right. Perhaps she should be careful. She tries, 'Sorry, you're right, it's whatever you want.' She smiles, but it is thin now.

Even more forced.

'Whatever you're after is fine, then you can drop me back, all right?'

'No.'

She laughs and it is tinged with hysteria.

He stares at her, surprised at how calm he is. He hadn't meant for this.

Hadn't wanted it.

He'd just been driving.

But he'd never forgotten about the last one. The first one. The one who changed it all, and now it didn't seem consequential.

He leans in and whispers, 'You're rubbish and your children are better off without you.' Then his hand goes to her throat and he presses evenly and hard. There is a click and he thinks something may have broken. It reminds him of the delicate wishbone on fresh roast chicken.

Inside, that's all she is. Just the same. The innards to all living things are so similar. Most people have evolved past that stage.

Animals.

Though not all.

She is making a sound, almost like clucking too, a click-click strained groan and then she is quiet.

He undresses her, then he drives and drives, and he starts to smile as he pulls up at a refuse disposal site. It's almost like he's bringing her home.

Chapter Eighteen

November 1963

Mortlake

It was cold. The sort of biting bitterness that England served up during its darker months. Even though it was the middle of the day, there was a sheet of grey overlaying everything. Like someone had covered a camera lens for effect. Jimmy had read about them doing that in the pictures. A sort of blurring to denote tone or mood. Bleak would be today's mood. Which was in good keeping with the scene before him.

The builder who had discovered her, in the most awful of ways, was standing to one side talking to Cal. His face was tear-stained and he was clenching a cup of tea, which wobbled precariously in his hand. He had been digging here and when his shovel had met resistance, he had pushed down harder. The result was the awful scene they were now faced with.

A woman.

Naked, exposed, rotten, and in two parts.

Her head resting just shy of her body. Not the man's fault of course, but not something he would forget in a hurry either. Jimmy imagined the combination of the physical feel of it, coupled with the image, would cause the poor bloke many a sleepless night to come. She had been well hidden, and from the state of her, she'd been there a while. The man couldn't have known, would never in a million years have guessed that what he was butting against was a human body. His job was just to level the site, which is exactly what he'd been doing.

The site was for refuse. A rubbish tip. This woman, bare except for one sad stocking hanging forlornly from her right foot, had been abandoned. At the dump. Jimmy couldn't help feeling it was a reflection of the disdain felt by whoever had left her there. What sort of a person did something like this?

He watched Cal stretch out a hand to the poor man, who nodded his head.

A young WPC, Merilyn, was on hand, leading him away. She was good with anything involving sensitivity, and despite her youth had already proven she had a good stomach for the awful aspects of their job. She would drive him home and, Jimmy hoped, he would be allowed a few days off. To gather himself.

He headed over to Cal, eyebrow raised.

Cal said the doctor would be doing a post-mortem later.

Jimmy nodded. He would be there. He felt a certain responsibility towards her, though why, he had no idea.

Post-mortems were strange. They felt simultaneously impersonal and like a total invasion of privacy. It was a body not just stripped bare, as this one had already been, but opened up, dissected and taken apart. It was an inhuman process, Jimmy always thought. And though he liked the pathologist, Dr Daniel Eart, well enough – and he did, the man was insightful and quick – he also wondered at someone who would choose this as his profession. Daniel must have started out his medical training wanting to save the living. At some point, that focus became analysing the dead.

A useful job, vital if they were to uncover the secrets that bodies hid, which was the role of the police after all. But still, Jimmy found it an odd choice. Dragged out to horrific scenes – even the accidental deaths and roadkill weren't pretty – and then ferreted away here in the basement, which always smelled of disinfectant and bodily finality. You needed a strong stomach. When there was a fresh body, or entirely un-fresh as in this case, it was hard to repel it. The smells assaulted Jimmy and Cal.

Cal lit a cigarette, passing the pack to Jimmy, who took it gratefully. It dimmed the odours somewhat, though not nearly enough. The waft of sulphurous, rotten egg, decomposing flesh permeated not just Jimmy's nose, but everything in and on him. He knew from experience that he'd wake still thinking he could smell it over the next few days.

The worst thing about the whole ordeal was Daniel's announcement that she'd been dead for weeks, and that she was pregnant. So, two deaths.

Weeks that woman had lain there with a babe in her belly. The already sad, already unlucky pair heaped in with peoples' waste and refuse. Weeks where no one had come looking. A young woman. A mother already, according to her body, which the doctor said had given birth twice. It was unthinkable. And yet it was so.

Jimmy and Cal left and neither spoke for minutes. Granting her awful end the respect of silence. Trying to process it all. Jimmy felt perfectly at ease around Cal Doyle. He thought about how they'd met in a similar circumstance to this one. Liza Plum. Cal had given Jimmy some instructions that day, a few things to follow up on, and had been impressed with the way he'd handled them. He'd taken Jimmy under his wing after that, making his progression up the ranks much faster than it otherwise would have been.

They walked back to the station, side by side. Everything looked off-kilter. It was a bleak winter. The streets were quieter than they had been in previous months. People hurrying from one place to another, heads down. Coats on with collars up.

Jimmy cleared his throat and spoke what was on his mind, 'This is like Liza Plum.'

'The Dukes Meadows girl?'

Jimmy nodded, swallowed thickly, trying to make his voice remain even and untroubled. 'My first murder case.'

Cal said, 'I remember it.' And added, 'They stay with you.' Placing a hand on Jimmy's shoulder.

Jimmy felt a rush of relief. Four small words and a touch so fleeting that if you'd blinked, you'd have missed it. But these things meant the world to Jimmy.

Cal meant the world to Jimmy.

At that time, he often wasn't sure which of his feelings were reasonable, what were the right responses for a man. He assumed it was the lack of a father figure during his formative years. He'd always found himself checking what was correct. What expectations were. What wouldn't make him the 'sissy sissy' of the playground bullies, laughing at him for being a mummy's boy.

Cal said, 'They're likely not related.' Adding, 'Prostitutes die all the time.'

'You know her, this one?'

Cal nodded, 'Geraldine Ross. Involved with Vella, of course.'

Jimmy grunted. All paths on their patch led back to that fucker. Rae's arrest had felt like a triumph, but he was only ever a symptom of the real problem.

Cal told Jimmy, 'She has a son that we suspect is his, though he'd never admit it. She once tried to make off with more than her cut and Marshall had her beaten half to death.'

Jimmy asked, 'The mother of his child?'

Cal nodded, 'Like I said, he'd never admit it, but she was pretty certain, by all accounts. It's a dangerous job.'

There was a pause while they both thought about that.

Then Cal offered, 'This could be an abortion gone wrong. The poor cow already has one child who lives with her sister and the son Marshall denied. Being pregnant a third time probably wasn't ideal.'

'Why was she all the way out there, though?'

Cal shrugged, 'The abortionist might have panicked. Not known what to do.'

Jimmy said, 'Not fucking likely, though, is it.'

Cal smiles, 'Nope, not fucking likely, son.'

Jimmy said, 'Sorry.'

And Cal placed that calming hand on his shoulder again. Jimmy felt another wave of emotion, a longing for things he'd never had. Mothers were golden of course – he'd been lucky enough to have one of the best – but fathers served a necessary role. He saw that enough in the lives of the people he arrested, who often had just as little fatherly influence as he had, for one reason or another.

Jimmy would have been a good policeman anywhere, but he did better under Cal's watchful eye. With the encouragement, someone to learn from, to look up to.

That day, he held his peace, but there was something about her, Geraldine, and something about Liza. Not just the rudely bared flesh or the glassy vacant eyes. Something about the simmering, controlled anger. Something that to him seemed personal.

Cal said, 'We'll need to go and see Marshall.'

'Yes.'

'But we don't need to go this second. Come on, let's get a pint.'

And Jimmy nodded, having never heard a better idea.

Chapter Nineteen

Vella's

Marshall was livid. He wasn't in Vella's much in those days and I was grateful for that, as it had become my domain. I no longer did the books at home to have them collected by Rae. I had my own unofficial desk in the office. But today, Marshall had come in and was taking up all of the space. He'd been there for about an hour already, storming around the office, smoking, drinking, making phone calls and generally getting in the way. I was perched on the edge of Vincent's desk; Marshall had taken my seat, with merely a flick of his hand for me to move.

Vincent was looking at his father with open disdain and I fully understood his exasperation. There was no love lost between father and son. Marshall had, I thought, seen bringing Vincent back as a statement to Rae.

They had the same dark colouring, but that was where the similarities ended. In all other respects, they were like different species. Marshall had married a woman who was almost aristocracy and I assumed that's who Vincent got his manners from. He'd also been sent to the best schools money could buy. I knew, and could even understand to some degree, that Vincent's attitude might rankle his dad. He was a know-it-all and took a superior attitude with most people he had dealings with. But he afforded me respect, and maybe if Marshall wasn't such an idiot, Vincent wouldn't look down his nose at him so much.

I couldn't go so far as to say I warmed to Vincent. He was charming certainly, but he wasn't a cuddly kind of person. He was polite and, perhaps most importantly from my point of view, he was fair. He gave me the job at Vella's not because he liked me, but because he thought I'd benefit the business. And I did.

I reckoned Marshall was sorry now that he'd brought his son back to London, but he couldn't really get rid of him. Vella's income had almost trebled since Vincent took over. Though that was in large part down to me. Vincent didn't have any particular passion for the club – he intended to run a few car showrooms in town, which was his pet project and which Marshall was disdainful of. He'd asked me if I had any ideas about Vella's while I'd been in doing the books and I'd had plenty. I hadn't expected to see them taken up, but Vincent had listened, made changes, offered me a proper job, and now the place was changing.

Marshall slammed down the phone, got up from my chair and flopped his considerable self on the small settee between Vincent's and my desk and scowled at me as I took my place again. 'What you fucking staring at?'

Vincent said, 'Is something the matter?'

Marshall glared at him under a haze of cigarette smoke. 'Fucking old bill hassling me.'

Vincent looked more alert at that. 'What about?' He prided himself on keeping things, at least on the surface, above board.

Marshall shrugged, 'Some fucking slag.'

Vincent shut his eyes and rubbed his fingers across the bridge of his nose. When he opened them, Marshall was stamping out his fag. Still looking glum.

He said, 'Silly bitch turned up dead.'

'What's that got to do with you?' Vincent asked.

'Bugger all, son, which is my point exactly.'

He seemed about to say something else and I braced myself for one of his long rants – I had heard plenty of them over the years – but we were interrupted by Rae and Frankie coming in.

Marshall asked, 'All done?'

Rae nodded. I dreaded to think what 'all' meant.

'Right, drinks on me then, eh?' Marshall grinned.

Rae ruffled my hair on his way out.

I slapped at his hand, rolling my eyes and told him, 'Take it easy, yeah?' to which Rae and Marshall laughed uproariously. I realised that my brother was already reasonably drunk.

Frankie nodded on his way to the door and I felt a wave of sympathy for him, and relief at Marshall's departure. It was like there was air in the little office again.

Cocaine definitely made Rae more unpredictable than ever. And Marshall, for that matter, though Frankie suspected that man had always been a few sandwiches short of a picnic. He was a lunatic, Marshall.

Rae was sitting with the big man's arm clasped around his shoulders, sipping champagne and doing lines. Surrounded by girls who were hanging off Marshall's every word.

Frankie was tired – he wanted to go home, get out of here. They were in an awful, dingy club that had definitely seen better days, down a nothingy little street hidden in the bland industrial estates of London. A shitty little brothel that Marshall's 'associate' ran and somewhere they went more and more often since Vincent and Faith had all but cleaned up Vella's. Frankie would have preferred to stay there with his sister. But here was where he was expected to be and he was, after all, just a man who did what he was told.

Sitting there, under the dim artificial lights, he felt a wave of hopelessness threaten to overwhelm him, and crushed it with a long slug of his drink. A pretty blonde smiled at him and he looked away. He might be interested if this wasn't work for her.

Marshall and Rae had no such reservations, and Marshall had shunted Rae along and now had women either side of him. Frankie felt the usual swell of disgust he always did around the man.

Eventually, Marshall went to the bar and Rae slipped into the seat beside his little brother, 'Penny for them, Frank?'

Frankie shrugged.

'Come on. What's wrong?'

'Nothing,' adding, 'I might go home soon.'

Rae said, 'Marshall won't be happy.'

'Fuck him.' The words sounded hollow even as he spoke them.

Rae laughed. 'Last time I did that it cost me prison time, mate.'

Frankie saw something then on his brother's face. A tightness in his jaw, a heaviness around the eyes. He felt a rare wave of sympathy for Rae, who, in his own cack-handed way, had attempted to break out and away from Vella. He asked, 'So you'll just do as you're told?'

Rae shrugged, 'For now. What choice we got, eh?'

Frankie knew he had a point, but he was still annoyed. Plus, he didn't know whether to feel relieved that Rae was obviously just toeing the line for the time being, or absolutely terrified. He often thought about how life might have been if it had just been him, Shirley and Faith. It always came back to one thing: Bass would still have been there that night, and Frankie hadn't been the one who'd acted. Hadn't even known what was happening.

Hadn't had the guts, a nagging voice whispered in the back of his mind.

He felt bitter, grateful and sad just thinking about it. Bitter that it was Rae who'd stepped up, been the hero. Sad that there even had to be one, that there was no parent who might have come to Faith's rescue. To any of their rescues. Grateful that Rae had done what he did. Despite it bringing Marshall to their door.

Rae stood suddenly, knocking Frankie's drink as he went. Frankie was about to complain when his eyes followed his brother's and clapped on Roxy McCann. She looked stunning and smiled at Frankie, who returned it easily. Frankie had seen a fair bit of Roxy over the past year. She was back working for Vella, in one of his houses, and tending bar here, as she had been since Rae had gone down. Frankie collected from the house she was situated in. She always had a smile for him, and he'd taken to stopping in for a chat. Had found out the horror of her situation. That her own mother had put her on the game at fourteen. That her father was in and out, with nothing resembling a job. That she had two younger siblings she wanted to protect.

He also knew that she was shit scared of Rae, who took a deliberate step towards her. The smile dropped instantly from her face.

For fuck's sake.

Frankie stood, bracing himself for trouble to come.

Rae reached out a hand, grabbing her arm and pulling her in to him. Frankie couldn't hear what he was saying, but Roxy was shaking her head.

He stepped closer and said in a light tone, 'What's going on here, eh?'

Roxy looked at him and he saw pleading in her eyes.

'Come on, Rae. Let's let Roxy get on, eh?' Frankie said.

Rae frowned, 'I don't see why she doesn't want to sit and have a drink with me first, though.' His eyes were dark, foreboding.

Roxy murmured, 'I'm working.' Her voice strangled. Frankie was pissed off as well as frightened.

Rae said, 'The boss won't mind.'

Frankie felt more than a little sorry for Roxy. Being the object of Rae's affection rarely went well.

Marshall came back, setting a tray of shots on the table and grabbed Roxy's arse. 'Looking lovely, darling.'

Roxy smiled – what else could she do? But she looked even more nervous.

Marshall lit a fag and Rae said, 'Stuck-up little cow reckons she's too good to join me for a drink, Marshall.'

Marshall looked at her, 'That right, Rox?'

Her eyes filled with tears, 'I'm working. That's all I said.'

'And who do you work for, darling?'

She looked down at the floor. 'You.'

'Me. And Rae is my associate. A valued one at that. Why not join him for a drink, like he asked.'

Roxy said, 'I don't want to.' In a voice so quiet, Frankie wondered if he heard right, and kind of hoped he hadn't.

Marshall kept staring at her, smoking, appraising her like one might a smear of dog shit on the sole of one's shoe. 'That so?'

She nodded, looked up. 'I've got customers anyway. I should go.'

Rae looked outraged. Frankie watched his brother's fists clench, shoulders hunch, face twisting in horror.

Marshall looked at Rae, then back at Roxy. He grabbed the girl roughly by the shoulder, pulled her in. It wasn't until Frankie smelled a terrible burning that he realised Marshall had stabbed his cigarette into her

93

shoulder. Roxy was yelping, wriggling in pain. Marshall let go of her, dropped the fag, drank the three shots and clicked his fingers at Rae to follow.

After the two men were gone, Frankie leaned down, reaching for Roxy, who was sobbing in a heap on the floor.

Then Rae's head poked back through the door. 'Frankie. Now!'

And he mouthed, 'I'm sorry,' and headed out into the night, full of impotent rage.

Chapter Twenty

Vella's

I helped Devlin clean up after the last customers left. It had been a good night – busy, and the tills hadn't stopped ringing: music to my ears. I was pleased to note that the clientele at Vella's was changing as the place evolved. I'd managed to persuade Vincent to let me book live acts, even though they cost money, and it had paid dividends. The dance floor had been teeming with people, all of them having a good time. I loved it. The feel of the place, the buzz. The people, the smells and the noises. Vella's needed a face lift, that was for sure, and I was optimistic it might happen. It wasn't urgent, but every night I looked at it with a critical eye after the doors had closed and the lights came up. Devlin and the team wiped sides, picked up glasses and discarded pieces of clothing. You could see that it was shabby and run-down, but it still looked all right when the lights were low and the occupants were pissed.

I handed Devlin an envelope with an extra cut in – the man never stopped working; I'd be lost without him. Then I paid all the bar staff and put the amounts down neatly in the books. This month was the first one ever where there was only one set. No books for the Vella girls because they were no longer on the premises, or if they were, they were doing business that was theirs and theirs alone.

I was moving towards getting them out altogether and if I caught a girl once, she got a caution. Twice and she was out. They'd all been offered bar work – not a move Marshall was pleased about, but, as Vincent had pointed out to him in a slow voice as though dealing with someone very stupid, the girls in the club were well past pasture and could only pull in punters pissed out of their minds. The main girls, the young ones who could draw a wedge, were out in the houses, three that Marshall had left. Vincent put it to Marshall that taking the old dollies off the floor and putting them behind the bar was good business sense. And it was, but a few still attempted to have the best of both worlds, which I wouldn't stand for.

Before this, I'd never given much thought to what I might do with my life. I did what Rae told me and my main focus was survival. You got used to living in a constant state of fear. But the club game – well, I was good at it. I loved it and my head was thrumming with ideas. For the first time, I let myself dream little dreams.

Women all over the country were working now, many found they'd enjoyed it during the war and didn't want to go back to the kitchen. And who could blame them?

I was quickly pulled out of these thoughts by the arrival of Frankie, worse for wear and visibly upset.

Devlin rushed to him and I could see even from across the club that he had to hold my brother up.

'Frankie?' I called, rushing towards them.

To my absolute horror, his face crumpled, and for a terrible second I thought maybe he was about to cry. But he seemed to catch himself at the last second. I looked at Devlin, who shrugged, as bewildered as I was.

'What's happened, Frank? Is it Rae?'

He laughed at that, the sound echoing around the empty club. 'Isn't it always bloody Rae?'

I looked over his shoulder at the door, 'Where is he?'

'Still with Marshall, God knows where they've got to. I've had enough, Faith. Enough for tonight. Forever.'

'All right, mate, easy on the dramatics, eh?' I was grinning, trying to get him to smile too, but he wasn't having it. With a sigh, I said to Devlin, 'Let's get him upstairs.'

In the office, Vincent had been packing up, ready to leave for the night. When he saw Frankie, he stopped.

'Sorry, Vincent, family stuff,' I said.

Frankie laughed, 'Your family too, mate. As bad as my lot. Worse, even.'

I snapped, 'Frankie.' Then, to Vincent, 'I'm sorry, he's drunk.'

But Vincent waved a hand at me. 'If he's talking about my father, he's likely making a good point.' He smiled at Devlin, 'Leave us to it, old chap? Lock up on your way down.'

Devlin nodded, no doubt curious, but not the type to poke his nose in where it wasn't wanted.

After he left, I put the kettle on, pouring scalding water over coffee granules and putting the mug in front of Frankie. He studiously ignored it. I was hoping Vincent might just leave, but instead he shifted the coffee aside, poured Frankie a whisky and slid his cigars over, which Frankie gratefully accepted.

'Haven't you had enough?' I said to Frankie, side-eyeing Vincent.

Vincent shrugged. 'He looks like he's in shock. Thought it'd calm his nerves a little.'

Frankie nodded his agreement, sipped the drink, lit a cigar and told me, 'I don't think there is enough booze in the world to save me tonight, sis.'

Vincent sat down opposite my brother, his face the picture of sympathy, and said to him, 'Tell us what happened.'

The entire time Frankie spoke, slurring and jumbling his words, my heart sank. I flicked glances at Vincent, who sat listening to Frankie's tale of woe, nodding and murmuring agreement. Encouraging him to keep going.

Vincent disliked his father's womanising, which he himself seemed to be well above – something I respected about him. It seemed unusual to me for a man in his position to show any restraint. I knew he had a wife, though that wasn't a barrier, Marshall proved that, but even the most loyal men in our circles took the odd extra girl on. Vincent never tried it on with me, either, for which I was eternally grateful.

Frankie calmed down as he talked. I felt like kicking myself for not paying more attention to him. With Rae away, Frankie had still been roped into a lot of jobs for Marshall, but he'd sunk into the background of Vella's precarious firm. I'd thought he was safe. But since Rae came home, he was dragged back into the thick of it, along with Rae who was firmly front and centre again, working for a man Frankie didn't like any more than I did.

As Frankie's story unfolded and he reached the part about Roxy, my stomach flipped in revulsion. When I looked at Vincent, I noticed his jaw was clenched.

He asked Frankie, 'The girl?'

Frankie sighed, 'She'll live, but she's shit scared of Rae.'

I told Vincent, 'Roxy McCann was Rae's girlfriend, of sorts, before he got locked up.'

Frankie looked at his feet and I felt a wave of pity for him. He and Roxy had started talking a lot, especially of late. I suspected he was soft on her. Of all the girls to get a crush on . . .

Vincent asked Frankie, 'She works for my dad?'

Frankie nodded. 'Has done since she was fourteen.' He let that sink in and told us, 'Edith, her mother, pretty much shoved her out the door to earn for the family. Her dad is a useless wanker.'

It was a familiar story, but no less sad for being common. I thought of Shirley. Too young to have us, beaten – literally by men and metaphorically by life – and she'd never have considered selling her own children.

I was unusually speechless; angry at Rae who would

heap more shit on this girl's door, at Marshall who was a pig, at myself for not being able to do much about any of it.

'My father messes with my life, your brother seems to be messing with yours?' said Vincent.

Frankie nodded. He was steadier now, despite the whisky. His shoulders had dropped. I wondered how many nights there had been where he felt like this, with no one to talk to.

I was somewhere between a rock and hard place when it came to my brothers. I loved them both, and whilst I could now admit to myself that life was better without Rae in it, I wouldn't ever say it out loud.

I sighed and told Frankie and Vincent, 'It's Marshall's influence; he's never been good for Rae.'

I'm not sure I even believed the words as they spilled out of my mouth.

To my surprise, Vincent responded with a vehemence I'd never heard from him. 'He has a habit of injecting poison into everything he touches. I have no trouble believing it is he who is leading Rae astray.' Then to Frankie, 'And you are doing work you'd rather not?'

Frankie shrugged, 'I collect money from pimps, but yeah, I'd prefer to avoid that aspect of business.'

My heart went out to him. All I saw when I looked at him was the little boy who'd wake me in the night, begging me to check Shirley was still breathing.

It was a long, hard slog to adulthood in the Diamond house. Who could blame Frankie for forming an aversion to the skin trade? Yet here he was.

Vincent poured drinks for us both while Frankie drifted off on the settee.

'I'm sorry,' he said. 'For my father.'

'He's not your fault any more than Rae is ours.'

Though I'm not sure I fully believed it.

Rae was protecting me when Cal Doyle came and took him away. That awful night that changed the course of all our lives, especially Rae's. Borstal hadn't done anything to rehabilitate my brother. What he'd needed was help. Being locked up with other damaged boys had only fuelled his dark side. In a murky world where battles were won by brute force, Rae was nothing other than King. He came out of there harder, more brittle, no longer a child. And Marshall had been waiting, ready to harness Rae's demons to his own ends.

As if reading my mind, Vincent said, 'Your brother never really stood a chance.'

'Rae?'

He nodded, 'When my father takes a shine to someone, they're pretty much doomed.'

I thought about Shirley and knew that was true. Though I wasn't sure Marshall had taken a shine to her so much as stumbled upon a very convenient situation.

Then I thought about Rae's fixation with Roxy and the thought that like attracted like crossed my mind. I pushed it away, took a sip of the drink in front of me, feeling the warmth spread down my throat. I could see the appeal. Could easily understand the choice someone might make to give themselves up to it. Alcohol, drugs, gambling.

Not me, though. Never me. My most terrifying childhood memories weren't the thumps from people, or the
police knocking on the door, but Shirley, drunk, her
face so blank it was like she'd vacated her body. My
mum, but not. Once she had a drink in her, she was as
good as gone.

She barely remembered those times, but I could never
forget them. Nor could Frankie or Rae, though certainly
Rae was happy enough to follow in her footsteps. I was
almost one hundred per cent certain that most of the
crap he got up to was done whilst he was half-cut. I'd
vowed not to go there. Not to be her. But I understood
the temptation. The easier path.

I put the drink down, still mostly full, and pushed it
away.

'You've done well here. Exceeded all my expectations,' Vincent said.

I smiled, then, 'I'm glad for the opportunity.'

'I know that. I took a risk on you.' He nodded to
himself, 'It angered my father, too, and I won't patronise
you by pretending that wasn't a bonus.'

I laughed. He didn't often talk about anything beyond
business. He was a private man and tended to duck
in and out of the club, less and less as I became more
trusted. He oversaw all of Marshall's properties as well,
but Vincent's real interest was cars. He had started to
piece together a showroom, which Marshall thought was
stupid, but Vincent knew his stuff. He himself collected
them. Expensive ones, too.

He said, 'It's hard being the strong one.'

'Is that your role in your family?'

He nodded, 'My mother is an amazing woman, but . . .' He shrugged. 'She's been humiliated by him for many years.' He was talking, among other things, about Marshall's long-term affair with Shirley.

I told him, 'My mother never had a choice, you know.'

Vincent said, 'No one ever does where my father is concerned. And that becomes very tiring, doesn't it?'

Chapter Twenty-One

December 1963

The White Hart, Acton

The more Jimmy learned about Geraldine Ross, the sicker his heart felt. Her life had been brutal. She'd spent it lurching from one calamity to the next, whilst children sprang up, unwanted. An occupational hazard, along with the diseases that riddled her body. She'd never have made old bones, but she should have had more time. The baby inside her should at least have had a chance, no matter how flimsy that chance would have been.

All roads led back to Marshall, and Jimmy felt his anger rise with every new discovery. The Vella brothers had run a successful, albeit dangerous, vice ring. Marshall had carried on in their absence with the same level of terrible brutality, but earned less and less with each passing year. Though the big man flashed cash around like it was going out of fashion, the books told a different story. It was Vincent and Faith who had saved Vella's nightclub from extinction, and as far as Jimmy could ascertain, they had little to nothing to do with the prostitution side of the business anymore.

Jimmy had been out speaking to women who knew

Geraldine, who loved her and mourned her. He'd travelled out of London to visit her tearful sister. The woman who was raising her daughter. Jean told Jimmy that Geraldine never stood a chance. Their father had been a cruel man and their mother just the same. Jimmy didn't question it – believed fully that in order to do the kind of work Geraldine did, something had gone very wrong somewhere along the line. Jean was married and credited her husband with saving her from a similar fate. She told Jimmy through her tears that she'd tried with Geraldine. Tried to give her and her daughter a home, a chance.

She'd shrugged, 'She drank, brought home different men every night. What could I do?'

And he agreed that she could have done very little. By the time Geraldine ended up in London, she was beyond help.

But she still didn't deserve to end up in a dump, cut in two, with a bellyful of arms and legs.

He'd sat on the train back into town, staring blankly out of the window. The sprawling English countryside, beautiful, but no less dangerous than London when you didn't have anyone to keep you safe. Jimmy hated the refrain 'money can't buy you happiness' – poverty almost certainly guaranteed you misery.

He was lucky, he knew that. James Rose had provided for Jimmy and his mother, leaving a pension behind him in death. Lilly had been good with money, too. Jimmy was by no means rich, but for a man orphaned young, he'd never wanted for anything, and now with a decent salary, the worries of many had never been his.

He had felt nothing but contempt for the Diamonds. Even Faith, since she'd gone to work for Vincent . . . he'd managed to go so far as to feel disdain for the pretty girl he'd thought too often about only a few years ago.

But now he was delving a little more deeply into the club's recent activities, poking around, trying to see if Vella could be tied to Geraldine or Liza via his club. What he had discovered was that Faith was trying to build something new. Something separate from Marshall and all the awful pies his fat fingers were in. Something real.

And he felt almost sorry for Frankie, plodding along in Rae's shadow. Jimmy heard about what Marshall did to Roxy McCann – burning her like a human ashtray – and knew that Frankie had tried – failed – to stick up for the poor girl. He was stuck in one big, sick situation, with Marshall at the helm and Rae Diamond not far behind.

Jimmy met Cal in The White Hart, knowing his boss was concerned about him. He ranted about Marshall and Geraldine, and Cal gently pointed out that the two may not even be linked. Jimmy nodded, but he still burned with hatred for Marshall. That woman had given birth to his son, no one knew where the poor kid was now, and his eyes hadn't even flickered at news of her death.

The fat fucker.

He said to Cal, 'Liza Plum was one of his.'

'The Dukes Meadows girl?'

Jimmy nodded.

Cal sighed, 'Half the girls around here are on his

payroll, or have been, and most of them aren't headed anywhere good, Jimmy.'

That may be so. But it didn't mean it was right.

Jimmy kept his opinions to himself. Filing away the information for now.

Chapter Twenty-Two

Roxy McCann's home

Roxy McCann's place was awful. The stench hit me first. Rotten and mouldy – a combination of damp nappies and stale body odour emanating from too many people. It was comprised of two tiny rooms in a bigger block, which, I discovered, housed Roxy's mother Edith, and Roxy's two siblings: a girl in her early teens and a baby boy still in nappies. I wrinkled my nose as I went through the door, trying not to gag, but it was vile.

There were blocks like this all over London. Buildings made of sad little rooms filled with as many bodies as could squeeze in. Unbelievable that there were four people living here, five if you counted Roxy's dad, who seemingly came and went whenever he fancied.

I stared at Roxy's mother and wondered at the mess people made of their bloody lives. She must have been pushing forty, obviously didn't have a pot to piss in or a bloke to rely on and still she'd gone and added another kid into the mix. It was nothing short of madness.

I knew that Roxy was one of Marshall's top earners and as such she'd have been pulling in an enormous amount of money for him, yet here she was living like an animal. Despite the grottiness of it all, I could see that someone here had done their best to keep the place clean and tidy, but no amount of scrubbing and bleaching could improve this situation. Honestly, all that building was good for was demolition.

Edith, a thin, pinched woman with a long nose and a heavy frown, watched me through wary eyes with the baby on her hip. Looking at her, I wondered where Roxy had got her good looks from, and the others for that matter. The baby was a bonny child with Roxy's wide-set eyes and a quick smile, but I couldn't help but feel sorry for the poor little bugger, growing up the same way I had.

Shirley, Rae and Frankie had lived in one room before I arrived. The house on Sunningdale Avenue was rented to them by the council after I came along. I had started to make sure the place was slowly getting done up. Things were all right for us now, but they hadn't always been. Shirley must have felt the desperation, starting out in a tiny space like this with two small children.

The baby cooed at me, stretching out a hand and catching my hair. I had very little interest in them as a rule – children. I'd watched the women around me dragged down by years of child-rearing and the men they ended up tied to for life. No thanks. But I could see how they were appealing to some. He was a cute little thing.

I smiled at Edith. 'I'm Faith.'

The woman nodded. 'We all know who you are.'

Adding, 'I knew your mum.' Her tone was sharp, laced with disgust. Looking down at others from the gutter.

'I'm here to see Roxy.'

Edith sighed, 'She's down at the shop.'

I kept smiling, walked over to the kitchen table and said, 'I'll wait.'

There was a teenager sitting there already. A girl on that teetering cusp between child and adult. She looked at me open-mouthed and said, 'You're like a film star.'

I laughed, 'Thanks. Beverly, right?'

She nodded, blushing, 'Bev.'

'Your brother?'

The baby was walking towards us on wobbly legs. Beverly reached down, snatching him up and presenting him proudly, 'Tyler.'

Edith stood, scowling, arms folded.

I was relieved when the door opened and in came Roxy.

I watched a look pass over Roxy's face that could only be fear. She was carrying a paper bag which slipped slightly. She made a grab for it, but I got there first, taking it and putting it on the table in front of Beverly.

Roxy looked close to tears. 'It's about Rae, isn't it.' She wiped a hand over her pale face. 'I didn't mean to cause any trouble, I'm sorry, honestly . . .'

Edith snorted, 'Trouble's your middle name, my girl, and now we'll all go without.'

I frowned, 'What's that mean?'

Edith patted her hair. 'She lost her job.'

'And you ain't got one?' Knowing the answer, under-standing that Roxy not being able to earn affected the whole family.

Edith didn't say anything, heading towards the table, pulling out a pack of cigarettes, lighting one and brush-ing off the little child as he reached up for her.

'Well?' I demanded, and Edith at least had the decency to look away. 'Come on, Roxy, let's go for a walk.'

Beverly was also looking scared now, picking up on Roxy's demeanour.

I put a hand on the girl's shoulder and winked, 'Everything's all right, love. I'll have her back in an hour, OK?'

Beverly looked from me to Roxy, who nodded.

We walked out of the stuffy rooms and down onto the street. I said, 'Families, eh?'

And Roxy allowed the ghost of a smile. She was a small woman. Petite like Shirley, I had a good few inches on her, but anyone could see the steeliness run-ning through her. Young though she was, you didn't last a day in Roxy's life without being tough.

I said, 'We'll nip to The White Hart, eh?'

Roxy agreed, though she looked petrified and would probably have agreed with me even if I'd suggested a night walking over hot coals.

Once we were in the pub, I ordered two rum and Cokes and took Roxy to a quiet table in the corner.

Pretty much everyone in there knew me – a lot of wary glances were exchanged. I got a lot of 'Hi's and grins and bluster. The blessing and the curse of a Diamond. Find yourself related to one terrifying maniac and they tar you with the same brush.

There were new rumours about me spreading through town. That I was getting a little bit too big for my own boots. That I must be sleeping with Vincent – why else would he have a woman pretty much running the place alongside him? I ignored them. No fucker was crazy enough to say it to my face, but the Vella girls liked me, liked my mum, and gossip always got back to me. I made a mental note of who said what and left it there. For now.

Sometimes having a reputation could be useful and certainly it was better than the way we were treated as children. 'The whore's kids' was commonly slung at us and those words still echoed around my mind. You could understand why Rae had spent his life kicking and punching. Defending himself, and often us, to anyone who dared step out of line. Not that it made it right, and it wasn't how I was. Wasn't how I wanted to be, which is what had bought me to Roxy's door in the first place.

Roxy sipped her drink. I lit a fag, passing her the box. She took one with a shaky hand.

I said, 'I came to apologise.'

And she frowned so hard it was almost comical.

I added, 'Frankie told me what happened. Marshall . . . you know, burning you.' Just saying it made me wince.

Her face softened for a moment, 'He's a nice guy.'

'Frankie?'

She nodded and I smiled.

'He is, yeah.'

Her matching smile dropped as she told me, 'I was out of order, though. All Rae wanted was for me to sit and have a drink with him.'

I didn't smile this time when I said, 'You and I both know that's not all he wanted.'

Tears filled her eyes.

I said, 'You were living with him, when he went down.'

She shut her eyes and took a few deep puffs on the cigarette. When she stubbed it out and looked at me again, her eyes were clear and met mine levelly.

She said, 'Can I speak plainly?'

'Please do.'

'Everyone's talking about you of late.'

I grinned, 'Oh really?'

She nodded, not smiling back, 'Edith and her cronies, saying you act like a man and have too high an opinion of yourself.'

I laughed at that: proper belly-laughed. I knew what people were saying. That I did what I wanted, slept around, which was a bit of an exaggeration – but I did do what I liked with whomever I liked, it was true.

I asked her, 'What do you think?'

Roxy shrugged, 'You're well dressed, beautiful, seem to be making cash without lying on your back. But you work for Marshall and you're Rae's sister.'

I nodded, 'Two black marks against me.'

'Fuck, you can't choose 'em can you – family? Who the hell would have picked Edith?'

I laughed again and this time Roxy joined in. The

pair of us laughed so hard, tears streamed down my face. Half the pub was looking whilst pretending not to, but I didn't care. It wasn't often that I let go and relaxed like I did then, and in that moment, a bond was forged between us.

When we stopped laughing, there was a momentary lull in conversation.

I said, 'I'm sorry, though, for my brother.'

'I don't mean to be rude,' she said, 'but you've nothing to apologise for, I don't even know you and you've done me no harm. But you've come knocking at my door, now I'm here. I'm already shit-scared since Marshall's sacked me and who knows if that'll be the end of it. Your brother, no disrespect meant, terrifies me, for reasons I won't bore you with, and I've got no idea what you want from me, but I've fuck all to give you.' The little girl with the face of an angel and the steely grey eyes. She sounded tired, she sounded battered. She also sounded like someone who'd had her fair share of shit and was close to having had enough of it for one lifetime.

I could relate. I'd gone looking for her to apologise, perhaps even to bung her some cash. Dirty money, blood money. Something to assuage my misplaced guilt because I always felt at least a little responsible for Rae. I'd expected her to suck up, grab the money and to be relieved to be rid of her. Frankie said she was decent, but Frankie was a sucker. I had expected a strung-out mess, like most of Vella's girls, including a whole lot I'd had to chase out the club. I could see how they'd got there, could understand it even, and certainly I empathised, but they were done. Washed up. Useless to everyone, even themselves.

Roxy wasn't like that, though. She hardly even touched the free drink and she spoke to me quite plainly. In a way most people wouldn't have dared to. She had a quiet dignity that I warmed to.

As I asked her about her mum and how Roxy had ended up with Vella, she relayed the terrible tale in an even tone and I liked her even more. She wasn't a moaner.

Life had served her poorly, but when I asked what she'd do next, all she said was, 'Whatever I need to do to keep Beverly and Tyler fed.'

So I offered her a job.

Chapter Twenty-Three

Christmas Day 1963

Sunningdale Avenue

It was midday and Rae was absolutely wankered. Not just content with being pissed as a fart, he headed off into the loo every half-hour to shove lines up his nose. Over the past few months since he'd been home, he had become an absolute wreck. A new cocaine habit hadn't improved matters. Rae's downward spiral, coupled with Marshall's increasing instability, meant trouble was definitely afoot. Anything that man touched turned to shit.

Me and Vincent had just about saved Vella's from an obvious death, though how it had managed to get into such a state remained a mystery to me. I mean, how fucking hard was it to peddle tits and booze?

Most of Marshall's girls had run away up west to the Soho and East End gangs who were taking over everything. Which was fine by me. I wanted fuck all to do with the skulduggery. But it pretty much made Marshall obsolete and everyone could see it, except perhaps my idiot brother. Marshall's golden boy, who sat at Shirley's kitchen table that Christmas morning, ignoring the food we'd spent all morning putting together and making digs at all of us in turn. Even me, which was unusual for him.

He had the hump about Roxy, which I'd seen coming, of course. But I wasn't sorry about it, either. Devlin told me she was doing a terrific job behind the bar and the punters loved her. She looked the bomb and she could turn her hand to anything that was asked of her. Besides that, I liked her, and it was nice having another woman about the place. I'd slipped a few extra notes in her Christmas pay packet, to which Roxy had looked almost tearful. Whilst I found emotion like that a bit awkward, it made me pleased that I'd nagged Vincent to do it.

Rae was going on at Frankie, laughing at him for turning down Rita Antan's advances at Vella's the night before. The whole debacle had been a shambles. Whilst I had to accept Rae and Marshall setting up camp at Vella's whenever they pleased, it didn't mean I had to like it. When they arrived, the whole atmosphere changed, and every stride forward I felt Vincent and I had made seemed to fall away.

Frankie muttered that maybe he didn't have to pay for things like that, and the table fell deathly quiet.

Shirley stood, reaching for Rae's glass with a too-big, too-bright grin, 'I'll get you another beer, son?'

He said, 'I'm all right, thanks.'

Shirley laughed — a thin, humourless sound. 'Don't be daft, it's Christmas.' And I recognised her technique. I had seen my mother do the same thing many times before, most often with Marshall. Feed them enough booze and they'll eventually pass out. But Rae was no-where near that yet. The coke would keep him awake and at it for hours – days, even. As far as I could see, he was just getting started.

Rae's eyes were still on Frankie, who was hunched over his plate. The same way he'd sat at every meal with Rae since they were little kids. 'What did you say, Frank?'

And Frankie sprang up, then. I was so startled, I actually jumped, sliding my seat backwards. But Rae was up too, staring him in the face.

Frankie didn't waver. Didn't look away. Didn't sit. His voice was firm and clear, 'I said, I don't have to pay for it, mate.'

Rae's face was red. 'Neither do I. *Mate*.' The last word was laced with menace, but Frankie wasn't back-ing down.

I stood, calmly putting a hand on Rae's arm. 'Come on, Rae.'

He shook it off and my stomach lurched in the way only Rae could make it do.

'Think you're better than me, Frankie?'

Frankie shrugged, a grin on his face.

Rae swung then, as I'd known he would, and I watched the scene as if in slow motion. The beer glass Shirley had just been holding clattered to the floor, smashing into pieces, sparkling dangerously in the light. I had the fleeting thought that I ought to sweep them up and wrap them in paper. Put them in the bin.

Frankie stepped back as Rae lurched forwards, off

his head. He hadn't aimed a punch that landed and so his whole body swirled forwards in a pirouette that was almost comical. He staggered from the recoil unsteadily, little glittering pieces of glass sticking to his feet.

Frankie spat, 'You're pathetic.' And left the room.

Shirley looked at Rae, her face pale. She went to speak but stopped herself, and instead went after Frankie.

Rae sank back into his seat, red-faced. His head dropped into his hands.

I knelt in front of him, feeling a sharp prickle on my knees and moving onto the balls of my feet, placing my hands on his arms. 'Rae.'

His head snapped up quickly, looking left to right, then finding me. His expression was blank, looking at the spot Frankie just vacated.

'Rae.'

His unfocused eyes met mine and gradually came back to life. Ignited by a fiery anger that made his lip curl and his forehead crumple into a frown. 'He's my fucking brother.'

I nodded, 'He's worried about you, Rae. We all are.'

'Worried about me? Fucking worried about *me*?' Spit flew from his mouth. His eyes blazed. Good-looking Rae Diamond – a beautiful monster when his temper got the better of him; all too often in those days, and getting worse. 'That cheeky little cunt wouldn't be anything without me, none of you would. All she's good for is spreading her fucking legs. And you two wouldn't have made teenage years without me. I saved you from him. I gave Frankie something to do, a fucking name to build on.'

'Rae.' He was standing now. The rant livening him up, the same thing driving him that had for far too long. The real issue underlying all his rage. *Victim*. The world was against him. It wasn't fair. The same shit he'd been going on about half his life. The same shit that got him into trouble over and over.

'Come on, sit down, let's talk.'

'Talk? Why am I fucking talking to you? You're a fucking traitor, too. You . . .'

There were tears in his eyes, which gave me pause. Made me feel that familiar agony of guilt. I'd done nothing wrong. I knew it logically. The way he and Marshall had treated Roxy was abominable. And yet . . . he'd saved me, hadn't he, protected me. And I loved him. But how much could you let someone get away with?

'If you mean Roxy, I gave her a job, that's all.'

Rae shook his head, 'Disrespecting me. You, her, Frank. Everyone's fucking laughing at me . . .' And he went on and on, gearing himself up, working his whole being into a mess, like a tightly coiled spring. I could feel the awful energy coming off of him in waves and then he was running out the room, taking the small flight of stairs in two steps, half dragging Frankie back down them, with Shirley in hot pursuit.

He was screaming at his brother, yelling in his face, 'Outside, Frankie, see who wins this one, eh.'

And for the first time ever, out on the doorstep of Sunningdale Avenue, Frankie got the first punch in, then the second. Then Rae was kicking, hitting, fuelled by a virulent fury. Much bigger than his inebriation. Cutting through the drink and the drugs. Focused solely on causing pain.

They went at it until both were worn out, gasping. Frankie not letting up, lashing back, giving as good as he got. It was only seconds, minutes at most, but it seemed to go on forever, each thump breaking my heart.

My brothers were left standing staring at each other whilst I stood by and watched. Chilled inside.

There was blood streaming from Rae's nose. Frankie's clothes were torn and there were red marks that would later blossom into angry bruises on his face.

The curtains twitched as the neighbours looked out. Just like old times. The Diamonds giving everyone something to talk about.

I felt a peculiar urge to laugh, then. But it soon went away as I watched Rae run off down the street, still shouting, kicking at things as he passed them. Bins, a bike.

A madman on a rampage.

I glared at Mrs Malone and she quickly dropped the nets and poked her beak back inside. Then I took Shirley in my arms, her poor little body shaking with silent sobs, and I thought to myself, yet another merry bloody Christmas.

With Rae gone, it felt like the house itself breathed a sigh of relief. I hated to think it, but he was the cause of so many of our problems. *But, also,* a nagging voice reminded me, *he was the reason some of our problems weren't worse*. The day Rae stabbed Bass, he'd saved me from a fate that may have been worse than death. Shirley had been at her absolute rock bottom, almost at the point of giving up. Rae's terrible actions woke Mum up to what was happening, they saved me from a predator of the worst kind, and they paved the path for all of our futures. Frankie may have resented Rae – and I didn't blame him – but Rae had propelled us from abject poverty to better times.

At a price, of course.

Everything came at a price.

Rae had always had a dark streak – one Frankie didn't share. But he *was* tough, Frankie. We all were. Some of my earliest memories were of fighting other kids, ones who talked about Shirley, or made fun of our ill-fitting clothes. But where me and Frankie had entered survival mode, Rae relished the violence. Eventually the teasing had stopped because everyone was too shit scared of Rae to bother.

After Bass, and once Rae was in with Marshall, our family became untouchable. Even though every fucker still had an opinion, they at least kept them to themselves. Because if they didn't, Rae came knocking, armed with his bag of tricks and a terrible smile on his handsome face.

Me and Mum cleaned Frankie up. I watched my mother wince as she put TCP on patches of raw skin where Rae's boot had made devastating contact. So many times over the years we had done this for one boy or another. But this was the first time the wounds had arrived at each other's hands.

I felt a stab of fear that day at what was to come. I knew Rae couldn't go on how he was, even if he was the last to realise it.

Sometime later, the doorbell rang and I was surprised to find Devlin grinning, holding out a bottle of dark rum. One look at my face and the smile dropped.

'What happened?' His accent was musical with uplifts and lilts I had always found comforting. A gentle, kind man.

I sighed, 'Rae, mate. Same old, same old. Come in though, Mum'll be glad to see you.' Then added, 'Careful where you step, mind.' And finally went and got the dustpan and brush. Collecting up as many of the glittering shards as I could.

I carried on putting together our dishevelled downstairs, eventually sending Frankie to bed before he passed out. He was acting like he was unscathed, but every time he moved, he winced. I settled him down with a glass of whisky next to the bed and told him to shout if he needed anything.

When I came back downstairs, Shirley was sat at the kitchen table, smoking and chatting with Dev. It was an unusually happy little scene, not at all in keeping with the rest of the day, and the juxtaposition jarred my mind. I felt the walls of Sunningdale Avenue closing in on me; the ghosts of yesteryear pushing at my mind. Eventually, I made my excuses and nipped out, over to Roxy's for a few hours. Just to catch my breath.

I enjoyed the time I spent with my new friend and the girl's younger siblings, even if Edith evil-eyed me the whole time. Not much the old bitch could say, really.

By the time I got back in, though, my heart sank to see Rae passed out on the settee. Creeping upstairs, I found Shirley moving around in the bathroom. I checked my wristwatch: two in the morning.

'Mum?' She was tending to her own scrapes and bruises. I gasped when I saw the state of her, 'What the fuck . . . not Rae?'

Shirley shook her head, nodding to her bedroom.

I went in to be greeted by the sickening sight of Marshall, naked and snoring like an overstuffed pig.

I asked Shirley, 'What happened?'

'He got here just as Dev was leaving, started going on, Faith.' She pressed a cold, wet flannel to her face and winced. 'I told him Dev was a mate, just popped in to say Happy Christmas.' I took the flannel, sat my mum on the toilet seat, and held it there for her. 'Should have heard the things he said to him.'

I could well imagine. Marshall made no secret of his dislike for 'coloureds'.

'Shit, is Dev all right?'

Shirley nodded. 'Silly sod wanted to stay. I managed to get him to leave, said I'd be fine.' She wiped away a stray tear.

I asked, 'Frankie?'

'Still dead to the world, I gave him a sleeping tablet. Thought the poor sod could do with a rest. Rae came in with Marshall, but he was well gone. Doubt he'll remember much of this tomorrow.'

'Lucky him, then,' I said and felt a wave of bitterness that Rae might be able to forget this awful day that would be burned into my mind forever.

'Jesus, Faith, it's been so long, he's left me alone. I dared to hope that was the end of it. That my time and my body might be my own for the first time ever.'

She cried then. The sound was so heart-breaking and so wretched, it caused me physical pain. And behind that pain was a growing rage that I vowed to put to good use.

Chapter Twenty-Four

February 1964

Lavender Hill Police Station

It was the start of February and Jimmy wondered if he would ever see daylight again. Even in the afternoons, it was dark. Street lights came on by four-thirty. The sun didn't rise until after seven and his head was fizzing with the dismal grey that had descended on the city for months. Coupled with the dismal arrival of another dead woman.

He was standing outside Lavender Hill Police Station speaking to Alfie Kenzie, a reporter for the *Acton Evening News*. Alfie was pushing him on yesterday's news, a case that Jimmy wasn't involved with, really. Or likely shouldn't have been, but, when he'd heard it radioed in, he hadn't been able to keep away. Another Geraldine, another Liza.

She had a pair of her own knickers, semen-stained and torn, stuffed into her mouth for good measure. Nude, like the two before her. Bare and exposed. The disrespect was what got him. The utter contempt for human life.

Jimmy told Alfie they'd found a woman, naked on the shore of the Thames.

Alfie sighed, but didn't look shocked. His patch was Acton, Shepherd's Bush, Hammersmith. Violence was an everyday occurrence and he wasn't surprised at a dead body showing up.

He said to Jimmy, 'Prostitute?'

Jimmy nodded, 'Theresa Bell,' adding other words in his mind: mother, daughter, friend. He would not – could not – boil these women down to just their awful jobs. He refused. He knew they were treated differently. Viewed as less than, a scourge on society. Figures to be looked down upon, at best to be pitied. He understood that, he supposed. The pity. He'd spent the past twenty-four hours with the team here trying to comb over Theresa Bell's life and it was a bleak, sorry and well-told story. They were ten a penny around here, these desperate, sad women. They came to London too young, too poor, too unloved for anything else.

This wasn't his case. Wasn't strictly his bit of town. He was assisting here, that was all, and he thought that he'd need to tell Cal later. He knew really that he should have done it first, but he hadn't wanted to be instructed to keep his nose out.

He lit a cigarette and said to Alfie, 'She had four children.'

Alfie nodded, 'Sold one, as I recall. *The Times* ran the story.'

'Yes. For £20.'

The story had had a blaring headline and she'd been vilified over it, of course. Plenty of people did it, though. What was an unmarried woman with no real income to do with a child, for god's sake? But she'd made the mistake of taking out an ad after changes to Children Regulations had already been passed to put a stop to private arrangements like that, which, before then, were common and rife.

Three boys, she'd given away. Three sons, one after the other. She had a little girl, whom she'd kept. A child now without a mother. Left only with the father who, it seemed, had been poncing off Theresa for years. He was listed on two of the boys' birth certificates as well as the girl's. The first child had been delivered before she arrived in the city. Who knew where the poor little bugger had ended up by now?

Jimmy said to Alfie, 'A terrible, difficult life with a wretched end.'

Alfie agreed. He'd put a small piece in tomorrow's paper. Dead prostitute was hardly big news around these parts.

Chapter Twenty-Five

He finds it surreal reading about her in the Acton Evening News. *He had hoped she might wash away. Foolish in retrospect. The Thames was not the sea, after all. Its murky English waters were fine for concealing for a short time, but never entirely removed things. He knows that from years of watching rubbish floating along its surface. He'd seen an entire pram go by once.*

Anyway.

She'd been found bobbing about by the landing stage of the Corinthian Sailing Club. Not far from where he'd left her at all. It had been easy again; he suspects this is the sort of thing that once done before becomes embedded somewhere in the soul. Now the entire act feels familiar, comforting.

Right.

Each time the same, but different. He knew this one. Not very well, but more than he had the others. He'd thought it might make it harder, or maybe even easier. Different, at least. But, actually, it wasn't. It was the same.

They were all the same.

He knows that others too would be glad to see the back

of her. They'd never credit him, of course. Nor would he wish for it.

He's lost in these thoughts when the door opens, almost making him jump out of his skin.

Work, work, more work.

The new girl, whose name he can't remember, comes in and puts a coffee down on his desk. He'd forgotten he'd asked for one and now he resents her presence.

She smiles at him, and he forces himself to grin back. She's here to do some odd jobs, that's all, but she's definitely after a bit more. She's all eyes and smooth hands that flow over his shoulders and down his arms like silk.

She nods at the paper, 'Oh, I read about that earlier.' She shudders dramatically, 'It's awful, isn't it.'

He nods in agreement, 'It is, yes.' And he feels a sort of splitting.

He is the man who did this.

Punched that wretched little woman repeatedly in the jaw and stuffed her mouth with her own filth.

And he is also here smiling at this little number and expressing shared horror.

Horror.

He makes his face look sad, and she nods with him, that hand reaching out. Any excuse to touch him.

She only sees pound signs, of course. He feels a faint waft of anger, then it's gone.

Best to send her away now. He waves her hand off him and goes back to the paper. Letting her know she is dismissed.

★

Girl in the Thames is identified.

Scotland Yard fingerprint experts today identified the girl as Theresa Bell. She came from Northumberland, lived in a South London flat and was a frequent visitor to the West End.

David Hench almost choked on his beer.

Shit.

Fucking hell.

Then he was running along to Agnes down the hall, asking her to watch the little one 'cause he needed to make a telephone call, or, better yet, get down to the station.

Jesus wept.

He'd wondered where the fuck Theresa had got to.

Chapter Twenty-Six

Notting Hill Police Station

David Hench was Theresa Bell's partner. Jimmy took an instant dislike to the man, so strong it was almost physical. He had persuaded the officer in charge to let him sit in on the man's interview, telling him that he was interested in the case. Jimmy was a senior officer, plain clothes, a member of the Flying Squad and, more than that, his reputation as Cal Doyle's next in line made him well known around town. Other officers respected him, came to him for advice on things. There was no way they'd refuse him a seat at the table, even if they didn't quite understand his interest.

David Hench was a small man in every way. From his short stature, his skinny body and his beady, screwed-up little eyes. The first thing he did was complain about being left with a child, adding that when Theresa had last walked out the door, her parting words to her daughter had been, 'How would you like a new mother?'

This might have sounded shocking, but Theresa and Hench had been arguing about a woman he'd been seen out and about with. 'A nice lass,' as David put it, the implication being that Theresa wasn't. Jimmy resisted the urge to point out that a *nice lass* may have struggled to keep him, as Theresa seemed to have done for years.

The officer ascertained that David and Theresa had been 'together' for a long time. David claimed, laughably and somewhat piously, that Theresa worked as a waitress.

Jimmy slid himself forward across the table and smiled at David.

David, who was neither a bright nor an intuitive man, grinned back as though they were sharing some kind of joke.

'The boys were yours, were they, Dave?'

He frowned, 'Well, it's my name on the certificate.'

Jimmy nodded, his face serious, sympathetic even.

David added, 'But I suspected they weren't.'

'Why's that then?'

He sniffed, shrugged, 'Woman like Theresa, could have been anyone's.'

'Like Theresa?'

He nodded, 'You know, you know.'

Jimmy looked confused, 'Know what, Dave?'

'She was . . . you know, did things for money.'

'What kind of things?'

'With men.'

'A prostitute, Dave?'

He nodded, serious-looking, wide-eyed.

Jimmy smiled again, 'Not a waitress then, Dave?'

His face changed expression as the trap laid by his own words dawned on him. He spluttered a bit, 'Well.' He opened his mouth, shut it. Then said in a whiny voice, 'She just left me with the kid.' As though that was the bloody point.

Jimmy leaned further forward, kept smiling, and finally David was reacting to it appropriately. Looking at the big detective with the baby face, he saw that there was something else there too. Steel, determination, disgust.

David looked away. A weak man of poor character, he knew what he was but liked to live in the delusion that others didn't. The way Jimmy Rose was looking at him now shattered any illusion he might have had about that.

Jimmy said, 'You, Dave, are a ponce. Lower in my estimation than the woman you've lived off.'

'Now, hang on, I've just lost my girlfriend, mother of my children.'

'And you seem truly heartbroken.'

David didn't say anything. Eyes firmly on the table.

The other officer remained silent, fascinated, watching Jimmy Rose work. He was a young man still, moving up through the ranks at a rapid pace, and his reputation was already legendary. He'd brought down Rae Diamond, albeit briefly. That story had run on front pages for weeks. Better than that, he was well respected. He helped Cal Doyle to train the night-duty officers and never expected those of a lower rank to do all the grunt work. The senior officer on this case had been disgruntled at Jimmy's intrusion but had allowed him in to question Hench because he was known and liked and, who knew, perhaps he might help.

Watching him in action, the young PC could see where his reputation stemmed from. Not that they were dealing with Einstein, of course. But still. David Hench had gone from playing the innocent to laying bare the truth of his relationship with Theresa for all to see.

Jimmy picked up a pen. 'Names, Dave, of anyone we might need to speak to.'

He reeled them off and Jimmy took it all down. Putting Theresa's pimp – Marshall Vella – at the top of the list and underlining it twice.

When they had finished, he smiled at the little man and said, 'Now, me and PC Jacobs will drive you home and nip in and have a look around, eh?'

The little man looked so forlorn that PC Jacobs almost felt sorry for him. He deserved it, though. Ponces were the pits. Like lazy pimps, and pimps were bad enough.

As they accompanied David to Jimmy's car, PC Jacobs found himself suppressing a giggle at Dave's sorry hang-dog state.

Jimmy, for his part, kept up a stream of cheerful conversation, carrying a strong threat of menace underneath.

Jimmy walked into Vella's. The place still looked pretty shabby in the daytime, though it was his understanding that it did a roaring trade at night. These days, the once-brothel was, for all intents and purposes, a legitimate nightclub, complete with performers, trendy clientele and, most importantly, a late licence.

He was not overly hopeful that Marshall would be there. Word had it that the man did even less work than ever since his son had arrived, and also it was still early evening – basically first thing in the morning for someone like Marshall, who everybody knew kept night-time hours only.

Roxy McCann was behind the bar cleaning glasses, and when she saw Jimmy, her eyes widened. She raced into a back room and came back with Devlin Rowan, who nodded at Jimmy.

'Can I help?'

'Looking for Marshall.'

Devlin shook his head, 'Ain't here, man.'

'Vincent then.'

Devlin's eyes narrowed, but he said, 'Wait here.'

Jimmy sat at the bar, grinned at Roxy and said, 'New job, Rox?'

He'd had the misfortune of having to pick her up once or twice. Always felt sorry for the kid.

'What do you care?'

'Just being polite, love.'

Then Vincent was there, and Roxy's face dropped the scowl. 'Hello, Vince, can I get you anything?' she asked brightly.

Vince, eh.

The man – who looked nothing like his father – smiled widely, 'I'll have a tea.' Then he turned to Jimmy and said, 'Detective?'

Jimmy was surprised to be asked but told Roxy, 'Coffee for me, two sugars, don't spit in it, eh.'

Vincent wrinkled his nose. 'I'm sure my terribly efficient bar girl wouldn't dream of doing anything of the sort.' He nodded to her and Devlin, who was back behind the bar, then gestured to Jimmy to follow him.

He picked a booth in the corner of the club, far from Roxy and Devlin.

Vincent said, 'What can I do for you, Detective?'

'I was looking for your old man.'

'Ah well. I can't help you there. No one's seen him for days.'

'Doesn't he work here?'

Vincent shrugged, 'Not really, which is much better for Faith and I.'

'Is she here?' Jimmy tried to sound disinterested, but he had wondered on his way over whether their paths might cross today. Though why he cared, or even *if* he cared, was a bit of a mystery, and one he didn't want to prod too hard at.

Vincent shook his head, 'No, she'll be in in a few hours, just before we open. I tend to slope off about ten.'

'Not one for the nightlife?'

Vincent grinned. 'Not really, no.'

'So where do you think he is, then? Your dad?'

Vincent shrugged, 'Your guess is as good as mine, but perhaps there's something I can help with?'

Roxy arrived at the table, putting down a cup of coffee in front of Jimmy and a tea in front of Vincent, who smiled warmly at her. 'Thank you, Roxy.' As she left, Vincent told him, 'She's very good. Works like a dervish and nice for Faith to have another gal about the place.'

'Can't imagine Marshall was pleased though. He'd sacked her, from what I heard.'

Vincent grinned, a twinkle in his eye, 'No, I don't think he was pleased, Detective.'

Jimmy let that sink in, took a sip from his coffee, which actually wasn't too bad, and weighed up what to tell Vincent. He'd heard rumours and was getting the distinct impression that Vincent didn't much like his father. But blood was blood.

He said, 'You and Marshall aren't close, are you?'

Vincent's smile dropped. His face arranged itself into a serious expression of thinly veiled contempt. 'Are you close to your father, Detective?'

Jimmy shrugged, 'He died in the war when I was young.'

'I'm sorry to hear that.'

Jimmy didn't respond. Didn't tell this man that losing James before he'd ever really got to know him had left a huge hole in his soul that made him bitter and raging for years. That he had lost all faith in the God Lilly had still so staunchly believed in. He wasn't here for a heart-to-heart, after all.

Vincent said, 'My father,' and he spat the word out, 'dodged the draft, which tells you all you need to know about him.'

Jimmy said, 'You don't even like him.' More a statement than a question.

Vincent let out a single laugh, which sounded like a bark. 'What's to like? He's a villainous oaf. He told my mother he was a businessman. Met her when she and her parents were rather down on their luck. Vulnerable, you might say.' He added, 'She married him in good faith and he's dragged her name, her family's name, through the mud.'

Jimmy sipped his coffee. Fascinated by this insight into Vincent's view of Marshall. Cal was adamant that Nora Vella wasn't much better. She came from old aristocracy, but her father had made some poor investments and lost everything. It was commonly believed that she knew all about Marshall's nefarious activities but the lure of money was enough for her to turn a blind eye. Jimmy wondered if Marshall knew how much his son looked down on him, whether his wife had the same attitude.

Not that he could ever bring himself to feel sorry for Marshall. Not at all. He deserved nothing other than contempt and disgust. He was a repellent man. Everything that could possibly be wrong with a person wrapped up in one foul package. But, so far, he'd evaded any real consequences and that bothered Jimmy. Bothered him a lot. Even more so as he thought about those three nude women left out like rubbish to rot in the elements. All linked by one thing – Marshall bloody Vella.

He decided to just lay his hand out. 'We've found a girl. Theresa Bell. Dead.'

Vincent frowned, 'Another one of his?'

Jimmy nodded, pulled a folded *Acton Evening News* from his pocket and slid it over to Vincent. He let the man read, then asked, 'Did you know her?'

Vincent shrugged, 'I knew of her.'

'There are two other girls, Liza Plum and Geraldine Ross.'

Vincent looked surprised. 'You think he had something to do with it?'

Jimmy said, 'He's the thing that connects them all.'

'Can you prove it?'

'Not yet.'

Vincent finished his tea. Jimmy drank his coffee.

Jimmy asked, 'This place,' waving a hand, 'is in your name?'

Vincent nodded, 'Yes. He put it in my name the day I turned eighteen.'

'Always had plans for you to run it?'

Vincent grinned, his small, even teeth glinting in the light, giving him the appearance of a Cheshire cat. 'Quite the opposite, I'd say. Marshall thought it would be a good way to make sure it remained in the family if he ever got into trouble.' He shrugged. 'I have no record.' Adding quickly, 'Because I am, in fact, a law-abiding citizen. Like I said, my mother is a good woman and I'm pleased to report I take after her more than I do my father.'

'But now you're here?'

The grin widened, 'Now I'm here. A rather hasty reaction to what he saw as Rae Diamond's betrayal.'

'They've made up, I hear?'

Vincent nodded, 'They have.'

'But you're still here?'

Vincent smiled, 'It's driving him mad, I think.'

'You don't seem overly upset about that.'

The smile dropped and Vincent said, 'I make light of it, but the pain, the embarrassment, he has caused over the years has been immense.'

There was a long pause that stretched. Jimmy absorbed what Vincent had said, filing it away for further use, but for today there was nothing much left to say. He needed to find Marshall.

He stood, shaking Vincent's hand, and said he'd see himself out. He was halfway across the empty dance floor when Vincent called out to him, waving him back.

Jimmy walked back, Devlin and Roxy watching from the bar.

Vincent waited until he was close enough for them not to be heard and said to Jimmy, 'The world would be better off without him.'

'It would, yes.'

'And, actually, I might have a way we can make that happen, Detective.'

Chapter Twenty-Seven

Vella's

I arrived at Vella's just before nine. I was glad to see Devlin and Roxy taking charge of the team behind the bar. Glad the team had expanded, and hopeful that in the future there would be even more employees.

I suspected even then that Marshall had made a grave mistake keeping some of his businesses in Vincent's name and I was to be proved right in a way I could never have imagined. I assumed he thought that blood would always be thicker than water, but I don't think he ever really understood how much Vincent disliked him. How much he resented him. Marshall, at a glance, looked like a successful career criminal, but it had been his brothers who'd made the Vella girls a success. Vella's itself had been taken from the previous governor by force when Marshall thought that pimping out of a club would be easier than managing a load of houses. It was a messier way to do it, though, and people willing to pay big money preferred privacy.

It was an idea borne out of laziness on his part, of course, but he was a stupid, useless drunk, who rarely made good decisions. He'd got to where he was by accident, not design, and everything he did was ill thought out and chaotic. I don't think he ever considered that Vincent would be working there properly, full time, though he'd come down to London sometime earlier, in the late fifties, and been given an overview of Marshall's concerns. Rumour had it that the two had argued over most of it and that Vincent had gone back to the countryside exasperated. He'd also married around that time, so had his own reasons for leaving London. I think when Marshall called him back to the city again, he really didn't think it through. The move had been to spite Rae, of course, but it had backfired on him considerably. How little he now came to Vella's was proof of that. He had been relegated to a back seat and he had no one to blame but himself.

I headed up to the office, expecting to catch Vincent just in time to say goodbye, and was surprised to find him seated at his desk, hanging up a phone call and not looking like a man getting ready to leave. We'd got into a kind of pattern here – he worked the daytime hours and I stepped in and took over at night, or action time as I thought of it. Vincent didn't put a foot wrong, I couldn't fault him, but he also wasn't what I'd necessarily have called a people person either. He didn't enjoy dealing with the staff or the punters, whereas I thrived on it.

He said, 'Ah, Faith?' and I felt a shiver of nerves. He pretty much left me to it during opening hours; something I realised in that moment that I'd started to take for granted – enough to think of it as my place. It wasn't, though: it was his. The deed was in Vincent's name. He asked me, 'How's it looking down there?'

'Like it's going to be a busy night. Dev's about to open the doors and we've a queue of people out there already.'

Vincent nodded, 'The place is doing well.'

I smiled my agreement and slid into the seat behind my desk. He got up, poured two drinks, and settled one in front of me. Neither of us were big drinkers, and though our relationship was polite – complimentary, even – we didn't have many moments like this. The last time we'd had a drink together had been over Frankie's passed-out form. My momentary relief at his comment about Vella's doing well was replaced with another spike of anxiety. No matter how comfortable I might have felt, I was here at his grace and, in reality, I knew very little about him.

'It's down to you,' he said, 'the success here. You've got a talent for it. You can spot trends and you've a good head for business.'

I didn't know how to respond to that. Praise wasn't something I was entirely used to, especially from someone like Vincent. I wouldn't go so far as to say I liked him, but I had learned a lot from him. He'd guided my work and left me to it when he saw I was capable.

I took a sip of my drink, trying to muster the right words. Eventually, I said, 'Us, Vince. And it's your name over the door, isn't it.'

He nodded his agreement. Sipped his drink, waited for me to do the same.

Then he said, 'What if it wasn't?'

Getting through that night proved challenging. There were so many thoughts rushing around my mind and so much . . . hope.

Painful hope.

I didn't dwell on the past, didn't see the point. I knew that Rae spent a lot of time looking back, maudlin and regretful, and it didn't do him any good. What was done was done. You couldn't change the past, but I was learning then that you could certainly shape the future.

I managed the club that night with my mind racing, thinking of all sorts of things. Thinking of possibilities.

Three times, Roxy asked me if I was all right and, each time, I nodded, sat at the end of the bar, smoking, greeting people, checking on everyone. Looking around the place, thinking *what if*?

Diamonds.

That's what I'd call it, of course, and I'd give it a proper facelift too. And a big grand opening night. That's not where my vision ended, either. It would be the first of many. And it was just within reach, my fingertips were resting gently on the reality of it.

But it would come at a price, and it wasn't just me who would pay. Not just me who would be involved.

Rae and Marshall came in in the early hours of the morning and I watched them both carefully, Marshall in particular, unable to keep his hands to himself, sneering at Roxy. Eventually I went over and told the poor girl to head up to the office.

I took her place behind the bar and Marshall asked me how Mum was, a faint sneer on his rubbery lips. The truth was, Shirley wasn't good. She'd been shaky since Christmas; every time the phone rang or the doorbell went, she jumped out of her skin. She'd turned Devlin away twice, and flat out refused to leave the house, other than to go to the shops and back.

Rae, on the other hand, had been in and out of Sunningdale Avenue as though nothing had happened. And although he and Frankie were speaking again, there was still tension. They were forced into a truce they had little choice over, as Marshall had the pair of them running all over town together, collecting money, evicting non-payers from his falling-down, squalid buildings. Frankie told me that the number of people Marshall was able to cram into just one room was appalling. He targeted immigrants, charging more and kicking out long-term tenants who understandably felt resentful, though they misdirected their anger at the poor sods moving in. He took delight in fuelling the already ripe tension everywhere. I knew my youngest brother was weary, tired of it, and I also knew he had his limits. Christmas had proved that.

We were all stepping around the issue at heart carefully, trying to avoid Marshall, but the truth was we were all still living very much under his shadow.

I said, 'She's all right, thank you.' My voice as tight as my heart felt.

He laughed at that and I felt a swell of hatred and disgust for him. He leaned forward, slipping a hand over mine on the bar. My skin crawled; all I could think was that it must be a thousand times worse for Shirley.

He said, 'You tell her – I'll nip in soon and say hello.'

'Will do. Any idea when?'

He laughed, 'Nope, it'll be a surprise.' Then he grabbed Rae by the arm and the two men headed off, my brother waving casually back at me as he went.

I left Devlin in charge and made my way up into the office, where Roxy was sitting on the settee, smoking and pale-faced.

'Have they gone?'

I nodded.

'I'm so sorry,' Roxy said.

'Stop. It's not your fault.' She stubbed out her cigarette and I asked, 'Shall I call you a cab?'

Roxy shook her head and stood. 'No need if they're not here. I'll finish my shift, if it's all right with you?'

I smiled, 'Course it is.' As Roxy went to leave, I asked, 'You like it here?'

Roxy shrugged, 'I love working for you, Faith.' But her voice wobbled.

I said, 'It's hard for you when they come in.'

She nodded and bit her lower lip, 'I'm not complaining.'

I shook my head, 'I know that. I get it.'

'Sorry.'

I put a hand up. 'Really, you've nothing to apologise for.'

And I meant it. She wasn't the problem and I wanted

to believe that without Marshall, maybe Rae wouldn't be a problem either.

I went home, planning on sleeping the day away, hoping that by the time I woke up, I would have come to a decision about what Vincent had suggested.

I couldn't sleep though, and in the end, I sat up in bed, smoking endless cigarettes and thinking until my brain hurt. There were so many reasons to say yes. So many real and valid reasons. But – and it was a big, huge, fat but – it was still grassing. Did I want to be that person?

I thought about it – about who I'd become. Who Rae had become and who Frankie had become. None of us had got to choose. There was always a shortage of choice. Of control.

But this . . . this was in my power.

After hours of agonising, I knew what I had to do. Especially if I didn't want to live with regret for the rest of my life.

I called Vincent as night was closing in again. Before I had time to rethink anything.

'I'm in.'

Chapter Twenty-Eight

March 1964

Sunningdale Avenue

I sat, looking expectantly from Frankie to Shirley. We'd had a few family meetings in the past. Sprawling, chaotic events, usually called to action by Rae, who was notably absent today. But there'd never been one like this. Normally, they were long, drawn-out events held purely for Rae to boast about his latest escapades and tell the rest of us what we were meant to be doing. Usually in Marshall's absence.

This one was different and, I hoped, would mark a change to the way things were to be.

I carefully laid out everything Vincent and I had discussed. The things that by then we had already set in motion. That I would still have been willing to stop if either my mother or Frankie told me to. I was not one hundred per cent sure how they would react, but I was desperately hoping it wouldn't come to that.

Frankie said, 'Fucking hell.'

And Shirley muttered, 'His own dad.'

'Who's a prize cunt,' I snapped.

Shirley looked at me and I looked squarely back.

Unwilling to apologise for having spoken the truth, as much as we all liked to sidestep around it. Then she started laughing. Frankie and I exchanged a pointed look. She went on and on until tears ran down her face. Then she stood up, came over to me and wrapped her arms around my shoulders.

'Faith, my daughter. I loved you from the second I held you in my arms.' She looked at Frankie then, too. 'I love you all so much.' Then she turned back to me, 'You are my girl. You're stronger than I ever was.'

I started to protest then, to tell her she was wrong, but she silenced me, pressing a finger to her lips.

Then she smiled, 'Imagine how much it'll sting when he knows it was you who brought him down.'

I felt a wave of relief and looked at Frankie, who nodded.

Then I said what had to be put out there in the open: 'It's grassing, though. Whichever way you look at it.'

Frankie shrugged.

But grassing wasn't to be taken lightly and it was the part of the plan I struggled with the most.

I told them, 'That policeman thinks he's got something to do with the dead girls.' I was trying to justify something I clearly didn't need to.

Frankie said, 'Look at what he's done to Mum over the years. That fucker is capable of anything. You don't even know the half of it, Faith. He keeps a lot of his girls in worse conditions than you would bloody animals.'

I said, 'But they still choose to work for him, Frank.'

Frankie laughed, 'Like Mum chose to work for Rae Senior, or chose to be Marshall's fucking mistress.' I saw Shirley flinch, but Frankie carried on. 'Or Roxy chose to be Rae's toy of the fucking year?'

'I know, Frank, and I'm with you, but . . . still.'

We were all silent then, all thinking our own thoughts.

My brain raced with all the things me and Vincent had started doing. I had all sets of books now, including the ones with Vella's old accounting, back when they traded in skin. So arrogant, or perhaps so drunkenly careless, was Marshall that he'd left them in the safe at Vella's. They were now neatly ordered, highly incriminating, and ready to go to Jimmy Rose at Vincent's suggestion. There was also paperwork proof of serious fraud, and we had two witnesses saying they'd seen Marshall and associates carting away Clemont Barrington Abra – aka Babyface – a pimp who'd taken more than his cut and went missing, never to be seen again.

We'd also made sure neither one was going to mention the fact that Rae had been with Marshall at the time of Babyface's disappearance. That was irrelevant in these circumstances and both witnesses were guaranteed ongoing employment and no prison sentences if they stuck to the story. This part was the thing that would make sure Marshall served a proper lump of time. The fraud and money laundering would get him years in double figures, but there would still be the possibility of him living long enough to get out. But the pimp's kidnapping and the whereabouts of Clemont Barrington Abra's remains (a disused industrial estate just past the

Heron Trading Estate) would be the crowning jewel for the police.

Jimmy said to Vincent that he would make everything run smoothly and we'd experienced no hitches so far, but it was me who would be handing in the books and signing sworn statements along with the other witnesses. Vincent was ready and willing to do his part, but testifying against family members could be tricky and he would, of course, inherit everything Marshall owned. The falling-down buildings, a few empty, long-since abandoned shops . . . Jimmy had stressed to Vincent that in order to convince a jury, and the courts, they needed me onside. I had no criminal record, had been in charge of the business side of the club and would back up the claim that Vincent had been the owner only in name until he'd come down in 1963 and taken over the helm.

We would weave a tale of surprise and outrage. One which ended in us doing our civic duty. Even managing to uncover the ins and outs of Babyface's murder. It was a tuck-up, obvious to anyone who knew, but it would mean Marshall went down for the rest of his years. The fraud and the books at the club wouldn't be enough. They needed him on the murder too, or he'd be free to walk the streets and that would put us in grave danger.

As it was, Vincent and I had turned most of Marshall's workforce to our way of thinking. It hadn't been difficult. No one liked the fucker and his staff were miserable, underpaid, overworked and abused. They could see that a restructure would mean better lives for them in the long run. I was confident the few people we'd given any detail would keep it quiet.

And I felt good for having finally told Mum and Frankie, but nothing was ever perfect.

I sighed.

'The only problem we have is Rae.'

I had ways of taking my mind off my family, and that afternoon I found myself in the grotty bedsit of my latest distraction. I rolled off Jake Hawseley and reached over to the side table for my cigarettes. I lit two, passing one to him and slipping out of bed. I stood naked and stretched with a shiver.

'Bloody freezing in here.'

I looked around, noting the fact it was also a mess. Like the bedroom of a petulant teenager, rather than somewhere for a grown adult man to live. The ceiling was covered in woven scarves and blankets, picked up on his travels, which he never tired of boring me with. *India, man.*

He grinned, 'Come back to bed, then.'

I laughed, 'Some of us have jobs to do, mate.'

He frowned at that. 'I work too.'

I smiled at him, resisting the urge to roll my eyes. He was very good-looking, excellent in bed and didn't give me any real hassle. 'I know, love, but I have to be somewhere, don't I?'

He said, 'We're playing tonight.' Defensiveness in his voice.

I nodded again, not wanting to get into an argument

about it. His band were good enough, he had a nice voice and I'd been happy to give them a Saturday night spot at Vella's.

I liked him, but he was a spoilt little puppy. One of those trendy kids rebelling against parents who'd never put a foot wrong because he really had nothing better to rail against. But, ultimately, if things went pear-shaped for Jake, he'd just go back to his mum and dad's Surrey house and get a little job at Daddy's company. I wasn't much older than him, but I was often reminded we were worlds apart. I marvelled at kids like him. He spoke to me about his mum and dad with an unwarranted bitterness – as far as I could ascertain, their only crime was that they were boring. What I wouldn't have given for a bit of boredom.

Still, if everything went according to plan, my family would be doing fine in no time at all, and all thanks to me. I tried to shush my mind. I'd come here to switch off and honestly thought after meeting with Mum and Frankie I might have felt a bit better. But it turned out I was in a state of perpetual adrenaline-laden excitement. Waiting, hoping against hope that everything went according to plan.

It was a tense time.

Jake looked sulky and I felt a bit sorry for him. He had, after all, helped relieve the stress and tension building within me, if only for half an hour. He was putting out his fag, reaching for the cigarette papers and rolling a joint.

I slipped my dress over my head and pulled my

knickers on underneath, then sat on the edge of the bed. I smiled, reached for his hand, and he looked at me, all cute eyes and pouty lips.

'I'm working really hard, Faith. It's difficult when you've got a dream, you know?'

I nodded, still smiling, but also suppressing a laugh. Like I didn't have dreams myself. Slowly becoming one of the richest women in London being the main one. Dreams I hadn't even known I was allowed to have and that I'd fought for. Dreams I was finally making come true, despite the terrible odds stacked against me.

I picked up my bag, kissed him full on the mouth and stepped out with enough time to nip home, get changed and go and open up at the club, leaving the man-child getting stoned and likely thinking only about himself.

Chapter Twenty-Nine

Vella's

Vella's was filling up and everything felt surreal but under control. Jake and his band were on stage. I gave him a nod across the dance floor, glad when he winked but carried on working. I'd made it clear to him that privacy was important to me, that this was my place of work and he needed to behave sensibly when we were there together. I was aware by then, though, he wasn't, that we were reaching our end date and I knew I'd need to have that conversation with him soon, but I felt like it could probably wait. With everything else I had going on, his hurt feelings weren't something I was keen to manage alongside.

I headed up to the office. *My* office, as I had allowed myself to start thinking of it. Vincent had certainly been there less and less of late, and he wasn't there that night.

I sat behind the big desk which was normally his, lit a cigarette and rested back on the chair, allowing myself a moment of satisfaction.

But it was cut short by the door opening and Marshall Vella walking in like he still owned the place.

The first thing he said was, 'That's Vince's desk.'

'Vince isn't here.'

'Left you in charge, has he?'

'Something like that.' I stubbed out my cigarette.

Marshall came and stood over me. Trying to intimidate me. It was working.

I felt like that scrawny little girl again. Paralysed with fear in my own bed. My heart hammered in my chest, but I refused to give him the satisfaction of knowing I was rattled. I pulled a stack of papers together, clipping them in the corner, pretending to be engrossed by the contents of bills from breweries, and still he stood over me. I could smell his breath. Rancid and warm. It took all I had not to jump and run.

'My son is a fucking idiot.'

I willed my mouth to stay shut. We were so close to it being over, at a point where I would never have to worry about this man again.

He went on, 'Women aren't meant to be here doing our work. You think you're better than your mother, but you're all the same. Only good for one thing.'

Something in me snapped then, at the mention of Shirley. My poor mum, who had put up with so much from this absolute fool. We all had. But Shirley Diamond was worth ten of him, at least. What Shirley had done was far more honourable than anything Marshall and his brothers had ever achieved. They were lazy fuckers who'd made a fortune built on the misery of others. The backs of the women they so profoundly looked down upon.

I pushed the chair backwards so hard it toppled down behind me, and before my brain had a chance to engage my mouth, I said, 'I'm doing better here than you ever did. Mate.'

His face turned a peculiar shade of puce. Not unusual for Marshall, for whom any sort of physical exertion produced an almost immediate response. Honestly, I was surprised he hadn't keeled over from a heart attack already.

But his colour right now denoted something else. Anger.

I looked at the door, mentally planning how many steps it would take me to leg it over and out.

But before I had the chance, he lunged at me, his big meaty hands grasping at my throat. He leant in so close that his halitosis became overpowering. The reality of my situation forced up a swell of nausea, acidic and vile in my throat, and real stirrings of fear.

He pushed me back onto the desk and I felt the clips from the paperwork dig into the tops of my thighs. He released the grip on my throat and I swallowed thickly, acid burning the back of my tongue. I attempted to push a knee into his groin, but he had me pinned just by sheer size. I couldn't move. Couldn't breathe. I grasped at his hands, clawing with my nails.

I was a little girl in a small, damp bed with a large man running hands along my legs. I was horrified, and frightened, frozen. Myself, but somehow not – paralysed by terror and revulsion as I felt him reach to his belt and begin unbuckling it.

No.

I was not that child.

This wasn't meant to happen to me.

I lashed out, limbs flying like a wildcat. Scraping at his face, his neck, smashing my fists on his arms. My hands meeting with doughy resistance.

He laughed at me, at my futile attempts, his face on mine, his cheek pressed to my cheek, and when he pulled back to look down at me, a nasty grin on his awful face.

I spat at him. Because he was going to take me down no matter what, but I wasn't going without a fight.

'You fucking bitch.'

I heard a bang behind us. The door, it was the sound of the office door opening, but I couldn't move, couldn't look, couldn't get free. I could only shout – horrified at the softness of my voice that of all times needed to be loud.

'What the fuck?'

It was Rae.

Marshall pulled back and he and Rae stood eye to eye for what must only have been seconds, but felt to me like forever. I was still across the desk. Shaking and soaked in my own sweat. My throat hurt from where his hands had squeezed it and my breathing was uneven and forced.

Marshall pulled himself together, levelled one last look at me, finger stabbing in my direction and said, 'I'll see you.'

Then he was gone and Rae came over to me, tears

sparkling in his eyes. 'Faith. Faith, are you all right? Faith?'

I pushed him aside, ran out to the kitchen and threw up in the sink.

When I turned around, Rae was behind me and I was so disorientated, so messed up by what had just happened, that I screamed in surprise, jumping, feeling trapped, scared by the male proximity. I held my hands up, trying to push him away, but he stepped nearer, folded me into his arms and held me until I stopped flailing and stood still. My arms curling around him.

I could feel his breath in my hair and he told me, 'You're all right, Faith. It's all right.'

Over and over again.

We stood like that, the way we had so many years ago, and he whispered his soothing words and my breathing slowed, my heart stopped pounding. I didn't cry, but I took in the familiarity of my brother. So big and so solid beneath my arms. He would have been able to throw Marshall off. My attempts were futile and weak. I was smarter, better, but when it came to brawn, men had the upper hand. Standing there, I had the dim thought that if that was their advantage, it was weak in its own way. A lazy dominance based on an old survival system which needed to be put to bed.

I felt dampness on the top of my scalp and realised that Rae was crying. There had been so much trouble with him, so many dramas, that I could forget how very much I loved him. Despite how fucked up he was underneath the brawn and the bluster. Brute force, but not inner strength. I had it, Shirley had it and I saw it in Roxy, too. A steely core. Rae had heavy fists and big feet, but inside he was jelly. Soft and bruised.

Eventually, I pulled back. 'I need a fag.'

We went into the office and I lit up, looking at the mess on Vincent's desk and feeling anger replace my fear.

The fucking pig. How dare he come in here, touch me? The nausea threatened to return and I pushed it from my mind. Pressed a hand to my mouth.

Rae was watching my every move.

As I sat down, he asked, 'Did he . . .?'

I shook my head, 'You got here just in time, Rae.'

He held his head in his hands. 'Fucking hell. Fuck. Faith.' And his voice was pleading, desperate. His face tear-streaked. So many things I was uncertain of with Rae, but one thing I knew for sure above all others: he loved me. Perhaps I was the only person in the world for whom that was true, but it made me think he wasn't all bad. He had the capacity for love. Even if those natural urges had been warped and bent out of shape.

I told him, 'I hate him so much.'

And he looked up at me with clear dark eyes so like mine and he said, 'Me too.'

The conversation that unfolded between us that day was a revelation to me.

He reminded me that he'd tried to break free and where it had got him.

Eventually he said, 'He owns us. Owns me.' His face sad but accepting.

161

And I grinned at him then, the last piece of this jigsaw. The bit that had been nagging at me, a niggling doubt. Not what it seemed.

And I told Rae, 'Not anymore.'

Chapter Thirty

Sunningdale Avenue

Rae drove me home to get myself together ahead of the night shift. Shirley knew something was wrong and she followed me up into the bathroom, watched me running water into the tub and said, 'OK?'

I shook my head, but smiled at her nonetheless. 'It'll keep. You all right?'

She kept looking at me, but eventually nodded agreement.

I told her to go and make Rae some food and a cup of tea, and she went.

I washed without thinking, scrubbing at my thighs, where his hands had been. Shutting my eyes against the memories that mingled with Bass, and of men over the years whose hands had slid across my mother's body like poison spreading through water.

I shampooed my hair, brushed my teeth and sprayed on perfume, but still I thought I could smell his disgusting breath.

Years Shirley had had to put up with him.

I got into the kitchen and leaned down, squeezing

her little body to mine, inhaling the familiar smell of her hair. One of the good things that stuck in my memory, along with all the muck, like a jewel in a tin of shit.

I asked her where Frankie was and she said she didn't know. Rae told me he'd been sent to the other side of London to collect money and that he was due to meet him in the next few hours at Vella's. I said I'd go with him, though the last thing I wanted to do was walk back in there. That made me cross. Vella's had become my haven. I couldn't let Marshall ruin that. Rae nodded.

I called Vincent and told him, extremely briefly, what had happened. All I said was that Marshall went for me and Rae stopped him. As I spoke, I saw Rae's fists curl on top of the kitchen table. Shirley gasped, covering her mouth.

When I hung up, I hugged Shirley again and said, 'I'm fine. I'm OK.' Adding, 'Rae was there.'

She had tears in her eyes. I was grateful she didn't shed them. There could be no more tears over Marshall Vella.

She leaned across the table and took Rae's hand in hers. He startled when she did, and their eyes met. She told him, 'You've always been a good brother to Faith, Rae.'

Things had been strained in our house for so long by then, but that day it could have been years ago. When Rae was a small, bolshy boy and I had thought he was king of the world. When Shirley had been half drunk most of the time and all we'd had was each other.

He picked at a chip on the underside of the table and

I looked at my mum. She'd confided in me over the years. One woman to another, I suppose. Had told me all about Rae's awful start in the world. That his father used to mock him, even when he was tiny, with his words and his fists. That the second she'd brought him home from the hospital he'd been in danger. That as soon as he was old enough, he used to tell Shirley he'd take care of her. Of all of us.

I could remember him saying it, too. And he did. He had. Mum hadn't been up to the job. Until the terrible night with Bass, she'd simply switched off. Leaving us to fend for ourselves. How were we to get it right? How was Rae?

Shirley said to him, 'I'm proud of you, son.'

And Rae looked directly at her. His eyes softer than they had been for a long time. And he said, 'I'm sorry, Mum.'

For what in particular, I didn't know, and I don't think Shirley did either. Maybe Rae himself didn't even know what the apology was for, but she stood, went to him, took him in her arms. He was twice the size of her, but he leant into her and cried.

She told him, 'You saved her, son. Just like you saved me once before.'

And he had. Rae's arrest had woken Shirley up. Cal Doyle had checked in on the family while Rae had been away too, and I understood he was keeping an eye on her. She rose to it. Social services were gone from our lives quick enough. Bills were paid and business never took place in our home again.

Until Marshall. A poisoned chalice if ever there was one.

Cal Doyle spoke to Mum about our situation, I think. I overheard them talking a few times. Shirley told him she was ashamed. That she came to, not knowing what had happened. That I'd looked like a little angel from a horror film in my bloodied nightgown while Rae was dragged off, handcuffed, into the night. I felt sorry for her, but she was at least partly responsible for Rae and she knew it. They had a difficult relationship. Much more so than Frankie and I had with her. We were naturally more forgiving, but, of course, we never bore the brunt of the abuse in those early days. It wasn't either of us who'd ended up caged before we were fully grown.

I knew it all caused her shame in a long life pock-marked with endless humiliations. Rae going to Borstal had been the big one. But a wake-up call, too.

Rae had indeed saved Shirley from herself. Just as much as he'd saved me from Bass, and now Marshall.

I smiled at him and Mum and let myself feel a moment's peace.

The calm before the storm.

We drove back to Vella's in silence. I smoked and watched the city whizz by outside. I guess we were both thinking our own thoughts. Both trying to come to terms with the evening's horror. I think, by then, Rae was more shaken than I was. His face was pale, his knuckles tight around the steering wheel.

I only felt relief.

Relief that he wasn't in Marshall's thrall. That his loyalty sat with me — *us*, the Diamonds. I reassured myself as we drove that he and Frankie would find peace with one another again. I'd always been a channel between the two and I'd carry on being that.

I was impressed by how well Rae had played the part of Vella's willing sidekick. Reminded once again what a wonderful actor my brother was. He was a chameleon of sorts, Rae. But when he lost control, which he always did, it was never good. The facade would slip.

I pushed aside any worrying thoughts about him, clamouring for attention. He would be fine as soon as Marshall was gone.

I had one goal.

One focus.

We would be independent.

As we got out of the car, I took Rae's hand, squeezed it and smiled at him. He smiled back and it was so sad and so sweet, my heart shuddered for him.

Vincent was waiting in the office.

He said, 'Tell me again, slowly, what happened here tonight.' Then he flicked a glance at Rae, apologetically, 'Sorry.'

Rae didn't respond. He slumped down on the sofa beside me and looked away as I began to talk.

He looked from me to Rae, who was still damp-eyed, sat limply, his hands hanging between his legs.

Vincent poured drinks and handed them around, sliding a box of cigars across to Rae. His nemesis in many ways. Or he could have been.

Everyone knew Marshall favoured Rae, but Vincent seemed to hold no malice towards him. He'd told me already he felt his father had been out of order to scout and recruit Rae so young and on the back of such a terrible tragedy.

Vincent wasn't above such things himself, though, I suspected. I had no proof, but I knew he wasn't entirely above board. He liked money too much to ever be poor, and with money in our world, there was always some degree of skulduggery.

Despite his good education, smooth voice and manners, he'd still jumped at the chance to come to the city and work this side of his father's business. Rumour had it he hadn't excelled in the business world as he might have hoped.

He started to speak. 'My father is an oaf. A terrible man, and all I can say, Rae, is that I'm sorry for your trouble.'

Rae met Vincent's eye, each man sizing the other up.

Eventually, Vincent carried on, 'I'm sorry for my father.' I'd told him Rae was with us briefly on the phone and Vincent was solidifying it now.

Rae said, 'Not your fault, is it?' a frown on his face.

'Nonetheless, help me get rid of him once and for all and we'll all have brighter futures.'

Rae grinned then and I saw Vincent allowed a faint glimmer of a smile to cross his face.

I allowed myself to relax.

Chapter Thirty-One

7 April 1964

Chiswick

She's a cheeky mare. That's what he thinks.

He's bumped into her quite by accident. Not planning anything exactly, but open to possibilities. He's out of sorts, has far too much on his mind.

He walks through them, the throng of human waste that they are. A blight on society. And yet, he feels himself tune into it, feels the filth sink into his skin, that peculiar charm they hold, exciting really. Like all things you shouldn't do. Shouldn't have.

It's dark out here, he has his hat pulled down, he's anonymous enough. Then she says his name and, really, he wants to hit her.

He doesn't, though. He smiles, realising she's drunk, loud, going on about a baby and needing money. He takes her arm, small and stick-thin under his hand which fits full circle around it. Hard to believe her sickly, diseased body could harbour life, but these girls churn out more children than seems possible. He piles her into the car, starts the engine and drives away.

Begging is her first tactic. She's half-cut. He can see that in the wobble as she leans into him as though they are old friends and she's confiding. She's no friend of his, but here she is, gabbing on about things that aren't his problem, things he doesn't care about at all.

He manages to get her to the car without a scene. He will drop her home. Or nearby, at least that's what he tells himself. And yet, as he starts his drive, he heads out towards the water. Where it is quiet and dark. He wonders what he might do and feels a thrill at it. So few things so unknown. So few things that bring that feeling.

Even as he parks up, he isn't sure if he will act on his impulses this time, but then she says something stupid, even for someone like her: 'I've still got the Polaroids.' Smiling now, 'I'll give them back to you. Wouldn't want to cause you any trouble.'

And he freezes for a moment.

She is threatening him. The bitch.

A red mist falls over his eyes, his hands reaching out to her, thoughts seeping away from his mind like tiny wisps he can't quite grab hold of. Like Stop . . .

He doesn't though. He can't.

After, he feels the usual jubilation and then he feels annoyed. He wanted the Polaroids. He could have got them easily, too.

She had to threaten him. Had to bring up payment, as they always do.

It's her fault, and now look.

Now. Look.

Chapter Thirty-Two

Chiswick, London

Jimmy watched as a woman so small she could have been a child was pulled from the Thames. She was less than two miles from where they found Liza and just 300 yards upstream from Theresa.

Dr Eart stood, face impassive, watching alongside Jimmy as she was lifted from the water.

There was a moment of gruesome suspension where she hung, unreal and macabre, in the cold, bright morning light. Jimmy looked away. Not because he couldn't handle it, but out of respect.

The Shepherd's Bush officers were there and PC Jacobs moved towards Jimmy, pale-faced, clearly unnerved. 'Same as the last girl.'

Jimmy nodded.

'What does it mean?'

'It means we've got to catch him, and fast.'

The other man ran a shaky hand across his face. Nodding agreement.

★

Jimmy travelled back to the mortuary and waited while Dr Eart fussed around, moaning about how busy he was. Bollocks. It had been a quiet week until now.

Jimmy knew better than to piss him off, though, and instead said, 'I really appreciate this.'

Dr Eart said, 'I can't get you a full report, I'm having a quick look, that's all.'

Jimmy nodded. 'Understood.'

They both turned their attention to the small woman laid out on the slab. Jimmy's eyes stuck on a small tattoo on her right arm. 'In memory Jack'. Someone who had meant something to her, someone she had mourned. A permanent reminder of pain that never left. In memory.

Twenty-five years old. Five feet tall. Bottle-blonde hair so bleached it was almost white and looked brittle and immovable. Yellowing candy floss above a silent face.

Pregnant.

Fourteen weeks or so. And had suffered from at least one venereal disease. So had the other naked, strangled prostitutes. An occupational hazard for the girls who walked London's streets. Unwanted babies, painful diseases. Insecurity. Indignity.

In memory . . .

Cal listened to Jimmy tell him that he was sure the murders were linked. Liza, Geraldine, Theresa, now Sandy Lakeheart.

He told his boss, 'All prostitutes, all worked for Marshall Vella.'

Cal sighed, 'There's no evidence; you can't get him on these.' But he didn't disagree, either.

Jimmy said, 'I know and I'm not after the glory.' Though he didn't know if that was strictly true. 'All I want is him off the streets. I want these women safe. And I think I've found a solution.' He outlined what he had planned with Vincent.

Cal frowned at the younger man. 'When were you going to mention this plan?'

Jimmy sighed, 'As soon as I was sure it was going to happen.'

'And you're sure now?'

Jimmy nodded.

Cal looked at him. 'The books themselves aren't enough for a substantial stretch.'

Jimmy knew that, though they were worth a good lump. He told Cal, 'We've got two members of his firm willing to testify to Babyface's murder and we've been given the location of his remains.'

Cal shook his head, 'You're kidding.'

Jimmy grinned, 'Nope.'

'And Vincent is behind this? Happily tucking his own dad up?'

Jimmy shrugged, 'Can hardly blame him.'

Cal said, 'Still.'

And they were both silent.

It wasn't often that people grassed. Not in London. There were a few firms, mostly tight. There'd always be holes, of course, or drunk idiots with loose lips, which Jimmy and Cal both relied on at times. Something like this, though . . . So organised and, according to what Jimmy was telling his boss, so many people willing to either sing or turn a blind eye . . .

Cal said, 'Marshall is really hated.'

Jimmy nodded, 'Absolutely despised, and if I'm right about the girls . . .' He let it hang there. Allowed his mind to think of their little naked bodies. Then he said to Cal, 'If I am right, I wouldn't say Shirley Diamond's exactly safe.' Then added, 'They all look like her.'

Cal mulled that over. He hadn't noticed before, but Jimmy was right, he supposed. He'd really felt for Shirley over the whole Marshall thing. He'd even go so far as to say he liked her. She'd stepped up after Rae went down. Really cleaned up her act. His sharp words hadn't fallen on deaf ears. He'd assumed her kids would be taken into care, separated before Rae's first year was up. But that hadn't happened, and for those two years, they'd not been called out to Sunningdale Avenue either. She'd kept working, but on the downlow, and out of the house.

He wasn't as convinced as Jimmy about the dead toms. They all worked for Marshall, sure, but all the girls around here would have been Vella's at one point or another. Everyone paid a cut to him somewhere along the line. Still, getting him off the streets would be good. Though some other fucker would probably step up. Vincent would struggle to retain power, Cal thought. He wasn't a part of this life like Marshall was. Pesky fucker though Marshall was, he'd stayed, remained and earned.

'And it's all in place? Everything?'

'I think so. I hope so.' Jimmy felt stupid now. What he'd wanted was to go to Cal with the books in his hand, the evidence neatly lined up, and signed and sworn witness statements. But he'd realised that in order to get it all done, he'd need his boss's help. He had envisioned himself coming out of this a hero. Now he was having doubts. Had he done the wrong thing? Was Cal getting the hump, or worse; would this put him out of line for the promotion everyone knew he was heading for?

Cal shook his head, but he was smiling. 'Fucking hell, Jim, fancy getting a capture on Marshall Vella.'

'You're not pissed off?'

'Only that you didn't tell me sooner. And you think he's doing these girls in?'

Jimmy shrugged, 'I don't know for sure, but he's the link.'

'You feel invested in this case?'

Jimmy nodded. 'It's the carelessness of it.'

Cal could have pushed him. Asked him to explain, but he didn't. Oftentimes, certain crimes became personal. You couldn't always say why. Another man in his position might have been annoyed at Jimmy. Sticking his nose in all over the place. But Cal saw his passion. Understood it.

And he told him, 'Go on. You'll want to hear what Eart has to say, no doubt.'

Chapter Thirty-Three

Vella's

Marshall knew Jimmy Rose was looking for him and so seemed to somehow remain elusive. I didn't see him again after that awful night, until his arrest. I hated to admit it, and wouldn't have said it out loud to anyone, but I was nervous. I hadn't been back to the office on my own since.

I sat at the bar, where I'd been for the whole evening, when Devlin leaned over, looking at me intently. I smiled at him, but he didn't smile back.

'Baby girl, why you down here?'

'Not up for my help tonight, eh?'

He smiled. It was gentle, almost fatherly. 'I don't mean that and you know it.'

I swallowed, but it felt thick.

'Are you all right, Faith?'

The desire to confide in Devlin was strong, but enough people had already been dragged into this. I didn't want anyone to know what had happened between Marshall and I, either. For reasons that escaped me then, I felt a mish-mash of emotion about it. Most surprisingly, shame. That I had somehow let it happen. Put my own safety in jeopardy. That it was my fault. I had no idea how Shirley had managed to hold her shit together for so many years. No idea how any of those girls with hard lives, hard insides and soft, pliable bodies managed to do their jobs. I was tough as nails. I'd made myself that way. But, as it turned out, I wasn't untouchable.

It was important then that we carried on as usual. Me, Vincent, Rae and Frankie. Shirley too, but no one was going to question her, unless Marshall turned up there, and even then I'd seen her lie to him many a time before, so she could do it again.

Rae was keeping an eye out. He seemed to have no trouble listening to Vincent. Vince had a way of making you feel like things were your idea and Rae responded well to that. They'd spoken on their own the day before. I'd been worried about how that would go, but when I asked Rae afterwards what he thought of him, he said he seemed OK. He was also sober, or not fall-down annihilated, which was a vast improvement on how he had been.

Drunkenness wasn't something Vincent tolerated and I assumed it had been spoken about. Though how he'd got through, I'd never know.

I smiled at Devlin, 'I'm OK. Honestly.' I put a hand on his arm and he squeezed it with his free hand, keeping eye contact. He'd have been good for my mum, but, I consoled myself, things were about to change. I grinned at him for real then, 'Really, Dev. Thanks for checking, though.'

He didn't fully believe me and that was all right. Dev knew when to keep his nose out, which was part of his appeal.

Vincent had told me the night before that we were ready to go, but everyone was freaked out about the girl in the Thames right now. Shirley had taken a personal interest in that particular case and I'd seen a few Toms coming in and out of Sunningdale Avenue for tea, gossip and endless fags since her discovery. It had been years since Shirley had dared have friends round. I'd forgotten how social my mum was. And how well liked and respected, too. She was a good listener. In the brief period where Rae had been locked up, Shirley had struck up a few of her old friendships again. Stepped, albeit tentatively, back into the loop.

I could have done without it to be honest – a house full of noisy prostitutes cooing over Shirley's curtains and cups and God only knew what else. It was an annoyance to me when I got in, usually early in the morning, exhausted from work and on tenterhooks.

I was also wary of Marshall, who I didn't want to give a reason to lash out at Shirley. If he turned up and found her entertaining some of his 'girls', he'd be none too pleased.

But the company had done wonders for her mood. On top of that, Frankie and Rae were finally getting along, or at least pretending well enough. I hoped it was all a sign of good things to come.

I spied Jimmy Rose come in and watched him work his way across the dance floor, low key but eyes darting around. Taking it all in. He was a handsome man; it was a shame he was a copper. I'd had a good time with him that night, but it felt like a lifetime ago now. A repeat would cause complications, and complications were exactly what I was looking to be rid of. Anything for an easy life.

He came over, nodding to me and I smiled, 'What can I get you, Detective?'

'Hello, Faith.'

'Beer?'

He shrugged, 'Why not?' I signalled to Dev to order our drinks and Jimmy lit a cigarette, sliding me the pack. 'Can I join you?'

'Please do.' And he took the bar stool next to mine. So close I felt the brush of his knee against mine as he sat.

Chapter Thirty-Four

Vella's

Now she was right there, sitting on the stool next to him, her impossibly long legs occasionally touching his, and he had no idea what to say next.

Luckily, she broke the silence and brought his mind back to business. Back to reality.

'Have you found Marshall yet?'

He frowned and shook his head. 'Went to see your brother, though.'

'Which one?'

'Rae, who's got a mouth like a sewer, by the way.'

She laughed at that and the sound was infectious. He was smiling too by the time she stopped.

She said, 'You went to talk to him about Sandy?'

He nodded, 'You knew her?'

'My mum did.' She was still smiling, but sadly now.

He said, 'Cal and your mum go way back.'

'They do, yeah.'

'He says she's all right.'

She nodded again, 'She'll be even better once we get this done.' And she looked at him, intensely now.

He knew this was work, the biggest pull of his career, most likely, but he allowed himself to momentarily get lost in her eyes, for different reasons altogether.

Then the singer ambled off the stage and over to them, staring daggers at him. He reached out a hand and slid it onto Faith's shoulder.

She jumped slightly, frowning at him. 'Can I help you, Jake?'

'Just seeing if you're all right.'

'Fine, thanks.'

The lad didn't move.

'Jake, Detective Rose,' Faith said eventually.

And the boy looked simultaneously relieved and puzzled. He said in a voice that didn't suit him, 'Old Bill hassling you?' and Faith rolled her eyes at Jimmy over Jake's head.

'Fine thanks, Jake.'

Jimmy almost started to feel sorry for him.

Then Jake said, 'I'll see you then, later, at mine yeah?'

Faith scowled but snapped, 'Sure, whatever.'

Jimmy looked down into his pint as Jake walked away.

Faith stood up and said, 'Vincent says I'm to come and see you?'

Jimmy nodded, not meeting her eye. Thinking unreasonable things about Jake. 'Yes, I think Cal will be in contact to arrange it.'

He stood as well. The moment was awkward.

Then he said, 'Well, have a lovely night with Jake.' His tone dripping with sarcasm before he could stop his stupid mouth opening.

She smiled coolly, turned and walked away.

Jimmy was left feeling like a prize dickhead.

Jimmy went back to the station, arriving at almost the same time as Cal. The two men walked in together, bringing with them the cold air of outside.

Cal had been out talking to the girls on the streets, and said to Jimmy, 'They're scared.'

Jimmy nodded, 'They should be.'

Cal said, 'The problem is, they know so many utter arseholes that it could be any number of people. They may be entirely unrelated and the similarities mere coincidence.'

Jimmy frowned, not sold on this theory at all. 'Could be.'

Cal asked, 'You don't think so, though, do you?'

Jimmy shook his head.

'All roads lead back to Marshall Vella, eh?'

'They do, yes,' Jimmy nodded.

Cal sighed, 'Call Vincent. Tell him to have the books brought in tomorrow. We have the statements on Baby-face. We need to get this moving and we need to do it now.'

The words were like music to Jimmy's ears. He had reason to celebrate – Marshall Vella was going down. Any awkwardness with Faith Diamond would just have to be forgotten for now.

Chapter Thirty-Five

Acton Police Station

I had no idea why Jimmy Rose's words stung me the night before, but they had. I felt his judgement and it made me prickly and annoyed. I prided myself on the fact I didn't give a shit what anyone said about me, but that wasn't always strictly true.

I didn't go to Jake's that night and was debating whether I even needed to bother having a conversation with him about where we were headed. I didn't like the possessive way he'd glared at Jimmy and I didn't like him butting into our conversation. It felt like a child interrupting the adults, and jealousy was not something I welcomed. Everything he did smacked of immaturity. The kind that a life of middle-class comfort seemed to bring.

I felt like Jimmy had somehow seen a bit of my life I hadn't wanted him to and made a dig about it to boot.

Worse still, I'd only been home five minutes the next morning, when the phone rang. Cal Doyle, telling me I'd been summoned to the station with the 'evidence in my possession'. Actually, the evidence was in Vince's possession.

I called Vincent and arranged to meet with him and Frankie at Vella's. I was still nervous – what we were doing was a big deal. A huge deal. But I no longer had any doubt that it was the right thing to do. Any lingering hesitation I had over grassing had been quashed when I'd felt Marshall's awful body pressed against mine. Now all I wanted was to have it done.

I was going to sting this man who'd been in and out of our lives for over a decade and I felt nothing for him other than contempt. There was no fondness or gratitude. Anything he'd given any of us had been earned a hundred times over. We'd all paid for our association with him one way or another.

Vincent helped Frankie and I pack the books into a cardboard box and load them into Frankie's car. When we got to the station, I told Frankie to wait outside, and headed in, the box heavy in my arms.

A young PC was on the front desk and she told me I could go straight up. I swung the door open and found myself in an empty corridor, stairs in front of me. I pressed my back against the door, feeling the weight of the files in my arms, and took a few deep breaths. I understood that in life you couldn't always avoid making wrong moves, wrong decisions. And I was generally OK with that. If you didn't decide things for yourself, didn't act on them, life would do it for you, and I didn't want to be that sort of woman. I refused to be. This wasn't a wrong move, but it was monumental. I allowed myself a moment to savour it in peace. There was a new age coming. I had choices. More than women of previous generations. More than Shirley ever had, and I would choose for myself.

I could have said no to Vincent; without my co-operation he wouldn't have got the lads to talk about Babyface's murder. My sweet-talking and credibility got those witnesses and I could have denied the books were the ones I'd kept. Could have stuck up for Marshall. I could have talked my brothers out of this. I could even have gone to Marshall. I would have been rewarded momentarily. Of that I had no doubt.

But I hated him. More than I'd ever hated another human being. He made slaves out of those who worked for him. Even Rae, who he claimed to be fond of. Marshall didn't see him as a person; he was a walking, talking, loaded weapon. He ruined lives without a second thought and I didn't like the way he carried out business. Not at all. Marshall was even worse than his brothers before him. He milked people for everything they had. The Vella girls were always out there, spending long days and nights on back-to-back customers with little reward and only the illusion of safety. Some of the stories Roxy had told me honestly broke my heart. He doled out drugs to them as a means of control and when they slighted him, real or imagined, he lashed out.

Marshall was furious at Vincent, not just for keeping me on to do the books, but increasing my responsibilities in the club. He himself hadn't thought to give specific instruction about me, a woman after all, who deserved no consideration. Quietly and surely, Vincent had given me new tasks, more freedom, positioned me as the face of the club. By the time Marshall realised, Vincent argued that he'd been doing what was best for the club, which was what his father wanted, after all. Marshall had swallowed it — had to, really. The club was Vincent's on paper, and as the months drew by, it was clear to everyone that Marshall was being muscled out in every practical way, too.

On his increasingly rare visits, he utilised every opportunity to swipe at me and Vincent. A petty man, as well as violent, abusive and stupid. I'd thought that Vincent was impervious to his father's attacks, but over time I noticed that after Marshall's visits, Vincent was different. Subdued, not quite himself. Marshall had a way of getting at his son. Usually sniping at his mother. His own wife. Marshall was a man devoid of feelings, who found other people's amusing. He honed his words with the most painful precision.

The WPC looked around from the side of the desk that gave her a view of the front and back of the door to the station and snapped, 'Are you going in or not?'

I almost snapped back, but then Jimmy was there, walking down the stairs towards me, frowning at the officer in charge.

'Are you all right?' he asked.

Chapter Thirty-Six

Acton Police Station

Jimmy thought he'd seen a nervousness on her. She hid it well and, as usual, was impeccably dressed. But she'd stalled at the door. Jimmy took her by the elbow, walked her in and talked her through what would happen next. Cal mostly stayed quiet, but he was making notes and asked the odd question.

They went through the books, Faith speaking calmly and clearly about what transactions meant what and where the money had gone. As they worked, Jimmy realised she wasn't just clever, which he'd known, but she was super smart. She grasped sums and numbers quickly and frowned at him when he couldn't keep up, which made Cal chuckle.

He told her everything that would happen after this. Sam and Will – their witnesses – had signed statements about Babyface. She nodded. He understood she had been instrumental in getting the two men to talk, and also that they'd be on her payroll in the future. None of this would have been possible without Faith's co-operation. It was unusual in the underworld of London to find criminals willing to sing on each other, no matter what had happened to them.

Jimmy could feel the anger pulsing from Faith when he spoke about Marshall, and he understood that this was incredibly personal for her, as well as practical. He'd looked over some of Shirley's old files. Over the years, Marshall had beaten Shirley black and blue. So he understood where Faith was coming from. And he was grateful to her. This would be the biggest capture of his career.

'You're doing the right thing, Faith,' he said.

She nodded, signed her statement and agreed that if she was needed in court, she'd be there.

He didn't think she would be needed. He hoped not. Sam and Will would have to stand up and testify about Babyface's kidnapping and subsequent death. Both were guaranteed no prison time for the kidnapping as a result. It would go down that they had been coerced with menace, which was laughable, but would do. That, along with the years of dodgy accounting in black and white before Marshall put the club in Vincent's name, would be more than enough. Marshall would never see the light of day again.

But as with all matters involving detail of this scale, it would take a few weeks.

Merilyn came in with a breath of excitement and said, 'There's a man downstairs claims he killed Sandy Lakeheart!'

Jimmy scowled at her, quickly leaving the room – and the lingering whiff of Faith's perfume – Cal in hot pursuit.

'Bring him up, then.'

189

Joseph Archibald was a tubby man with a wide, amiable face. Not a pretty face, but friendly, if slightly dozy-looking. He came into the interrogation room behind Merilyn, smiling happily at Cal and Jimmy, who remained seated and stony-faced.

Merilyn sat him down and left the room.

Jimmy and Cal let the silence stretch.

Joe started picking at the cuff of his jacket before eventually asking, 'Well, do you want me to sign something, then?'

And Jimmy asked, 'Like what, Joe?'

'I don't know, I don't know . . . like a confession. Or is it recorded now? On film, even?'

'WPC Jones said you had something you wanted to tell us. Let's start there first.'

The man frowned, 'Who?'

'The officer who brought you up here.'

He was grinning again. 'Oh yes, seemed a nice lass. An officer, eh. Girls doing everything everywhere now. Eh? Eh?'

Jimmy sat forward. 'Sandy Lakeheart.'

'Ah yes. Lovely little Sandy.'

'How did you know her?'

'Well . . .' He looked uncomfortable. 'What I say is confidential in here, right?'

'Unless we need it for trial, Joe.' Which was a definite no, but the silly man nodded and grinned.

'I'm a caretaker. At the tennis club.'

Jimmy said, 'Which one?'

190

'Mulholland Park, in Kensington.'

Cal made a note.

Joe added, 'Nice place.'

'A good job?'

He shrugged, 'Not too bad, but doesn't pay well. Know what I mean?'

He looked from Jimmy to Cal, who both nodded agreement that they did, in fact, know what he meant.

Jimmy said, 'So you're the caretaker there . . .'

'That's right. And I got keys and access to things like the bar and that.'

'All right.'

'Well someone approached me about doing some after-hour do's there.'

'Who would that be?'

He shook his head, 'Oooh, wouldn't like to say.'

Jimmy resisted the urge to roll his eyes but made a mental note to prod at that later.

'So, you're getting a bit extra to host some after-hours parties there?'

He nodded agreement, 'I am, yeah. Thirty quid a week extra, to be precise.'

Jimmy raised an eyebrow at Cal, who said, 'Not a bad wedge.'

Joe said, 'Well no, that's right. For doing nothing much.'

'You stayed for the lock-ins?'

He nodded, 'Yes.'

'Which is where you met Sandy?'

'Yes. Lovely little Sandy.'

And Jimmy wished he'd stop saying that. He shut his eyes momentarily and was bombarded by an image of her small body laid out on Dr Eart's slab.

In memory . . .

Jimmy said, 'Who supplied the girls?'

'Same man who paid for the space.'

'Vella, then?'

Joe nodded, then said, 'Shit. No, I mean. Does it matter? And besides, this is all confidential, right? So you've no need to say anything. Have you?'

'Vella sent you in here with this cock-and-bull story.'

Joe looked at Jimmy and smiled, 'Nope.' But his grinning lips said otherwise. This was a waste of bloody time and yet they'd have to see it through.

After that, Jimmy was too livid to really focus. He let Cal take over, recording a ridiculous confession from the man. Archibald signed it, everyone aware that it was all simply a waste of time. But still, this also told them that Marshall was scared of being done for the murders but seemingly had no inkling there might be anything else that he needed to worry about.

Marshall had paid Joe to come down here and make his stupid confession and he'd paid him to use the tennis club, presumably after Vincent had taken over at Vella's and stopped him doing a trade there. The thing was, Marshall wasn't only implicated in this one death, so he'd either assumed the police hadn't connected Liza, Geraldine, Teresa and Sandy or he honestly knew nothing about the first three. Jimmy doubted that. He was pretty certain Marshall was their man. And they would get him one way or another.

Joe's confession was an inconvenience, though, and would waste time.

So, it was with a grim smile that Jimmy left the station, amazed as always at the things people were willing to do for money. Joe Archibald would serve a long, rough sentence if he got done for Sandy's murder.

Chapter Thirty-Seven

24 April 1964

Brentford

He's panicking now and he must calm down.

Deep breath in, long breath out.

But it's no good and for a second he pauses, allowing himself to feel the sheer terror of it. A complete loss of control like he's never known before, and now look.

She is a mess. At one point, he hit her so hard, some teeth came away from her jaw and now lay next to her body, glinting like awful jewels in the dim light. He picks them up and slides them into his pocket, cramming everything else into the boot of his car, along with her body.

Then he drives.

His eyes blur as tears fill them and he punches his leg hard, flinching, but waking himself enough to get a grip.

Get a fucking grip.

He's not going to make it as far as the river and he desperately needs to get away, go home, leave this sorry affair behind him. At least for now.

Though he can't say he hasn't enjoyed himself. He certainly has.

But still.

He parks, opens the boot and looks down at her face. Blank eyes stare up at him. She is twisted at a peculiar angle, made to fit.

He lets himself stop, take a moment. Converse with what is left of her, murmuring things under his breath. Taking in the marks on her skin. That he made.

That he left there.

He isn't sorry for what he's done, but still . . . the timing. The rashness. The loss of control.

He leans her against the wall of an alley, where she almost looks like a mannequin – a peculiar, bruised mannequin. Comical in a way; an involuntary giggle escapes from his mouth. The sound odd and unwelcome but a reminder that he must go, and go now.

By the time he starts the car, gets moving, he is panicking again, and he takes a corner too fast, almost colliding with another vehicle. Then he is away.

Away.

Acton Evening News

24 April 1964

'Yard warn women'

Daily Standard

25 April 1964

'Giant Murder Hunt'

The Evening Herald

25 April 1964

'. . . The killer could be a man who hates women of the streets, or a new monster, like Christie . . .'

News Standard

25 April 1964

'Yard hunt Strip Killer'

Chapter Thirty-Eight

26 April 1964

Rae Diamond's flat

The papers were going wild.

Speculations were being made, and Jimmy and Cal were on their way to Rae Diamond's flat, where Marshall Vella was apparently sleeping like a baby.

Rae had walked downstairs from his flat to the payphone on the pavement and called into the station himself. Muttering non-specifically that he'd been with the big man for a while now. Jimmy felt annoyed that Rae hadn't called as soon as he had Marshall in his sights. He'd been trying to track him down unsuccessfully for days now. Joe had been let go after his flimsy confession wasn't backed up with any evidence, but Jimmy had felt incensed that Marshall had so obviously sent someone else in to take the fall. It was also only a half-arsed attempt at best, which proved Vella wasn't particularly worried. And he needn't have been. There was no way Jimmy could have got him for any of the girls' murders – or none that he'd found, anyway. Which didn't mean he wasn't going to get him at all.

Jimmy's mind was whirring with the details of this latest nude victim.

Kat Smart.

Another Vella girl, though long estranged from her pimp, from what they had gathered. She was well liked by many, frequented the jazz clubs of the West End and had been trying to make a go of it out there on her own. She'd had a child at nineteen that she gave away, but seemed to be finding her feet in London, even if life was hard. She'd been making the best of it.

The ferociousness of this attack was startling, even compared to the others, and Jimmy sensed the killer behaving rashly. His temper exploding into his crimes in a way it hadn't to date.

Marshall, if he was indeed their killer, knew that Jimmy was closing in and Jimmy wondered whether that kind of stress would be enough to fuel a maniac into new levels of violence.

Joseph Archibald had been a flimsy attempt to trip Jimmy up. Marshall didn't know one hundred per cent that Jimmy wasn't coming at him for the naked corpses. But even though he'd been concerned enough to plant Joe, Jimmy suspected the big man wouldn't be all that worried. He'd likely figured out that the police had little in the way of evidence when it came to the dead girls, and he was right.

But Jimmy was smarter than that, smarter than him.

He was coming and he would get him.

★

Rae Diamond was standing at the bottom of his block of flats, smoking a cigarette and looking for all intents and purposes like a flipping film star.

Hard life though the Diamond children may have had, they were a good-looking brood. Rae and Faith both had dark complexions, dark hair, though Faith's eyes were a deep blue – almost navy. Frankie was fair, but no less striking.

Rae had something else though, a dangerousness. An edge.

He reminded Jimmy of a wild cat as he stood there, watching the detective get out of the car through lazy, hooded eyes. As Jimmy drew closer, he grinned. Not with any warmth, but with menace. Just like Rae himself. He was a man Jimmy would never trust. He'd attended scenes where the savagery had beggared belief, all thought to be at the hands of Rae Diamond.

Rae was a henchman through and through. Despite his charisma and good looks he was, and likely always would be, a second in command. Having said that, Marshall was cut from the same cloth and he'd been head of his own enterprise.

When this day's work was done, it'd be Faith in charge of the club and Jimmy got the feeling she wouldn't stop there. He wondered if Rae would challenge her. He didn't suppose it mattered much to him either way what happened to any of the Diamonds once this was done. As long as they didn't cause any more trouble on his streets – at least that's what he tells himself.

Cal shook Rae's hand and Jimmy did too, trying not

to wrinkle his nose at the man who had, after all, delivered their target, hook, line and sinker.

Jimmy asked, 'He's inside?'

Rae nodded. 'Comatose, like I told you.'

'Drunk?'

Rae shrugged. 'Mostly.'

And Jimmy didn't push that point. They'd asked Rae to keep him there, but hadn't told him how to do it.

He asked, 'When did he get here?'

'Couple of days ago.'

'What day exactly?'

He shrugged, 'Friday?'

Jimmy frowned, 'Well, was it or not?'

Rae laughed, 'Yeah, Friday. Don't know what time. I got back in the evening. He was here.'

'He's got keys?'

'He owns this place.'

Jimmy looked at Cal. Their girl was dumped early hours of that morning. It was possible Marshall came here straight after.

Jimmy said, 'Where were you?'

'Out.'

'When?'

Rae's eyes narrowed. 'Thursday to Friday evening.'

'So he could have got here Thursday.'

Rae shrugged. 'Could have.'

'Who were you with?'

He laughed, 'With a couple of girls.'

'Where?'

'Notting Hill way. I'll give you their names, but let's

get this done – he's stinking my place out to fuck.'

Vincent had told them that Rae was unhappy with Marshall. Felt trapped by the man. But still, they'd worked together for years. Since Rae was a boy, really.

He didn't seem ruffled in the slightest.

Marshall Vella was like a beached whale on the settee, mouth open, a faint grunting coming from his direction, and Rae had been right, the smell was vile. Body odour, booze and fags. He looked like he hadn't changed his clothes for days and Jimmy thought hopefully that they may find some of Kat's blood on him.

He shoved him with his foot. Marshall slid slightly to the side.

Jimmy shoved a bit harder, and the big man blinked twice, opening his eyes. He sat up, rubbing his large hands over his face, wincing slightly. Jimmy reckoned he likely had the mother of all hangovers kicking in. It'd be a painful day in the cells for him. This cheered Jimmy up. By the time Marshall managed to focus, the detective was grinning.

Marshall looked at him, groaned and said, 'Fuck's sake, ain't you got Joe down for that girl? Surely you can leave me alone now.'

Jimmy said, 'He's only confessing to Sandy.'

Marshall looked puzzled. 'Well, who else is there? You're not still bleating on about that other cow from last year. I forget her name . . .' He clicked his fingers, shaking his head as though trying to pull his thoughts together.

That gave Jimmy pause. Joe had been adamant that he had nothing to do with Kat, and how could he, considering he was in police custody at the time. That had been the undoing of his − never very believable − confession. Marshall didn't seem to know anything about her, either.

But still, he was a career liar.

Jimmy said, 'I'm not here about the murders at all. Not those ones, anyway.'

Marshall looked genuinely puzzled now. Rae came in and Marshall nodded, 'All right, son.'

Son.

Rae didn't answer, but he'd chosen to be here, to watch the show. Jimmy and Cal had given him the option not to be around for it.

Marshall told Rae, 'They're on about some shit or other. Not the fucking tart. I thought he was here about Sandy.'

Jimmy said, 'Marshall Vella, I am arresting you for the murder of Clemont Barrington Abra, also known as Babyface.'

Marshall looked from Jimmy to Cal to Rae. 'What the fuck.'

And Rae was smiling.

'You're also charged with running a house of ill repute, living off ill-gotten gains, money laundering and fraud.'

Marshall smiled, confused, obviously in pain and likely seriously dehydrated, but still not quite grasping the seriousness of his situation. 'Yeah yeah, I'd like to see you prove it.'

Jimmy read him his rights, adding at the end, 'I don't think that'll be a problem. Do you, Rae?'

And Rae stepped forward, relishing the moment almost as much as the young detective, albeit for very different reasons.

'I don't, Detective. No.'

Chapter Thirty-Nine

Vella's

I could hardly believe it. I put the phone down, my hand tremoring, turned to Vincent and said, 'They've got him.' My voice was barely a whisper.

He looked at me blankly and for a second I wondered if he'd heard me, but then his face broke into a large, genuine smile. He started to laugh and then he was up, out of his seat and pulling me out of mine, clasping me in a hug. I was so startled by the unusual display of affection from him that I laughed, too.

I didn't think I had ever seen him look anything close to excited before. He was positively jubilant.

I'd been harbouring worried thoughts that he might change his mind at the last minute or be so wracked with guilt he'd fall apart. But he seemed happy, carefree and honestly looked better than I'd ever seen him look. Like a weight had been lifted. Which I suppose it had.

'Now, young Faith.' He pulled back, sliding open his desk drawer and taking out a large white envelope. 'In here are the deeds to Vella's.'

I felt a rush of want within me.

'I've had everything signed over to you, and the last thing we have to do is take it to my solicitor so he can witness you signing your part.'

I was gobsmacked:

That easy.

Or not, when you considered all that had gone before. But that day, that wonderful day . . . The moment that changed my life forever.

He said, 'Shall we . . .?'

I didn't hesitate, grabbing my bag and following him out of the club – my club – into the warm spring sunshine.

I had the deeds, I had the keys and I had the place to myself, for a few minutes at least.

I stood in the middle of the empty dance floor. Breathing it all in. Looking around at the place through fresh eyes. What I'd do here. The things I had planned.

The door opened and in came Roxy.

She smiled at me, 'Oh, hello. Dev asked me to open up – hope that's all right?'

I grinned back at her, 'Certainly is, it was me who asked him to get you here early.'

She frowned, 'Everything all right?'

'Better than.'

She nodded and headed behind the bar, taking down the glasses that had been drying along the back and lining them up in preparation for the night ahead. I watched her; diligent, methodical, careful.

I said, 'Did you hear about Marshall?'

Roxy nodded, wide-eyed. 'I did, yeah. Best news ever, if you don't mind me saying so.'

'I don't mind at all, Roxy. In fact, I reckon there might be better news still.'

She paused, looked at me. 'Oh?'

'You probably suspect that Vincent and I might have had . . . a part to play in Marshall's downfall.'

She blushed. 'I had heard, yeah. Since his arrest, a few people have mentioned the possibility.'

'What do you think of that?'

She stopped what she was doing then. Lining the last glass up and looking at me directly. 'I hated him, Faith.' She spat the words out like poison. 'The things he's done to me, the things I've seen him do to other people. We all felt for Shirley and how it must have been for you all. I'm not wanting to speak out of turn, Faith . . .'

I assured her, 'You're not. I'm asking you for your honest opinion.'

'Honestly? You did the right thing.' She shrugged.

It was all the evidence I needed and solidified the decision I'd all but made at that point.

'Glad you think so.'

Roxy smiled.

I told her, 'The club's mine now.'

'Fucking hell. Really?'

I nodded, 'Really, and I'm looking for two managers, someone to oversee the security side of things, deliveries and that.' I waved at the main arena. 'That'll be Devlin.'

Roxy was still staring at me, not speaking.

I said, 'I'll also need someone to oversee the night-to-night running. Someone who can keep the girls behind the bar in check, make sure everything is legit. I've got plans, Roxy, big plans. First, we're going to have a massive opening night.' I looked around, could almost see it in my mind's eye. I asked her, 'So, what do you say?'

'Me?'

'Of course you, you pillock.'

She burst into tears. Laughing and crying at the same time. When she came around the bar for a hug, it was probably a step too far, but I appreciated the gesture. I patted her awkwardly on the back. Scared that I might bloody cry, too. All the years of frustration, of keeping my feelings inside, and hidden.

I blinked once, twice. Composed myself. 'Flipping heck, Rox, calm down.'

But I was pleased. What I was offering her was a big deal. A huge deal. A life-changing opportunity for someone from our world. I didn't think I'd be sorry having her on board.

There was a new world order and I was at the helm.

Part Three

'There is nothing more deceptive than an obvious fact.'

– Arthur Conan Doyle, *The Boscombe Valley Mystery* (1891)

Chapter Forty

May 1964

Diamonds

The place looked spectacular and it was absolutely heaving with bodies. I stood on the balcony, looking out over tables, chairs, the dance floor and the stage. Triumph was an understatement. Devlin and his crew were literally turning people away at the door. Roxy and her team were serving non-stop. I could almost feel the money pouring in; each ting of the cash register was like music to my ears.

Diamonds.

The most buzzing club in London and – if everything went according to plan – the first of many.

Frankie stood at my side and let out a low whistle, 'Bloody hell, sis.'

I grinned at him, 'Not bad, eh?'

'Not bad at all.'

I asked him, 'Where's Rae?'

Frankie pointed to the bar, where Rae was standing alongside Vincent. I felt a momentary pang of annoyance. I'd asked him to come in early with Frankie. Vincent and Rae were like chalk and cheese, and I'd been surprised in the last month to see them striking up a rather peaceful association. Looking at them from above, I thought I could see more similarities between them. They held court at the bar, surrounded by a group of giggling girls. Whilst Vincent may not have had the rugged good looks that Rae possessed, he did have charm and class on his side. I'd suggested to him that he invite his mother and wife to the opening night, out of curiosity as much as anything, but he'd waved the suggestion away; apparently it wasn't their scene.

This past month had made me realise many things. One was that I didn't actually know all that much about Vincent. Despite working so closely with him over the past few years.

I linked arms with Frankie and we headed down the stairs and into the fray.

Roxy was flitting round, busy. I watched her work the room with smiles and arm pats, whilst simultaneously keeping an eye on everything.

I knew only too well that there was an odd combination of people here tonight. A fair few villains in the crowd, a lot of Vincent's friends and connections from the business world. Some minor and some more major celebrities – a cohort that I was very encouraging towards and who I paused next to now, gesturing to Frankie to get the local rag's photographer over to snap some pictures.

I'd also spied Cal Doyle and Jimmy Rose.

I headed over to Rae, who grinned and leaned down to hug me.

'Sorry we couldn't get here earlier, sis, something came up.'

I didn't want to know what that something was, so I didn't ask. Vincent's latest endeavours were moves into the motor trade. That had always been his plan and he was utilising the warehouses his father had once owned and, I had heard, actively looking to procure more. He was, he said, building car showrooms the like of which no one had ever seen before. Though I think Rae had been sent in to a few of the new properties to *persuade* reluctant owners to part with what was theirs.

I wasn't sure whether Vincent had changed over the past month or whether I was just noticing more about him that I didn't see before. I suppose he'd been my saviour of sorts. Not that I hadn't proved my own worth. I deserved the club. I was the one who'd made it a success, after all. He had signed it over to me and I'd been overwhelmed with gratitude for that. But since then, the dynamic between us had shifted; and I'd seen glimpses of things about him I wasn't so enamoured with. And heard things. Like that he was using Rae for muscle. Someone else taking advantage of my brother for all the wrong reasons.

Vincent beamed at me and I forced myself to smile.

He told me, 'Darling, this is wonderful, really. Bravo to you.'

'Thank you, Vincent.' I met his eye and realised I didn't feel indebted to him – or to anyone else – and in that feeling was freedom. I added, 'I heard you've been busy building your own empire.'

He grinned and nodded slightly but didn't offer any more than that. I didn't push. But I filed away his reluctance to be drawn. It could have been anything, of course. He was here to enjoy the evening, not to discuss business, but since my brother was working for him now, I considered it to be something I'd need to dig into.

I turned to Rae and saw him staring at Roxy. I slipped up alongside him and he smiled at me said, 'She's doing well here?'

I nodded, 'She is, yes. Really come into her own.'

He said, 'I keep asking her out.' With a grin.

I didn't respond. I was somewhat concerned about this situation. Roxy warned me he was persistent, and I'd promised to have a word. Knowing she was frightened of him, and really, who could blame her? He'd never treated her well.

I said to him now, 'Maybe you should learn to take no for an answer.'

He shrugged and waved to her with his glass.

Another conversation I'd have to have. But not tonight.

Chapter Forty-One

Diamonds

Rae watched Roxy. She looked like a butterfly emerging from her chrysalis and he had decided that it was a good time for him to make his move again. He was sorry about what had happened with Marshall, but no one could blame *him* for that, and besides, he'd sorted that situation out good and proper. And he was on the up now.

He was pleased enough for Faith, though he acknowledged the part of him that was jealous of her success. He loved his sister, probably more than anyone else in his life, but he didn't want her getting too big for her boots. She'd be nothing without him, and honestly he prickled a little bit at her 'advice' to leave Roxy alone. If he wanted Roxy back, he'd have her, and that was that.

As the crowd started to thin out, Vincent told him they ought to be off and he nodded, saying he'd do a few quick goodbyes.

He found Faith at the door, saying goodbye to the last trail of customers, some so drunk they had to be supported as they left. He hugged her from behind and whispered in her ear, 'You're a superstar.' And in that moment, he meant it. Changeable as his moods always were. Rae could go from blind rage to ebullient joy in nanoseconds. It was what made him so dangerous and was the part of his personality he was having to work on the most. In Vincent, he'd found a teacher of sorts. A man he wanted to imitate, and Vincent was keen on control. In himself and his workforce. Not in the sloppy way Marshall was. Vincent practised restraint and pause; his way was more effective.

Faith grinned at him and he said, 'Where's Frank?'

'Lugging beer barrels down to the cellar last I saw.'

It was cool down there and Rae was glad of it after the hot, sweaty evening in the club, with too many bodies pressed into one small space.

He reached the door of the cellar, aiming to say goodbye to Frankie before he left, but paused when he heard a giggle that he'd recognise anywhere. He'd been keeping his distance from her, asking her out politely and waiting before he did it again. He was trying to become calmer, as Vincent had advised him to, and that man knew self-control. He had manners and class; both things that Rae was keen to learn. But maybe tonight would be the perfect opportunity to clear the air.

He was about to push the door open when he heard another voice, low and murmuring.

Frankie.

He opened it, letting a crack of light spill out into the dingy hall – just enough for him to see them.

His brother.

With his girl.

And there was no mistaking what they were doing and how comfortable they looked doing it.

He let the door slide shut and stood listening as they reached the final moments. He almost exploded into the room right then and there, tempted to drag the pair of them out, to make them pay. But he didn't. He was learning new ways to be.

He forced his breathing to slow, feeling his pulse lessen as he did so. Clenching his fists hard as though they could contain the maelstrom of emotion welling up inside of him. He counted to ten. Back from ten. Then he made his feet move, ironed his face out into a relaxed expression.

He went and met Vincent, saying he was ready to go. Filing away his red-hot anger.

For now.

Chapter Forty-Two

Diamonds

Jimmy waited until the place was almost empty, telling Cal he'd see himself out and home.

He'd watched her all night, flitting in and out of the little pockets of people. Talking to punters, overseeing everything whilst looking utterly untroubled. She was saying goodnight to Roxy and Frankie, who were tidying up the bar.

Devlin came over to him and nodded, 'We're closing, mate.'

Jimmy said, 'I wanted to congratulate Miss Diamond.'

Devlin raised an eyebrow at that, 'Did you now?' and Jimmy felt almost foolish then. Caught out. He wanted to see her. Speak to her. But he had no reason to, and was about to turn around and leave when she came up behind him, almost making him jump out of his skin.

She touched a cool hand to his arm. It had been so packed and sweaty in there tonight that the air was still kind of damp. He reckoned he was reasonably dishevelled, but she looked fresh as a daisy.

She said to him, 'I was taking these to the safe, join me for a nightcap?'

And he nodded, trying to look casual.

'Devlin, the cleaners are just about to start, can you get some of your guys to stay put until they're finished?'

He nodded, 'Course.' He looked curiously at Jimmy. Devlin knew who he was, of course. But he didn't say anything and Jimmy was glad. He didn't want Faith to rethink the nightcap.

Even the office was different. Jimmy settled himself down on a plush white settee, while Faith put the takings in the safe, pulled a bottle of champagne out and set two glasses down on a low coffee table in front of him.

She said, 'I haven't had a chance to celebrate all night.' And he thought perhaps there was a question in her voice.

He smiled at her. 'That doesn't seem right.' She popped the cork, pouring it out, sliding one to him.

'Cheers, Detective.'

He held his glass up. 'To you and to Diamonds.'

She smiled, took a sip and put a record on. A slow, bluesy song floated out across the room.

She sank down next to him, kicking off her high heels and resting her feet on the coffee table. So close he could feel the warmth rolling off her.

They drank and she topped them up, lit a cigarette, waving the box at him in a question. 'It's been so busy, I haven't had a chance to stop and think.'

'I know what you mean.'

She laughed, 'I'm sure you do. Can't think London ever lets you rest.'

He smiled, 'Not often.' Then added, 'Some people are just better on the move.'

'Shirley always says the devil makes work for idle hands.'

They drank some more, smoked some more. Jimmy felt the music wash over him and found himself starting to relax.

He'd wanted to talk to her about Rae and Vincent. About things he had been hearing on the street. But he also didn't want this moment to end.

She leaned forward and stubbed her cigarette out. He did the same and their hands grazed.

For a second they were frozen there, faces so close he could just lean in.

Her voice was low and husky when she said, 'The thing is, Detective, all work and no play . . .'

He reached out a hand to her face, but the office door sprang open and Devlin was there. Looking bemused.

Faith grinned at him, 'You off, Devlin?'

He nodded, 'Want a lift?' If Jimmy wasn't mistaken, he'd say Devlin was playing the part of protective dad right now and he couldn't be more annoyed about it.

She looked at Jimmy, who stood, offering her his hand. She wobbled slightly and laughed. 'The bubbles have gone straight to my head. Yes please, Devlin.'

They walked down the stairs, out onto the street.

Devlin went to collect his car and while he was gone,

Faith turned to Jimmy, leant in and pressed her lips to his. 'Goodnight, Detective.'

Then Devlin was there and she was whisked away.

Jimmy stood, staring after the car like an idiot, for how long, he didn't know. Eventually he muttered, 'Goodnight, Faith.' And started to walk home.

Chapter Forty-Three

14 July 1964

Berrymeade Road, London

A voice calls out, 'Who dat dere?' followed by raucous laughter.

He looks at the two men in the van parked up by the pavement. Startled by them. By their presence. And frightened now, too.

He pulls up his collar, tucks down his head and scurries off, past the van and down the street, hoping the shadows are his friend. Perhaps he should wait, but everything in him is screaming to go, get out.

He climbs into his own vehicle and speeds off. Away.

But relief is only momentary as he sees a police car coming towards him. He is driving fast, but it will be more suspicious if he slows down, so he keeps going, heart hammering in his chest. He holds his breath tight beneath his ribs until the car has passed. And it does pass. Does not stop him.

Does not know.

Nobody knows. He is safe. It is all right.

He breathes in, breathes out. Thinks he can smell her perfume in here, in his car, but, of course, that isn't true.

Three days he'd spent with her and the only smell coming from her was the rotting of her flesh. They catch up with

222

themselves in death. Oh, everybody decomposes, of course, but these girls walk the streets like terrible rotten beings. Once the life is sucked out of them, their outsides start to match their insides.

He is rattled by the close call. This had been planned. Thought about. For weeks, he'd been thinking, deciding. He doesn't want to make mistakes, act in haste. Is scared, almost, of his rashness. He almost blacked out during the act itself. Every time. He had images. Glimmers of it all that he could play with and use. But sometimes even he is shocked at what occurred.

But still, he is hungry for more.

Still he longs for it.

News of the World

19 July 1964

'This is the story that will be read by millions, but I am writing it for only one man. And I know he will read it . . . you are a murderer. A multi-murderer. A modern Jack the Ripper who has caused a wave of terror among the street girls of London . . .'

Chapter Forty-Four

19 July 1964

Acton Police Station

Jimmy was aghast. Sat hunched over the paper. His head in his hands.

Cal looked at the younger man and felt a wave of pity. He knew Jimmy hadn't been one hundred per cent certain it was Marshall Vella killing these girls, but he'd believed there was a connection and that with the man's incarceration, the killings would stop.

Now they had Maria Teddy. Battered, bruised, naked, and two builders who'd seen a shifty man drive away quickly.

And this letter. A tawdry ridiculous thing from a newspaperman who'd never been a friend to the police and, despite what Cal hoped were good intentions, was not helping.

Cal put a hand on the lad's shoulder. 'Jim.'

And when he looked up at him, Cal felt even more pity. He'd been this way himself once. Still could be, he suspected, if a case grabbed him like this one had grabbed Detective Rose.

Jimmy looked up at Cal, shook his head, 'I got it wrong, Cal.'

Cal sat next to him, 'You didn't. You got Marshall fair and square.' He paused, 'And we'll catch this man, too.'

Jimmy nodded. But the big guns were headed down now. This investigation was going wide. With the press crawling all over everything, it'd go higher than Jimmy. Higher than Cal.

Jimmy wiped a hand across his face.

Cal said, 'Good news is, we've got undercover going out everywhere and people are taking notice.' He added, 'A lot of the girls are spooked enough not to take any chances.'

Jimmy nodded. 'That is good.' Then said, 'I don't know what to do with myself.'

Cal told him, 'The city's waking up for playtime.' Nodding at the clock that told them it was coming up to 11 p.m., 'You go and walk your patch, Jim.'

But Jimmy felt out of sorts. He walked through the streets he was meant to manage and felt a swell of misery. He passed a building with a sign reading 'No coloureds'. Next to it was one of Marshall Vella's slums. Once flats, they had been sectioned into tiny rabbit-warren rooms packed full of West Indians, who'd come here looking for a better life and ended up with this shit. On a wall across the road were painted the words 'Keep Britain White'. The street light above the wall flickered on and off. Illuminating the hateful words in a headache-inducing strobe.

Everyday people stepped out of those buildings to be faced with this crap. The white tenants in the 'No coloureds' building paying higher rents and already cross at the lack of space, the lack of resource and hope. Their neighbours baffled by this new place that told them to come and now screamed at them to go.

Vincent was supposed to be sorting his father's flats out. He'd promised Jimmy he would; that he'd do what he could to ease tensions. Jimmy would need to talk to him about it. Throughout the whole Marshall take-down, Vincent had been more than amenable, and he was still polite to a fault. But Jimmy had never warmed to him. Though Jimmy didn't warm to a lot of people. Vincent wasn't an out-and-out criminal like his dad had been. For all intents and purposes, he was a legitimate businessman. On the surface, at least. But Jimmy wasn't stupid; he knew what people were saying about Vincent and Rae. It had started to seem that if Vincent wanted something, he went out and got it. Jimmy had an eye on it, but he knew that his work meant carefully picking his battles. Lest he chose the wrong ones.

Like the nude girls . . . He tried to push the thought away, but it niggled at him anyway. That investigation had carried on and he'd stepped back. Assumed, arrogantly, that with Marshall out of the picture, that was the end of it. That his fellow officers were working a dead case, so to speak.

And now another nude.

Night-time had closed in and there were women everywhere, scantily clad and like a plague. Masses of them heading out for a night's work. There had been a team set up in Kensington that was supposed to specifically deal with the 'prostitution problem', but nothing worked. Nothing could be done. Every morning at West London Magistrates Court, there were women waiting, on all sorts of charges, but mainly soliciting. They saw it as a sort of tax, pimps even set aside money for it. The girls would come straight from work. Just an extra added bit of their shift. Until men stopped buying, they wouldn't stop selling. It had been five years since The Street Offences Act was enacted and it hadn't led to the hoped-for changes. Not so far, anyway.

Jimmy walked through crowds of people. They said hello to him, he said hello back. Reminded a few of the girls to stay safe, for all the good it'd do. One walked past, head down, and his arm went out, hand gripping onto hers. He recognised her. Roxy McCann's little sister. Fourteen years old at most.

'Where are you going?'

'Out.'

He frowned, 'At this time of night?'

She shrugged, 'No law against it.'

'I reckon there's plenty of laws against what you're planning.' His eyes narrowed. 'Does Roxy know where you're going?'

Her eyes filled, the bravado dropping, and she burst into tears. She shook her head, 'No, and I don't want to go, either. She and my mum have had a row, and Roxy said she was fed up funding her lazy arse. Mum said it was about time I pulled my weight.'

Jimmy processed this. He knew all about Roxy. Remembered the vivid bruises running up her thin arms when they'd gone to question her about her knowledge of the Pincasi scam. Bruises put there by Rae. When he'd asked her about them, she'd said she'd fallen down the stairs. The whole thing stank. The world was foetid and poisoned. But Roxy had done all right. Faith had seen her all right. Now here was Beverly – just a girl, for Christ sake. Dressed like a bloody tart.

He knew that Roxy's mother was a wrong'un. She'd put Roxy on the game and Roxy had done it, not for her mother, but for her younger siblings. She'd be fuming to see one of them off out to do the same after all her efforts to keep them safe.

He fumbled in his pocket, pulling out a handkerchief, handing it to the forlorn teenager. 'Right, come on.'

She'd asked twice if she was under arrest and he'd told her no on both occasions. He was walking at a brisk pace and she was struggling to keep up. He slowed down. There was no rush for him to be anywhere, he supposed. He'd felt lost tonight anyway. What was the purpose of it all? He walked his beat, oversaw his cases. Tried his best. Putting out small fires whilst bigger ones flared up all around him. The same stuff, over and over. He made arrests in social areas for pick-pocketing. A man the other night for stealing from cars, bold as brass, smashing windows as he went. A couple of lock-ups for drunk and disorderly and the almost constant moving on of women. It all felt pointless in that moment, so he wasn't bothered about not being on his beat.

He was depressed about the nudes. Generally, he could cope with the demands of the job, but there were times when it got too much. It had been bad after his dad died, of course. His head felt like it was being engulfed by a black cloud then. His feelings both muffled and painfully sharp all at once. He thought if he'd had any mother except Lilly, it may have got the better of him back then. Maudlin thoughts leading to more of the same and finally an overwhelming urge to be alone. To sleep and nothing else. But Lilly *was* his mother and she didn't allow it. She let him grieve his dad, but she didn't let him wallow. She let him sit in that mood for no more than twenty-four hours. Then it was out of bed, into action.

When he'd hit his teenage years, Lilly had sat him down and told him that his father had the same temperament. When he'd asked how he dealt with it, she'd shrugged and said, 'He learned it was a part of him and he worked around it. Some people feel things deeply, son, and you're one of those people.'

Which wasn't much use to Jimmy, who'd been heartbroken over Cynthia at the time.

He smiled at the memory and Beverly McCann asked, 'What's so funny?'

'Never you mind.'

'Where are we going?'

'Somewhere safe.'

'Am I in trouble?'

He stopped then and bent down slightly to look her in

the eye. Reminded again that she was just a child. That her mother was a monster.

He put a hand out to her shoulder, then snatched it back, not wanting the gesture to be misread, either by Beverly or any of the other people walking past who would see him, in plain clothes, and a girl in a tight top, a miniskirt and too much make-up.

'No. You haven't done anything wrong.'

Her eyes welled up again.

He muttered, 'Bloody hell, come on.'

And they kept walking, her taking two quick strides for every one of his.

Chapter Forty-Five

Diamonds

I was on the phone to a supplier who was making excuses as to why they were going to be late for a second
time and I wasn't impressed at all. I hadn't liked dealing
with him anyway. He called me 'darling', and when he'd
come to the club, back when it was still Vella's, had all
but refused to address me directly, always asking if Vince
was around.

I think he'd somehow got the idea that because I was
a woman, he could take the piss. Unfortunately for him,
that couldn't have been further from the truth. I'd already
had Roxy look into a new supplier, who I had lined up
ready and waiting. I took great satisfaction telling the
dumb-dumb on the phone that he wouldn't be getting a
third chance. He could stop begging now.

He was still talking as I hung up and I found myself
smiling. I'd given him ample opportunity to sort his shit
out. More fool him.

I picked up the phone and spoke to the new guy
Roxy had found. He was polite, agreed he could get
me what I needed and fast, and I said I'd be looking

forward to meeting him in person. I trusted Roxy and her judgement, but a personal touch went a long way and I was determined to treat everyone I worked with with respect. As long as it was afforded to me first, of course.

Growing up, I'd watched the men around me drive workforces into the ground and when we'd stitched Marshall up, finding people to rat the fat fucker out had hardly been a challenge. The people who worked for me didn't feel that way, I made sure of that. And those that did would get struck off the list.

I stepped out of the office, down the stairs and into the club's main arena. This evening, the lights were low, the bar was open and the glittery paint shone and twinkled.

Devlin was on the door and I could see him interacting with his crew via nods and hand signals, calling more men over when he needed to. Roxy was behind the bar serving expensive glasses of champagne and pulling pints. The crowd was different now from what it once was. A far cry from the plastic gangsters and wannabes of yesteryear. There'd be no trouble here. No discrimination, either – it had fast become known as a mixed club, which I liked, and a lot of the hipsters and trendy kids hung out here now. There were also lots of businessmen and entertainers. Influential people who I was keen to make associations with.

I walked out between the tables at the quieter end of the bar area, shaking hands as I went, nodding to Roxy's girls to refill glasses, 'on me'. I was greeted with air kisses and smiles and hugs. Photographs were taken and I stopped, smiling for the camera. Diamonds was the place to be and I was the woman to be seen with.

I checked in with Devlin, who told me all was well.

I headed past the dressing rooms, the singer from tonight's band giving me a grin that I returned easily, always a sucker for a good voice and a bit of charisma.

He called out, 'You going to watch our set?'

And I yelled back, 'If I can find the time.' Still smiling as I walked away, knowing he was watching me go.

I left the club floor and started to head back up the stairs to the office when I bumped smack bang into a tall man, firm and untroubled by my impact. I was about to lay into him when I saw with surprise that it was Jimmy Rose.

'Detective, to what do I owe this pleasure?'

'I'm looking for your colleague actually. Roxy McCann.'

I nodded, feeling a strange sense of disappointment. Ridiculous, of course, but I had always found myself drawn to this stable, solid man. An unlikely fit for me – laughable, even.

I smoothed my hair down, tied up in a long ponytail that stretched all the way down my back. Then I saw Beverly standing in Jimmy's shadow in some sort of vain attempt not to be noticed.

'Bev?'

She raised an eyebrow at Jimmy, who sighed and said, 'That's why I'm here.'

'Right then. You go up to the office, I'll grab Rox.'

I headed to the bar, signalling for Roxy to follow, and she came to join me. As we headed up the stairs, she asked, 'Everything all right, Faith?'

'I'm not sure,' I replied, and, opening the office door, we found Beverly sitting on the white settee, Jimmy stood awkwardly next to her.

Roxy took one look at the girl and stepped closer to her, eyes narrowed. Roxy wasn't more than 5'1", but Beverly cowered, shrinking back, and I didn't blame her. Roxy had fire in her eyes, focused solely on her little sister.

Jimmy put himself between them, 'Now now. I've already told the kid she's not in any trouble.'

He looked over Roxy's head to me.

I put a hand on Roxy's shoulder and said, 'Sit down.'

Much to my horror, the kid burst into tears. Roxy was up again like a lightning flash. This time folding the girl into her arms. I looked at Jimmy, who shrugged and sank down into one of my new armchairs with a sigh, lighting a cigarette.

As the story unfolded in Beverly's faltering, thin voice, her eyes downcast and shoulders slumped, I felt anger burn through my body.

I glanced at Roxy, whose jaw was also clenched.

She looked from me to Jimmy. 'I haven't given her any money for five days, for God's sake.' Then to Beverly, 'She should have loads of cash in the house?'

Beverly shook her head.

Roxy said, 'Where's it gone then?'

Beverly looked at her sister, her tear-streaked face emphasising her youth. 'Dad's been back.'

Roxy screwed her face up at that. 'For how long?'

Beverly shrugged, 'On and off for months. He comes over after you go to work, leaves before you get back.'

'She's been giving the money for you to Dad?'

Beverly nodded, 'She'll be angry that I told you.' She bit her lower lip.

Roxy tutted, 'Never mind that.' She sat beside her sister. 'Bev, why didn't you say?'

Beverly was all tears again. 'Mum said you'd be cross and would stop helping us out.'

Roxy got up, knelt in front of her sister. 'Bev, I'll always look after you and Tyler.'

'I told her that, but she said I was lazy poncing off of you all the time and should be bringing in something by now.'

Roxy laughed bitterly. 'That's rich.'

Beverly added, 'I felt guilty, you know? I'm still going to school and everything because of you. When you were my age, you was out earning.'

Roxy said, 'Is this . . . Have you?'

Beverly shook her head, 'This is the first time. I was meant to go round some bloke's house; she wrote down the address for me.'

The girl pulled a piece of paper from the pocket of her too-tight skirt and handed it to Roxy. She stared at it like it was poison and then looked over to me. I stepped in with a smile and took it, nodding at Roxy. One of my brothers could pay this man a visit. But the immediate problem was that Beverly and Tyler were no longer safe at Edith's. My mind raced as I weighed up the possibilities, until I reached the only logical solution.

Rae was in his flat and Roxy was spending more time at Sunningdale Avenue than she did at Edith's. I suspected there was something between her and Frankie, though they were going about it quietly enough.

I handed Roxy my house key and said, 'I'll get one of Devlin's men to drive you to ours, I'll come and sort it out after I'm finished up, all right?'

Roxy said, 'Don't you need some help here?'

'I'll be fine. Everything's done. All I've got to do is sit at the bar, have a drink, and listen to music.' I smiled to let Roxy and Beverly know it wasn't a chore, but my friend still paused.

She said, 'You shouldn't be out there on your own, though.'

I couldn't have cared less to be honest. Besides, I had a team of staff overseeing everything. But I knew Roxy felt like she was leaving me in the lurch.

I said, 'I'm sure the detective can join me for an hour, then I won't be on my own, will I?'

Chapter Forty-Six

Diamonds

It was an odd world that Faith inhabited and had somehow made her own. Jimmy knew the club – when it was Vella's – had essentially been a brothel. It was a far cry from that today. Everything had been thoroughly thought out and maximised on. Faith had an eye for trends and she lined up good acts to fill the stage. Crowd-pleasers. Certainly, when he'd been there for the opening, it had been an eclectic lot. Youngsters keen to spend cash in the capital. And it looked set to continue in the same vein.

Faith herself looked wonderful in a short dress, which sparkled even more than the walls of the club, and kitten-heeled sandals. She had her arm threaded through his and gestured to the girl behind the bar to bring them both drinks. He started to mutter that he ought not to, but, glancing at his watch, he realised his shift was over and he thought, *Why not?*

He recognised one of the men sat at the table and realised it was an actor he'd seen in a film he couldn't remember the name of.

Frankie was at the bar. He came over, looking slightly askew at Jimmy, but shook his hand nonetheless.

Faith leaned over and talked quietly to her brother. Jimmy heard snippets of her relaying the story about Beverly.

Frankie looked shaken and said to Faith, 'I'll drive them to ours, yeah.'

She nodded, 'All right, thanks.'

Then he said to Jimmy, 'You brought her in?'

Jimmy nodded.

He took Jimmy's hand – shook it with enthusiasm this time – and nodded as he did. Past animosity put aside. If it even still existed. That clear and divisive line between Jimmy and the Diamonds was, he realised, no longer in place. Not with Faith, anyway. Or Frankie. Jimmy felt a sort of thrill at that thought. Waved goodbye to Frankie and looked at Faith with fresh eyes and the stirrings of possibility.

Jimmy asked Faith, 'No music tonight?'

She replied, 'It's not even midnight, the evening's just beginning.' And, as if on cue, the lights went down on the crowd and up on the stage.

The first band played three songs. They were good. Very mellow rock and roll with just a hint of something new and a bit special. The singer was charismatic and Jimmy noticed Faith didn't take her eyes off him.

The next act was a small woman, accompanied by a man on piano. Her size was not indicative of her voice, which felt too big and too emotional for the space.

Faith didn't just have an eye for trends, but an ear too.

He knew people were talking about Diamonds all over town and he could understand why. Being here was an experience.

Jimmy watched along with everyone else in the club, transfixed. He was startled when the woman's set came to an end and he heard Faith whisper in his ear, 'Good, isn't she.' He nodded.

The lights came up subtly – the night was over. Jimmy was amazed to look at his watch and find three hours had passed.

Faith excused herself and took to the stage to thank everyone for coming. People filed out and she even thanked some of them personally. He saw her talking to the film star and other faces he recognised. A gang boss from the West End smiled at her and kissed both her cheeks. He watched her laugh and joke with ease. A powerful man to have on side. Jimmy understood that Faith was becoming a force to be reckoned with in her own right.

The lights continued to rise as the place emptied, until it was just Faith and Jimmy left at the bar.

She said, 'What do you think of my place then, Detective?'

He told her, 'It's a far cry from Vella's.'

She smiled. 'Isn't it just.'

'And this is all yours, nothing to do with Vincent, even?'

She shook her head, 'Or Rae. And I have plans for more.'

Jimmy said, 'Rae's working with Vincent now?'

She nodded, no longer smiling, and he wondered how much she knew. Vincent was a different breed to Marshall. He'd been born into wealth, had a titled mother, the best education money could buy, a trophy wife. But he had also learned a criminal cunning from Marshall; had chosen to come down here and run Vella's and subsequently the properties, and now he was realising his dream by properly branching out into the motor trade. All of this formed a deadly combination. Whether Vincent hated his dad or not – and Jimmy had to assume his feelings towards his father had never been ones of warmth – he was now employing many of his dear dad's methods in his own business. Jimmy had discovered that when Vincent set his sights on something, he was not above persuading people who didn't see things the way he did round to his way of thinking. And, just like Marshall, his main weapon was turning out to be Rae Diamond.

Vincent was smoother than his dad, silver-tongued and charming, but despite his education, his bloodline and what he thought of himself, Vincent Vella was still a chip off the old block.

Jimmy wondered how much Faith understood about him. But judging from the cool look on her face at the mention of her brother and Vincent, she wasn't totally ignorant. He was saved from having to ask when the lead singer of the first band sidled up to Faith and asked, 'Ready to go?'

Faith grinned, and said to Jimmy, 'Devlin will see you out, Detective.'

240

Jimmy nodded at Devlin at the door, annoyed to find his feelings hurt for a second time. He had no hold over Faith, of course; this wasn't exactly a date, for goodness sake. But he had been about to offer to see her home when the musician had come along and she'd dismissed Jimmy without even a proper goodbye. Just like he'd been about to kiss her on the opening night – about to imagine what might happen next – when Devlin had got in his way.

He knew he was being ridiculous, but sitting there, listening to music with Faith had, he realised, been the closest thing to fun he'd experienced in a long while. He definitely needed to get out more. He made a mental note to do just that. There were plenty of other women he could spend the evening with, and ones who were far more suitable than Faith bloody Diamond, too.

He headed to the station. His shift had finished hours ago, but he had no real desire to go home just yet and told himself he may as well look over the old nude cases before he did.

But he found the same thing he always did. No connection other than Marshall Vella. Even the latest casualty had at one time worked for him.

They all had sexually transmitted diseases, but then most of the girls in that line of work did. Most of the victims had unwanted children or pregnancies, but again, not uncommon. And they all had sad lives that met a terrible end. That was the main depressing factor.

Eventually, he started to put the files away and realised

the sun had come up and officers were beginning to arrive.

Cal said, 'Shouldn't you be home by now?'

Jimmy filled him in on the previous night's turn of events.

'Edith McCann has always been a horror. I remember her as a kid.'

'Do you?'

Cal nodded, 'Of course, the families round these parts have been here for generations. She has a brother who's been in the nick on and off for most of his life. Her mother passed away around the time she met Stuart McCann.'

'The dad?'

Cal nodded.

Jimmy asked, 'Flake?'

'Oh yes, without a single redeeming feature.' Cal laughed, 'In a lot of ways, they make the perfect couple.'

Jimmy frowned, 'They're not safe around their own children.'

Cal said, 'Often the way, son.'

It was. Jimmy knew this, but it still made him angry. It had been hard for Lilly, losing her husband so young. The only woman back where he'd grown up without a man at home. Her parents had both passed, but she'd put her heart and soul into raising him, and, goodness knew, he probably wasn't the easiest kid in the world.

Cal told him, 'Stuart and Edith McCann have been fighting as long as they've known each other. He'll occasionally nip back under the guise of seeing the children, and, more fool her, she opens the door every time. We were all sad to see Roxy end up where she did.'

Jimmy felt a fresh wave of indignation again. 'Beverly is fourteen and looks even younger than that. Her mother had someone lined up.'

Cal sighed, 'Yes.'

'We can't even go after him because we've no charge to get him on.'

Cal nodded, 'It's true.'

Jimmy thought about Faith and Roxy, who had that man's address and his name. He should feel guilty, perhaps. Should have taken it from Beverly himself. They'd send one of the Diamond brothers in after all, probably Rae. But he didn't feel guilty. He felt satisfied. Where angels feared to tread, Rae Diamond could trample through all he wanted. Sometimes it took the devil to get the job done.

Eventually, he did head home, dark thoughts passing over him like a thick, heavy blanket, suffocating his brain, sticking him to the settee. He sat very still and finally sleep came for a few fitful hours. And when his alarm clock rang, signalling the start of a new shift, he was relieved.

Chapter Forty-Seven

Edith McCann's Flat, Acton

The following morning, I felt as though my fantastic, carefree night at Diamonds had happened a long time ago. I'd allowed myself to switch off after Roxy took Beverly, knowing I'd have to face things today. I had Devlin by my side. I'd left Roxy and Beverly at Sunningdale Avenue, Rae had gone to pay the waiting punter a visit and I didn't feel a second of remorse or regret about anything. He'd make it out alive, because that's what I'd specified, but only just.

As I stood now at Edith McCann's door, I was full to the brim with hot, effervescent anger. It was worsened when Edith answered with a smile on her face that quickly dropped into a snarl. 'I thought Roxy was with you.'

My hand flew out before me, my fingers forming a strong cuff and wrapping themselves around Edith's neck. I felt nothing but satisfaction as I squeezed, watching the woman's shocked face as she was pushed back inside her flat.

Devlin stepped in behind me, closing the door quietly

after us, which proved to be pointless, because Edith — who I had thrown to the floor — was wailing like a demented banshee. She kept going, pulling herself up, using the wall for support — utterly over the top.

When she didn't stop screaming, standing there in her hallway, I stepped forward again, slapped her hard across her face, and put a finger to my lips, my face close to hers.

Edith finally seemed to realise that her theatrics weren't going to help matters. She stopped snivelling, and I smiled.

'Let's nip inside proper and have us a word, eh?'

Edith flicked her eyes towards Devlin and said, 'My Stuart wouldn't want a wog in here.'

I stared at her, gobsmacked, and looked at Devlin, who only rolled his eyes.

'Your Stuart will be grateful we paid a respectful visit rather than just eradicating you pair of sorry cunts from the face of the Earth. Now let's go through. Let's have a chat.'

The front room stank and there, sitting small and subdued on the settee, was Roxy's little brother.

I went over to him and knelt down. 'Hello, Tyler, remember me? I'm a friend of your mum's.'

The little boy nodded, staring down at his hands.

I reached out to raise his face and the poor little bugger flinched. I could see that he was filthy.

I said softly, 'I'm not going to hurt you, darling, I'm here to take you to Roxy.'

He looked up then, meeting my gaze with big, sad

eyes. He couldn't have been more than five. I was suddenly reminded of my own brothers. Neglected just as I had been, sometimes scalded, beaten.

I swallowed back the memories and said, 'This is my friend Devlin.'

Devlin came over, got himself down to the boy's height, smiling. 'All right, Ty?'

The little boy nodded.

I said, 'Why don't you go with Dev and get a few of your things together, eh?'

He took Dev's hand, dwarfed by him, and together they left the room.

Edith watched everything from hooded eyes, frown firmly in place. She had that kind of way about her, an amalgamation of righteous rage and self-pity. I had never warmed to her. Never forgotten what she'd put Roxy through. But I understood all the same why my friend felt such a need to protect her mother, to look after her. Full of the misplaced hope that she wasn't that bad, really.

I said, 'Detective Rose bumped into Beverly last night.'

And Edith's face paled. She gnawed at her lower lip but shrugged, 'So?'

'She said you were keen for her to get a job.'

Edith snarled then, a rabid dog. 'Roxy left me high and fucking dry this week. Me and Stu ain't even had enough to get bread and milk in.'

'A fucking week?'

Edith was still glaring, nostrils flaring with every outraged breath. 'Well, it's all right for you, but we're not all rolling in dough. Times are hard, you get a crust however you can.'

I resisted the urge to go and kick the woman from here to next week. Instead, I smiled, keeping my voice even and steady. 'When I was a kid, I hated my mum. One of my earliest memories is of walking into the living room and finding her there with her hand around Harry the butcher's knob. Remember him?'

Edith nodded that she did. He had long since passed by then, but once upon a time, everyone had bought their Sunday roasts from Harry, when they had enough in the piggy bank.

'He stood up pretty quick, handed me a shilling, scurried out the door and, *God*, I hated her. Why couldn't she be normal? Why did she have to do that?'

Edith sniffed, patted her hair and looked out of the window. Back in the day, she'd taken great delight in gossiping about Shirley. They all had.

I said, 'Thing is, that night we ate, and we ate well. What she did wasn't done for fun and wasn't done for herself. She had us, was younger then than I am now. An enormous weight for one person to bear. Three hungry, difficult little buggers. But she provided, Edith, and do you know, I don't think it ever crossed her mind that selling one of us instead would have been a better alternative.'

Edith opened her mouth to speak, but I pressed a finger to my lips.

'The reason, Edith, that it didn't occur to her, is because it's a sick thought. Fucking disgusting. Do you understand?'

Edith pursed her lips.

I said, 'Two of you. Two adults, with him in and out as he pleases, and you can't scrape together enough to keep 'em fed.'

I looked around the living room. On the table, there were bottles of booze, a pack of fags. The flat looked loads better than it had, and I knew that was because Roxy had had it decorated, bought pieces of furniture over the years, seen to it her siblings didn't go without like she had.

She said, 'Tell Roxy to come home, we'll sort it out.' And her tone was suitably deferential, pleading even.

But it was too little, too late.

I shook my head, 'Roxy will only be coming here to get her things, and Beverly's. Frankie will be with them, so don't bother with any of your shit. What you're going to do is pack them all up, neatly, and make sure they're ready for her.'

Devlin came back in with the boy and a small bag.

I stood up to leave and we headed towards the door, Edith in hot pursuit.

She didn't even glance at her little son. She just said, 'You can't just take my bloody kids.'

'Watch me.'

Back at Sunningdale Avenue, Shirley had the kettle on. Beverly was sitting in the living room with Roxy and Frankie, who seemed to be making them both laugh. I poked my head around the door with Devlin, the little boy between us. Tyler's face lit up when he saw Roxy and he went barrelling straight towards her. Beverly, sat beside her sister, joined in on the hug.

Shirley came in with a tray full of cups of tea, which she delivered around the room. Then her eyes fell on Tyler. She went over to him, leaning down and smiling, 'You must be Tyler?'

He nodded, overwhelmed, maybe, by the sheer number of people in the room. I could so easily forget what it was like for newcomers to be surrounded by my family.

'I'm Shirley. I'm hoping you and your sisters are going to come and stay here with me for a bit?'

I closed my eyes in relief. I hadn't expected much resistance from Shirley, but I was glad at her obvious pleasure at the new arrivals.

The boy smiled, nodded, then put his arms around Shirley for a hug.

My mother beamed, cradling his little body to hers, then she picked him up and suggested he helped her get biscuits for everyone.

Once she was gone, I said to Roxy, 'Take Bev up to my room, she can borrow some of my clothes, then Frankie will take you over to Edith's to grab some bits, all right?'

Roxy stood. She paused at the door of the living room, then surprised me by pulling me in for a hug. I patted her awkwardly on the back, just like last time – not great with displays of affection.

Roxy said to me, 'Thank you, Faith.'

I shrugged. 'You're family to us, Rox.' Roxy's eyes

shone with tears and it was more than I could take. 'Go on now. I'm sure Frankie needs to get on.'

Frankie and Devlin were both grinning at me.

I snapped, 'What's so funny?'

'You are, sis. Under that iron exterior, you're all heart, eh.'

I glared at them both, but they were right. I had to be tough as nails about life for many reasons. Though, this past year, I'd felt mostly numb. Like the calm after the storm.

At that moment, stood in the living room on Sunning-dale Avenue, I felt properly connected to my brothers for the first time in a long time and that warmed me a little. Frankie just for being Frankie and Rae . . . well, he might have had his flaws, but I wasn't above utilising them and I knew he'd see that man off, as well he should.

Iron exterior indeed.

I went into the kitchen to find Shirley. My mother was heading into her middle age, but watching her there that day, sunlight streaming in through the window behind her, she could have been a young girl. She turned, saw me and smiled crookedly. This was a big ask of her. The boy was a small child and Shirley had already raised three of them.

I said, 'Thanks, Mum.'

Shirley shook her head and said, 'Thank you, Faith.'

I frowned, 'What for? Saddling you with more little nippers to raise?'

'For giving me a second chance.'

'What do you mean?'

'I wasn't a good mum, worse at some points than others, and I can't change any of that, can't make it right. I didn't know any better.' She stood straighter. 'But now I do, and helping your friends is the least I can do.' She picked up the biscuits and left the kitchen.

Leaving me staring out at the little patch of grass beyond our house, bombarded by memories and somehow unable to tell my mother that I knew she had done her best. That I'd always known that.

Chapter Forty-Eight

Arthur Stockwell's bedsit, Acton

Jimmy had known what would happen, of course. He took young Merilyn with him when the call came in, heading to the same address that Beverly had had scrawled on that piece of paper. The one that Jimmy had given Faith. That Faith had given her brothers.

The first thing he noticed when he walked into the room was the smell.

Metallic, ripe, bodily. Blood.

The bed was soaked in it, along with smears of shit, where Arthur Stockwell had soiled himself. And who could blame him? Rae Diamond turning up in the middle of the night armed with his macabre bag of tricks was enough to empty anyone's bowels. Jimmy would dare any man to remain calm in such a situation.

Arthur himself was currently in the hospital, where, due to the severity of his injuries, it was likely he would remain for some time.

Jimmy and Merilyn took photographs of the scene and then started working through his room methodically. They found two Polaroids of a teenage girl, which

Jimmy took and sealed into an evidence envelope. They also found tickets to a few local strip clubs and, of all things, Vincent Vella's business card. Jimmy slipped that into his trouser pocket, unseen by Merilyn. There could be any number of reasons for Arthur to have it, but Vincent would need to be questioned, and everything was so finely balanced since Marshall was put away, Jimmy thought it might be better for him to deal with it on the down-low.

Merilyn was holding her nose as they left the awful, grotty little place. One of many bedsits in a not-so-bad block.

Jimmy grinned at her, 'Not the best start to the day, is it.'

She shook her head, 'So that's the man Beverly McCann was on her way to?'

Jimmy nodded grimly.

Merilyn said, 'My guess is the girl gave the Diamonds the address and they sent Rae in.'

Jimmy nodded, 'It's a reasonable guess.'

Merilyn was silent whilst they walked out and climbed back into the car, heading out towards the hospital. She still hadn't spoken by the time they arrived, which, considering she was often given to more talking than strictly necessary, felt distinctly off.

Jimmy eventually said, 'You all right, mate?'

She shrugged.

Jimmy pushed, 'Come on.'

'I know Arthur is a sick fucker . . .'

Jimmy smiled. Merilyn rarely swore, but when she did, she meant it, 'That he is.'

'But Rae Diamond's not exactly an angel, is he?'

Jimmy sighed, 'No, he's not.'

'And he's likely going to get away with this, isn't he?'

Jimmy's thoughts stretched through his mind like tentacles. Beverly's thin legs in a too-short skirt. Rae's face – always calm, but with a hint of menace. Faith Diamond, beautiful and efficient. Roxy McCann all those years ago, claiming she'd fallen down a flight of stairs. He tried to gather them together enough to answer Merilyn in a way that would satisfy her.

He understood – God knew, he did. He'd started out with such firm, unshakable ideas of right and wrong. Two sides. Black and white. The goodies and the baddies. But life just wasn't like that.

He turned to Marilyn and said, 'Sometimes I think it just has to be a case of deciding which is the lesser of two evils and going after the big one.'

The smell of antiseptic and disinfectant hit them as soon as they stepped into the building. Jimmy hated hospitals with a passion. He'd spent hours in and out of Kent, visiting Lilly. As she got sicker and sicker, her stays got longer and longer. Until the final stint, where all they could do was 'make her comfortable'. In the end, Jimmy had brought her home. He couldn't see the point in her being there. They'd warned him it would be round-the-clock care, and whilst she may only last a few days, it could be weeks. Jimmy had shrugged. What did a few weeks matter after the lifetime she'd given him?

It had turned out to be just a week in the end. She'd been in huge pain for most of it, the morphine working less and less as the disease ravaged her entire body. But they'd talked. He'd sat in the garden with her. She'd told him endless stories about James, about their early days together. How excited they'd both been when they knew Jimmy was coming. Their elation on the day he was born. Lilly told him, 'It's the happiest I ever saw him, Jim.' And Jimmy had grabbed onto that with a desperation and a longing he couldn't put into words. Instead, he'd just held her hand and she had nodded at him, rubbed his forehead as though he was the one in need of soothing. And perhaps he was, because even in death, she shone bright.

Now he was on the ward at Acton Hospital, Merilyn trailing behind him, wondering whether his mum would be proud. Whether his father would be. Jimmy knew from other officers that his father had been both friend and foe to the people on his watch, but he wasn't sure how much of that Lilly knew. He told himself, as he stood at the foot of Arthur Stockwell's hospital bed, the man's face swollen and protruding like a mangled caricature of a human being, that she wouldn't have understood.

But he knew she would.

She just would have made different choices.

Standing there, he felt closer to his dad than he ever had. The secrets that James did keep from Lilly, things that Cal had alluded to . . . The thin blue line dealing out punishments on the occasions they saw fit. Doing things for the greater good. Things like this, Jimmy told himself, even though his stomach was churning with an uneasy nausea.

The man on the bed wheezed.

A nurse arrived and leaned over him, 'Mr Stockwell, the police are here to see you. Do you think you can sit?'

He nodded, and she helped him into a more upright position. It took many painful seconds. Merilyn was studiously looking out of the window, but Jimmy forced himself to watch. He had handed the address to Faith, had sealed this man's fate. The least he could do was acknowledge it, warts and all.

One of Arthur's eyes was swollen completely shut. The other was surrounded by a burgeoning bright bruise about to dance through a spectacular array of colours over the coming days.

The nurse held water out to him, which he sipped through a straw, wincing with every swallow. She nodded at Jimmy and Merilyn, then left the room.

Merilyn hung back and Jimmy asked Arthur, 'How are you feeling?'

'Oh, just magic.'

Jimmy reckoned the man would be frowning if the swelling had left any room at all for expression.

Jimmy said, 'Surprised you've the energy for sarcasm, Arthur.'

He didn't respond.

Jimmy pulled up the hard-backed hospital chair and settled himself into it. He had spent hours sitting on chairs just like these, and he knew they eventually left you numb from the hips down. He shuffled himself now, leaning towards Arthur, 'You're good friends with Edith McCann?'

He kept looking over Jimmy's shoulder. 'Stu and me was at school together.'

Jimmy grinned, 'And you took a shine to his daughter?'

Arthur didn't say anything.

Jimmy asked, 'What happened to you last night, then?'

He sort of guffawed, 'Like you don't bloody know.'

'Enlighten me.'

Arthur clenched his jaw, causing himself a short, sharp shock of pain. He hissed through his teeth and Jimmy found that he was actually enjoying this moment. He suspected then that Rae got a lot more job satisfaction than most.

'Fell down the stairs.'

'You were found in your bed.'

'Walked back up them, then.'

Jimmy shrugged, 'We'll go with that, shall we?'

Merilyn said, 'We didn't see any blood on the stairs and considering the state of you . . .'

Arthur snapped, 'I walked carefully.' Glaring at Jimmy as he spoke.

Jimmy tore off the written statement, handed it to Merilyn and told her, 'Head down, I'll follow.'

She hesitated, but only for the briefest of moments.

Once she was gone, Jimmy leaned over Arthur and the man shrank back. Jimmy found that he was glad he was scared, though he didn't intend to hurt him. There were lines Jimmy wouldn't cross. Ones he didn't want to cross. 'Beverly McCann is a child.'

Arthur said, 'None of the girls in that family are children, look at her slag of a sister.'

Jimmy glared, 'Careful, Arthur, you don't want another visit from Rae.'

He let out that soulless laugh again – a sharp, high-pitched titter in the white, sterile room. 'And he's a fine one to bloody judge.'

Jimmy frowned, 'Rae doesn't hurt children though, Arthur, does he.'

Arthur held Jimmy's gaze long enough for questions to form in his mind.

'He doesn't hurt children, no.' He emphasised the word children. Then shrugged, looked away.

Jimmy took out Vincent's card. 'I found this?'

Arthur grinned then, his rubbery, silver-looking lips crusted white at the corners and cracking as he stretched them into a grin. The few teeth he had in his head were yellowing and thin. 'Me and Vince are old mates, didn't you know?'

Jimmy said, 'I doubt that.'

Arthur shrugged, 'Whatever.' His face was closing down.

Jimmy added, 'Rae works for Vincent. He'd hardly let his friend take a kicking off his lackey, would he.'

But Arthur was gone, eyes glassing over, settling back into the pillow.

As Jimmy left, he heard the man say, 'There are all kinds of friendships, Detective.'

Chapter Forty-Nine

Sunningdale Avenue

Two weeks had passed since Arthur Stockwell's savage attack, and lunch at Sunningdale Avenue had been going well until Rae turned up, half-cut and in the mood to pick fights wherever he could. I knew Shirley had been fussing all week about what to cook, who would sit where, and whether anyone would mind that Devlin was there. Up until Rae's wobbly, loud entrance, it had been a success.

Shirley had a new lease of life since the children had arrived and Devlin was the icing on the cake for her. For the first time in perhaps forever, they felt like a family. Not your average family, admittedly, but they'd all been chatting, eating, drinking a bottle of fizz I had brought in from Diamonds. Like any normal occasion. The sort other people likely took for granted.

Watching my mum carve meat, serve potatoes and wipe up spillages, I could see the woman she was always meant to be, and I was pleased. It was getting too crowded in the house for me by then and I was spending more time at Diamonds than I did there. I'd started looking for a place of my own, and I'd finally be able to do it knowing my mum would be all right without me.

But Rae had turned up after all. Late, despite the fact that I had stressed to him that it was important to Mum that he be there on time. He was playing with Tyler, who was too young to know what drunkenness looked like or understand its awful implications. But everyone else was tense. Rae was a big man with a big presence and he'd come in here in a foul mood, instantly changing the atmosphere around the table.

He slid down next to Roxy, grinning at her. She nodded back at him, eyes flitting to Frankie, who shifted along so she could, too.

Rae – not too drunk to not notice that – frowned, 'What, too good to sit next to me now?'

I said, 'Rae.' A warning in my voice.

He turned to grin at me, his face mellowing slightly. 'All right, sis.'

'Maybe you should have a little lie-down.'

He laughed, 'I'm all right, thanks. It's a bit early for bed.'

He turned back to Roxy, wrapped an arm around her and pulled her in close. 'Unless you fancy joining me, girl, old times' sake.'

It happened fast. Frankie was up, off his chair and yanking Rae from his.

Rae, who had not been expecting it, slid backwards, landing sprawled and awkward, banging his head on the floor.

Devlin stood quickly, taking Tyler by the hand,

ushering Beverly out of her chair. 'You two go out to the garden, yeah?'

Beverly paused, but only for a second. She could likely see as well as anyone where this was headed.

Shirley moved to her sons, standing in front of Frankie, reaching down for Rae, who smacked her hand away, getting himself up.

He looked at Roxy. 'No? Not even for old times' sake?' Then he looked at his brother. 'She fucking loved it once.'

And Frankie lunged.

They were a mass of fists and kicks. The table went over, Shirley screamed and Devlin, who'd just come back in, tried to split them up, getting a swift right hook from Rae for his troubles. I stood in front of Roxy, who was now in tears.

Devlin tried to go in again and was knocked backwards by one of them, it was impossible to tell which. But Rae was spiralling across the table, diving for something, and when he stood again, there was a glint in his fist. A deathly silence engulfed the room. Rae had the carving knife in one hand and Frankie in a tight grip with the other. His face was close to Frankie's and he looked at him with an almost loving expression. But the blade was pressed firmly to Frankie's neck.

Everyone stilled. I could feel Roxy behind me, shaking.

Shirley said, 'Come on, Rae.'

But he ignored her, eyes still glued to his brother. He said, 'Do you remember, Frankie, that fire truck?

Someone gave it me. Not Bass, one of the others before him.'

Frankie nodded, trapped by the blade, and I watched it dig in a little with the movement of his head.

'You loved that truck, but you waited, didn't you, until I was done with it.'

Frankie didn't speak, didn't move.

Rae said, 'I'd grown sick of it to be honest, plus I'd smashed it up a bit, none of the moving bits really worked anymore, the ladder got stuck. It was a bit shit by then.'

I was frozen, transfixed by the awful scene before me, my mind whirring.

'Thing is, Frank, I saw you playing with it and, all of a sudden, I remembered how much fun I used to have with it.' Rae paused.

A bead of blood trickled from a split above his eyebrow and he leaned into his brother, wiping the blood back along his hair, blinking it out of his eye.

'Mum told me off when I tried to take it back. Said I'd done with it and it was your turn.'

Faith closed her eyes. She could remember the bloody thing clearly, and also what had happened to it.

'Thing is, Frank, it was mine and while I didn't want it, that didn't mean you could just have it. Do you remember what I did?'

Frankie didn't answer, his mouth set in a grim line.

'You remember, Mum, don't you?' Rae was smiling again, that awful manic smile.

Shirley was crying. 'Let him go, Rae. He's your brother.'

But Rae kept hold, kept a firm grip on him. 'I smashed that fucking truck to pieces, Frankie. Remember?'

Then Frankie moved fast, throwing an elbow back into Rae's stomach and ducking out of his grip.

Devlin swooped in and grabbed the knife from Rae, who looked at him and hissed, 'Another man who doesn't mind his things second-hand.'

Devlin raised his fist, but Shirley jumped in just in time.

Rae sneered at him, kicked a chair that was in his path and turned to leave. He paused at the door and waved at Roxy, 'See you soon, yeah.'

Frankie went to run after him, but Devlin grabbed him before he could.

I put my hands on his shoulders with a loud, 'No.'

Frankie looked at me with tears in his eyes. 'He's got a screw loose, Faith.'

And I couldn't disagree with that. But he was still my brother.

I turned and followed Rae out onto the road, running to try and catch up to him. But he was gone. To where, I didn't know.

He worried me, Rae. As I walked familiar streets looking for him, my mind clouded with memories of him from over the years. He was his own worst enemy, of course, forcing himself to be separate, different. Apart from the rest of us. But I remembered him as a boy, crying when Shirley was cruel or one of her punters hurt him. Stealing food, money, making my life easier. And

Frankie's. I remembered the night he'd stabbed Bass and I'd found him, hands clenched around Shirley's throat. I remembered clinging to him tightly, both of us covered in blood. I'd held so steadfastly to my big brother that the police had had to prise me off him. Because, in those tumultuous years, Rae was safety. Rae was the one me and Frankie looked to when we needed help, and he had always obliged.

That was what would be hurting Rae as much as anything else. He loved Frankie, but the days where Frankie looked up to him were long gone and, again, that was Rae's own fault.

I'd guessed there was something between Frankie and Rox. Everyone knew really. I had known it would cause trouble eventually, and now look.

I gave up looking for him and headed home.

I knocked and Frankie opened the door. His face was steely, chin up and looking at me warily.

I said, 'No need for that, you could have told me.'

'What, asked your permission on who I can and can't fall in love with?'

I opened my mouth to respond. Realised he was right and shut it again.

My mum and Devlin were in the living room with the kids. I looked in and Shirley asked, 'Is he all right?'

'I couldn't find him.'

Devlin said, 'Leave him to cool off.'

And I nodded, following Frankie to the kitchen, where Roxy was sitting at the table, hands wrapped around a cup of tea, eyes red-ringed from crying. She stood as I came in, 'I'm sorry, Faith.'

I sighed, sank down into a seat and picked up a pack of fags, lighting one.

I looked at them both. Frankie next to Roxy, an arm slung across her shoulders. The marks from his brother's fists visible on his face, and I suspected his body would be covered too.

He said, 'Nice that you went after him.'

And I snapped, 'Well, I knew you'd be all right since you've got a whole crowd here.'

Frankie said, 'He's only got himself to blame.'

And I knew it was true, but still. I was the only person Rae hadn't pushed away really. Things had never been right between him and Shirley. Not after Bass. I knew our mother loved him, but Rae held resentments like they were precious gifts. He didn't have the ability to let anything go. I knew in my heart of hearts that he'd never forgive Frankie for this. My family was split, and I was stuck right in the middle.

I said, 'You must have known he'd be pissed off.'

Frankie said, 'He doesn't own her.' And his voice was a growl.

I wiped a hand over my face. 'I know, Frankie. I know that, and I know he's out of order.'

'But?'

'But he's still our brother.'

'And Roxy's my girl.'

I looked from one to the other. My friend, who had been through the mill more than once; my brother, who

265

had only ever really been able to come into his own in his brother's absence. Both deserved happiness. Of course they did.

Frankie said, 'We're moving out, I've got us a flat. We were going to tell him.' He added, '*Tell*, Faith, not ask.'

I nodded. 'And I'm pleased for you, Frankie.'

I looked at him. Searching his eyes for understanding.

He sighed, 'I know, sis.' Then he added, 'What a shitty Sunday roast.'

And I smiled, despite myself. 'Diamond family events, eh?'

Chapter Fifty

Rae Diamond's flat

I couldn't get my mind off Rae. The following week, I was still thinking about him. I went to his flat, feeling like a thief in the night. I unlocked the door, slid inside and waited, holding my breath. I didn't expect to see him there – word on the street was that he'd headed out to Kent with Vincent. None of us had really seen him since his and Frankie's awful argument. Whilst everyone else seemed glad to see the back of him, and I could understand why, I still wanted to connect with him. I couldn't believe that there was anything we couldn't overcome.

I shouted out, 'Rae?'

Visions of his hand, knife dangling from it, should have pushed a well of fear into me. But I wasn't scared of him. I refused to be.

Silence.

The place was a mess. Bottles, vials, cigarette packets. Remnants of half-eaten food. In stark contrast, in his bedroom hung three neatly pressed, steamed suits. He always looked smart as a pin, but I knew that the chaos he had evidently been living in was far more in line with Rae's insides than his polished outward exterior.

Rage. Drink. Drugs. Cocaine. I'd known he was back on the stuff and I hadn't acted. Hadn't done anything at all. Just like I'd known about Frankie and Roxy, known it would explode eventually.

I'd turned a blind eye and hoped for the best.

I'd felt disconnected from my family, had even wished for it in a lot of senses. Happy to let Shirley take over the day-to-day care of them all, and longing for a future for myself, getting to know new kinds of people, living my life. My job at Diamonds made me sought after. People were after me to buy their products, promote their band. Half of London wanted a job in my club or a spot on the guest list. I was photographed in the local press with all the celebrities who blew through my door, and I liked it. I was doing well, and honestly, I resented the petty dramas my brothers brought to my door.

But it couldn't be that way. Had never been that way. I wasn't a free agent. I had my mum. And Frankie and Rae, and now Roxy and the little ones to consider. I couldn't swan around doing what I liked without a care for any of them. I could have stopped this situation blossoming into what it had become. But I didn't. Instead, I'd been so wrapped up in my own plans, my mind heady with even bigger ideas. Foolish plans of freedom that would never come to fruition. No matter what I achieved, I was still a Diamond. They were still my responsibility, whether I liked it or not. And now look where they were.

I took a deep breath, headed into the kitchen, pulled out a large bin bag and a cloth and set to work.

I don't know why I felt I had to, certainly Rae wouldn't appreciate it, likely would barely notice the place had been cleaned. And threatening Frankie with a fucking knife was more than a step too far. But I couldn't abandon him.

I worked through the small, two-roomed place methodically. When I came to a set of Polaroids stuffed at the back of his bedside drawer, secured together with a thick rubber band, I almost laughed. Obsessed with naked women, my brother.

But one picture caught my eye. It was a face I'd seen before, but I couldn't think where.

Then, suddenly, I knew. And a cool, tremulous feeling winged its way through my guts.

Staring up at me, blank-eyed and naked, was a face I'd seen in the paper.

'Nude woman pulled out of the Thames just yards from the Corinthian yacht club . . .'

The headline flashed like a beacon in my mind. This could have been taken before the time of her death – it might not even be his. She might have been alive in the photo. But something about it made me think not.

The dark shadow around the woman's neck, the vacant, staring eyes, the grass underneath the woman's pale, naked skin, which could have belonged to the riverbank close to where she was found. It was slightly out of focus, though, and it might not have even been her . . . But even as I thought that, my own brain seemed to laugh at me mockingly.

There were three pictures. Of the same woman in the same place, with the same dark mark looped around her neck. I took the Polaroids with a shaking hand and slid them into my handbag.

I picked up the rubbish bags by the door to take down to the bins, locked up behind me, and left with my heart thudding, barely able to catch my breath.

All I could think of as I put one foot in front of the other was Rae, aged thirteen, his hands clenched round Shirley's throat and his face so eerily calm.

Chapter Fifty-One

August 1964

The White Hart

Jimmy was at the bar in The White Hart, listening to Merilyn chatter away. They'd both just finished their shift. She was a nice girl. Lovely, even. He'd known for a while she was sweet on him, and she was good-looking, bright, undemanding. He'd been planning on going home after work, but she'd persuaded him a beer was just what he needed. Now here they were, Merilyn smiling too much, talking too fast, trying too hard, and Jimmy trying desperately to keep up and not let his mind wander.

What the hell was wrong with him that what he actually wanted to be doing was looking over the files on the nude girls? The pathologist had found flecks of paint on his last examination, possibly from a grey car, the same flecks of paint had been found on Sandy Lakeheart, though never followed up, and he wanted to sift through the other cases to see if he found any mention anywhere else. The two men who had seen someone driving off in a rush in the Maria Teddy case had said the vehicle was either a large car or a small van, and grey. So, the flecks of paint seemed to tie at least two of the victims together, and Jimmy couldn't stop thinking about it.

There were other similarities: the missing teeth, the cause of death – though inconclusive – thought to be strangulation. Then there was the glaringly obvious link. The one he lost sleep over every night now.

Marshall Vella.

Who had been sentenced and would never see life outside of Her Majesty's four walls again.

He was pleased about that, of course he was. It was a good catch. *His* catch. And his career had been built on it. He would be going places within the force and that collar had cemented those prospects. Everyone knew his name.

But still. Still . . . Maria Teddy.

The latest girl. There was no way Marshall had done that, but Jimmy's gut said it was the same man.

Merilyn said, 'Jim.'

He looked at her 'Sorry, what?'

She sighed, 'Penny for them?'

'Sorry. Work, is all.'

She nodded, 'My dad was a policeman. I remember my mum complaining when he didn't listen, but,' she shrugged, 'it's different for me, you know, working at the station and all. I understand it.'

He smiled, resisting the urge to roll his eyes. That was half the problem with Merilyn; she was very under-standing. She'd not liked the Arthur stuff and he'd half expected her to say something about it, but after it was done and dusted, back at the station, she'd told him that he was likely in the right. She was agreeable. He could see that. But she just didn't hold his attention.

He was about to make his excuses, when the door to the pub opened and in walked Faith Diamond. He sat up straighter and noticed that his were not the only set of eyes on her. But as she searched around the crowded bar, her eyes eventually rested on him and she smiled, heading over and placing a hand on his arm.

'Detective Rose. Just the man I was after.'

He raised an eyebrow at that and felt Merilyn moving in closer, hand thrust out. 'Hello, Miss Diamond, we met at the station.'

Faith looked at her and nodded, then said to Jimmy, 'I'm sorry, I'm interrupting. It can wait.' And she smiled at Merilyn and started to walk out.

Then Jimmy found himself telling Faith, 'Not at all, we were almost done anyway. Weren't we, Merilyn?'

Merilyn looked set to say something about it, but Jimmy stood up, grabbed his coat and gave the barman a note saying to call the lady a cab home. Then he hurriedly kissed her on the cheek.

Chapter Fifty-Two

Jimmy Rose's flat, Acton

I felt almost sorry for the woman Jimmy left at the bar. He may have been oblivious, but I could see she was disappointed. I saw it all the time, women whose hopes and dreams were held up in the attentions of some bloke. That sort of thing invariably got in the way of a good life. You only had to look at Shirley to see that.

I knew most of my peers were keen to settle down – it was certainly where Roxy was headed and I was sure I'd enjoy being an auntie, which would no doubt be next. But I had no desire to be a mother.

Jimmy asked me, 'Where are we going?'

I said, 'Anywhere we can go to talk that's quiet.'

He hesitated for a moment and then said, 'My place.' Then hastily added, 'Or the station, if it's official, like.'

'I was rather hoping to speak to you off the record.'

He shrugged, 'All right then.'

We walked in silence and it wasn't entirely unpleasant. My day-to-day life was so noisy with the constant chatter of Tyler and Beverly at home. Frankie and Roxy were like lovesick puppies now that their relationship was out in the open, and Devlin was fast becoming a regular fixture, too. At work, it was the same. Occasionally, I might get a few hours in the office with no one bothering me. Asking what I thought . . . what they should do next . . . I loved it, but sometimes a bit of peace and quiet was good too.

We reached Jimmy's flat. It hadn't changed since the last time I was there. It was what you'd call sparse. The only personal touch was a photograph of a good-looking couple – the man unmistakably Jimmy's father – a record player and a stack of vinyls next to it.

He gestured to the settee, 'Take a seat.'

'Thanks.'

He nodded and ran a hand through his hair, making it stand up on end. 'Do you want a drink?'

'What have you got?'

He looked almost stricken at that. 'Probably not much.'

I shrugged, trying not to laugh at his obvious discomfort. 'Whatever you have.'

He came back into the room with a bottle of whisky and two glasses. 'Don't know how long it's been there.'

'It doesn't go off, though, does it?'

He sat on the floor opposite me and poured out short measures, sliding one glass across to me.

'To what, Faith Diamond, do I owe this pleasure?'

I grinned, 'Is it, Detective?'

'Is it what?'

'A pleasure.'

He blushed then, and I felt a wave of fondness for him. And attraction. He wasn't my type, and I was definitely the sort of girl to have one. Young, good-looking and stupid. He was certainly good-looking and he wasn't old, but Jimmy Rose wasn't stupid.

I took a sip of my drink, trying to iron out those thoughts from my mind. That wasn't why I was here and I didn't need to embarrass the poor bugger either.

'I appreciate your time.'

He shrugged, 'I'm not on shift.'

'But you were on a date.' He sighed at that and I asked, 'Was it not going well?'

He laughed, 'Even if it had been, I don't think there will be a next time.'

I said, 'I saw the way she looked at you. There'll be a next time, if you want one.'

'I know.' But he didn't sound happy about it.

It was my turn to laugh. 'Poor girl.'

He frowned, 'Right, well, now we've finished dissecting my love life, what can I do for you?'

'I wanted to talk to you about . . .' I paused and he waited. I said, 'The women, girls . . .'

'The nudes?'

I nodded and his face seemed to fall.

'Looks like I called that one wrong, eh.'

'Maybe so.' I felt a wave of pity for him and said, 'But we got Marshall Vella off the streets, didn't we?'

He nodded, a smile, but a thin one. 'We did, but while my back was turned, someone was still targeting those women.'

I asked him the thing I'd come there to ask: 'Who do you think it is?'

He laughed, 'If I knew that, Faith . . .' Then, 'I'd ask Vincent. He knew his dad's dealings as well as anyone, but he was as convinced as me that it was Marshall. The next person closest to him would be . . . Well.' He meant Rae, of course.

'Someone confessed, didn't they?'

My heart was pounding. I wanted him to say yes and that it was definitely that guy, he was going down, it was all over and my brother was definitely not a weird homicidal maniac.

'Yeah, but he was being paid by Marshall to open after hours. Marshall thought he would be good to take the fall, although it was flimsy – a proper half-hearted attempt.' He took a sip of his drink, wincing slightly. 'Honestly, I should have known then. Marshall didn't try and evade us particularly hard; even the fake confession was an afterthought, and he had no idea about Sandy Lakeheart. But I so wanted it to be him.'

I said, 'Me too.'

'Really.'

'Well, if not him . . .'

He watched me and it was my turn to colour, but not from embarrassment. From fear. Fear of what I could not say. Couldn't even believe I was thinking.

But Jimmy wasn't stupid and maybe a part of me was there because I wanted to tell him.

For what? Confirmation? Reassurance?

He said, 'Do you have any ideas?' and the air between

us seemed heavy. 'Someone you know, Faith?'

And I looked up at him, half wanting him to say it, half willing him not to.

'Rae?' he asked quietly.

I shook my head, 'It's stupid. He's not bad. But like you say, he's closest to Marshall. Maybe he . . . knows something.'

My lower lip trembled and for a terrible second I thought I was going to cry.

I pulled the whisky to me, swallowed it in one. And went to stand. I shouldn't have been there, shouldn't have come, and I knew that I should definitely leave.

I made to go to the door, but Jimmy stepped in my way. I braced myself for a fight, to tell him he was wrong, but I didn't get one.

Instead, he leaned forward and kissed me.

Chapter Fifty-Three

Farthing Park, Kent

I drove up to the Kent house. Nora Vella's home was a mansion, really. A whole estate. Apparently, Nora's family had lost pretty much all of their money, but had kept hold of this. A huge property on a large patch of land. I could see servants' cottages bigger than our family home on Sunningdale Avenue. And I thought to myself, not for the first time, what a difference birth could make.

I wasn't intimidated by it, though. When I'd first met Vincent, I'd been nervous around him, dazzled by his education, his accent, this different world which he came from. After working with him, I understood that the only difference between us was money and I could do something about that.

I rang the ornate doorbell, fully expecting a butler to answer the door. But it was opened by a pretty young woman with a watchful gaze.

'Can I help you?'

'I'm Faith Diamond. I believe my brother's here.'

The woman nodded, 'Rae?'

'That's the one.'

She swung the door open, and said, 'Do come in. I'm Hannah Vella.'

'Vincent's wife?'

She smiled, a wry expression, and I spotted something in her then that I recognised. Defeat. The same look Shirley had on her face every time Marshall knocked at the door.

'Yes. Vincent's wife. May I take your coat?'

I handed it to her and said, 'I thought you might have staff in a house like this.'

Hannah said, 'We have teams of people who do various things, but no one person in residence.' She added, 'My husband and mother-in-law are quite private people.'

'Good of him to let Rae stay then.'

Hannah sort of winced. 'I think my husband is very fond of him.' She turned to me, again with the forced smile.

I said, 'Well, I know he can be a right pain in the arse, so thanks for putting up with him.'

Hannah laughed at that and I smiled. Then she said, 'To be honest, I haven't seen him any more than I've seen my husband, which is hardly at all. In a place this big, it's easy to be completely alone.'

I thought of Sunningdale Avenue and the club. Places full of bustle and noise and life. Then there was this woman out here in the countryside. Married to a man who I knew spent most of his time in London and apparently ignored her even when he was home. A man I'd once respected. Less so now. It seemed to me he'd been on the charm offensive until he got Marshall locked up.

After his dad had gone down, and watching him take Rae on, I'd discovered that they weren't as different as I'd hoped, after all.

I said to Hannah, 'That's tough.' Because I thought it probably was. Loneliness wasn't something I'd ever had the opportunity to experience in a physical sense, but I understood it. I knew I was the strongest member of my family. The one that held everything together. That could get lonely sometimes, too.

Hannah shrugged, 'Life doesn't always turn out how you think it will.'

'Ain't that the truth?'

'They are out in one of the cottages. I'll take you across.'

We walked through several rooms and eventually reached a large back door. We stepped out into a stunning courtyard full of stables with actual horses in them.

Hannah saw me looking and said, 'Nora's, my mother-in-law. Quite the showjumper in her time.'

I nodded. Trying hard, but completely unable, to picture Marshall here in this setting.

Eventually, we got to a cottage. Hannah opened the door and we headed in to find Rae, Vincent, a man I couldn't place but was sure I'd seen somewhere before, and two women who I could recognise as prostitutes from a mile off. Good-looking but half-dressed, half-cut, and too loud.

So loud in fact that it took a moment for them to realise we were there.

My brother wasn't fully dressed and looked particularly

worse for wear. Vincent was in a suit, looking, as ever, cool, calm and collected. It was he who spotted us and said, 'Ah, Faith, you made it out to the country.' Unperturbed, it seemed, by his wife's presence.

I nodded. The unknown man turned away and started putting on his shirt. Rae tried to stand, but his inebriated state got the better of him and he fell back, a crooked grin on his stupid face.

Vincent patted the other man and nodded to the girls, 'Right, you lot, come on. I'll arrange your lifts back to London. My guess is that Faith wants to speak to her brother in private?'

I smiled tightly and Vincent returned it in kind, though it looked slightly mocking on him.

He grabbed at Hannah's elbow as he went. The poor woman was led away along with Vincent's unlikely procession.

I thought that Rae's mind was probably a bit befuddled. He seemed to look simultaneously pissed off and embarrassed.

He said to me, 'The party wasn't even my idea,' like he'd been caught out doing something naughty. Which I suppose he had, actually.

I said, 'Hannah seemed nice.'

Rae shrugged, 'Suppose.'

'This must be hard on her.' I waved my hand around at the awful detritus. When I'd worked with Vincent in London, it was understood that he didn't do strange and the fact he'd been the only one here fully dressed indicated he himself wasn't partaking in the fun. But this was his house and, I had to assume, his party. He sank even lower in my estimation.

I asked Rae about it and he told me in sloppy, elongated words that essentially Vincent provided girls for many high-profile men. I absorbed that information. Not so different from Marshall, but a better end of the business for the girls, and far more discreet.

Rae smirked at what must have been shock on my face. 'Didn't know about this side of Vincent's business, eh.'

I hadn't, and I wasn't happy with it. Though it was really none of mine. He'd given me the club. I had nothing more to do with him.

As if reading my mind, Rae said, 'Almost like your life's built on their backs, isn't it.'

I turned and hissed at him, 'It's nothing like that. Like you said, I didn't fucking know.'

He sighed, toyed with the paraphernalia on the table in front of him. I wondered if he was thinking about cutting himself a line. He didn't in the end. I suppose me being there spoiled his fun, just a little. He lit a fag, perhaps for want of anything else to do with his hands, and avoided looking at me directly.

Eventually I said, 'You've made yourself at home here, then. Not planning on coming back?'

And he shrugged.

I lit a cigarette of my own, sitting back and considering him through narrowed eyes. 'You look like shit.'

He laughed at that. 'Thanks, sis.'

'How long have you been awake?'

'I don't know, twenty-four hours, forty-eight. Time is a bit iffy out here.'

'In the countryside?'

He nodded. 'The air's fresh though, eh.' And he laughed at that, even though it wasn't funny. The last effects of the lovely high he had probably been in just moments ago.

I said, 'Who's that bloke? I swear I know him . . .'

'Politician of some sort. Martin Parsons.'

I raised an eyebrow and Rae looked at me.

'None of them are any different to us, Faith, they just hide it better.'

I didn't disagree, but I also didn't speak. I'd always been comfortable in Rae's presence, and I thought I was probably one of the few people he was ever at ease with. I sometimes considered the possibility that I was the only person he really loved. But this time, the silence stretched out like fabric pulled too hard, about to rip right down the middle.

'You come here to judge me, Faith?'

I sat forward, reached into my bag and pulled out the Polaroids, laying them on the table.

He said, 'Been snooping around my place, have you?' His words full of attitude, but tone wobbly and thin.

I told him, 'I cleaned it for you. It was a fucking state.'

He said, 'They've got cleaners here, can make as much mess as you like.'

'The Polaroids, Rae.'

He shrugged, but wouldn't meet my eye. My heart thundered in my chest.

'That girl.' I pointed a finger at one of the photos, pressing it down on the woman's face. 'Was it you, Rae?'

I was holding my breath, trying to catch hold of thoughts slipping around my mind like eels.

He mumbled, 'Was it me . . . What, did I kill her?'

His voice was incredulous now. He reached into his pocket for the little vial, taking it out, emptying more than he needed onto the table, trying to line it into shape and failing. Eventually, he just pressed his hand in, inhaling a lump right off the end of his finger.

'How's my traitorous brother?' he asked.

'Happy for once. Are you going to answer my question?'

He stood, 'No. And I can't believe you even fucking asked it. I'm going to get cleaned up and go out. My guess is, you'll be on your way, sis.'

Part Four

'And thus I clothe my naked villainy
With odd old ends stol'n out of holy writ;
And seem a saint, when most I play the devil.'

– William Shakespeare, *Richard III* (1597)

Chapter Fifty-Four

October 1964

Kensington

She wished she'd gone with the other bloke, but it was too late for that. She was in the car, smiling, but it was forced. All that was going through her mind were the screaming headlines, the faces of the women who hadn't made it, strewn over the front pages.

She'd paid attention, of course, but she was a tough little thing. Life had been kicking her about for so many years, she honestly thought it couldn't get any worse. But the way he was looking at her, and the way he was hurting her.

Deliberately.

It wasn't unusual, of course. A lot of the men who procured her services were less than gentle. But there was a difference between those who got carried away in the moment and this.

She squeezed her eyes shut, but he told her to look. She forced them open, just in time to see his fist flying out towards her face.

She thought she'd be OK because she knew him and he'd never been this way. Never really been any way that caused any concern.

She wondered how Tina was faring tonight, whether they'd

meet up soon enough and laugh about this in years to come, as they had many of the bad times gone before.

Her head was ringing with pain. He'd nearly finished and she did her best to smile at him, pulling down her skirt, sliding back on the seat and saying, 'All done then, lovely.' In a too-bright voice that didn't speak to the bruise springing up on her cheek, the faint ache between her legs and a wetness that she thought might be blood pooling there.

'Yes, lovely.'

And his voice was low and condescending and she realised as his hands closed around her throat that he was not all done.

Not all done at all.

And as her eyes closed for the last time, her final thought was of her children.

News of the World

24 Oct 1964

'Police have pieced together enough information to suggest the killer is middle-aged and hunts for victims between 5 foot and 5 foot 3 inches. He prefers the type of prostitute who is prepared to perform unspeakable perversions . . .'

Chapter Fifty-Five

Shepherd's Bush Police Station

Jimmy looked at the woman in front of him. Tina Munroe. Her shoulders shook with each sob. She was a tearful mess, and he couldn't blame her. She'd danced with death, that was for sure. She had every reason to be frightened, saddened. She'd been spared the killer's cruel hands, but her friend, Betty Preston, hadn't been so lucky. Tina filled Jimmy in on the sad details of Betty's life, which included three children, a bout of serious depression which had left her hospitalised, and now this.

Unfortunately for her and for their investigation, Tina had been so drunk that any details of the night Betty went missing were hazy at best. All she could tell Jimmy was that they were approached by two men. Betty went off with one and she went off with the other. She did think Betty had been familiar with them but couldn't say this for certain.

Jimmy sent her off to do a sketch composite. Feeling as frustrated as ever over the nude murders. His mind worked through various possibilities and landed, not for the first time, on Rae Diamond. The more he mulled it all over, the more he came to realise that Marshall Vella wasn't the only link to these girls. There were plenty of men who worked for him who would have had inter-actions with them. He'd drawn up a list of names, which included Rae and Frankie Diamond.

He knew that Rae had been out of London for a while, but he could easily have come back, and that would be the first thing he looked into.

The new victim also had the same paint flecks on her body, and the link to possible mechanics and cars fit Rae, too. He and Vincent were setting up showrooms all over London and they all had mechanics working out back. More than that, even his devoted sister didn't consider him above suspicion. She hadn't come out and said it, but when he'd thought it all through after she'd left, things had started to make sense. Rae had a history of violence, some of it towards women, Roxy for one.

He asked Tina, 'Did you see the colour of the car Betty went off in?'

She said, 'Ummm.'

'White? Grey? Black?'

She shrugged, 'Not black. Lighter-coloured.' Adding, 'It was dark out.'

And she had been drunk, of course.

He should have pushed Faith on her brother. Instead, he'd leaned down and kissed her.

Possibly the least professional moment of his life but also possibly the best.

She hadn't stopped him, had kissed him back, but she'd also left abruptly before it had a chance to develop into anything more. That *more* was something Jimmy thought about way too much and he'd wondered over the past few weeks whether she did, too.

He hadn't told Cal this, or that she'd come to see him, probably about Rae. Or that he'd slept with her all those years ago. In fairness, Cal wasn't as hung up on this case as Jimmy was, though he was working on it, along with most of the officers in the area.

They had undercover WPCs out on the streets. Merilyn was doing her fair share and had told him some of the horrors her evenings entailed on a few of their less-than-successful dates. He'd been hoping that she would grow on him, that he could build a good, sensible relationship with this woman, who was perfect for him. Really, the absolute right fit. But all he could think about was Faith and the litany of problems she came with. Not least her brother being perhaps Jimmy's only real suspect in this case.

There had been another connection found between Theresa, the third victim, and Betty. Both were connected to a married politician – Martin Parsons – had been sleeping with him in fact, who in turn was connected to a Harley Street physiotherapist, Steffan Capel, caught up in a great scandal. He'd been found to be connecting the services of women like them to powerful men who might be looking for such things – with discretion, of course. It hadn't ended well for him after the story made all the front pages, he'd committed suicide, and perhaps these girls were caught up in the same web?

Jimmy had found that connection buried deep in the

paperwork, and would have missed it, but something had niggled at his memory, and there was a reference on Theresa Bell's notes. Connections to Capel. Jimmy wondered if Capel had been connected to Marshall Vella.

He decided it was time to have a chat with Vincent and ask him about it. He had to track down Rae anyway, and he stepped out into the suddenly cold street, half hoping Rae was innocent for Faith's sake, and half hoping he was guilty for everyone else's.

Jimmy reached the car showroom in Chelsea where Vincent and Rae spent most of their working life and couldn't stop himself from feeling impressed. The front of the showroom was filled with beautiful, expensive cars.

He was pounced on within seconds by a well-dressed man, who saw him admiring a Jaguar E-Type and said, 'Isn't she gorgeous?'

Jimmy nodded, because the car was a thing of wonder, but it was also probably a few years' salary for him. Vincent was catering for those with money, that was for sure.

Jimmy got his warrant card out and flashed it at the salesman. 'Word with Mr Vella.'

The man smiled, utterly unruffled, and said, 'Of course, sir, follow me please.'

Behind the showroom was a desk with a receptionist, who stood as they arrived. The salesman told her who he was and she went to announce him to Vincent. Then she ushered Jimmy in.

He was surprised to enter a fairly sparse office, with two desks.

Vincent was standing, coming around his desk and shaking Jimmy's hand. 'Detective Rose, how lovely to see you here.'

Jimmy gestured back to the showroom as he took a seat, 'A huge operation.'

Vincent said, 'Yes. This will be our headquarters, but we've other showrooms ready to go and a large warehouse full of mechanics who can oversee everything up to and after sales. A significant part of our appeal is the fact that we see our customers through not only the purchase of their vehicle, but throughout its lifetime as well.'

'I suspect your customers often want more than one.'

Vincent smiled, 'Yes, the collector is the most valued customer of all, but we cater for many needs.'

Jimmy said, 'I heard you've been acquiring more properties across London?'

The question had an edge, because what Vincent had effectively been doing was offering money for the already occupied spaces, and if it was turned down, sending in Rae. A horrible practice and one Cal was pursuing in the hopes of getting one of the victims to talk on the record. As with all things of this nature, though, most were too scared to do so. And who could blame them?

A memory surfaced of Arthur Stockwell, swollen and bloody in his hospital bed, and Jimmy pushed it away. He was a nonce. He deserved it. But still . . .

Vincent didn't bat an eyelid and told Jimmy, 'We are

indeed expanding and the future looks very exciting.'

'What about Marshall's old properties?' He was still annoyed about the tenants living in such awful conditions.

Vincent nodded, 'I know. I know. They need looking at, sorting out. Honestly, I'm tempted to just sell the lot of them.'

'You've no interest in working as a landlord?'

Vincent sighed, 'None at all, and I'm not proud of how my father managed them.'

He sounded utterly convincing. So much so that Jimmy would have believed him, were it not for the reports of the way he and Rae were out there strong-arming innocent people. Those reports led Jimmy to believe that beneath the benevolent facade, Vincent was a dangerous man.

Jimmy said, 'You should hurry it up, people are living in those slums.'

Vincent shuddered but replied, 'You're right. I've been so busy and putting it off, but it's time.'

He smiled that Cheshire cat smile again and Jimmy felt like he was being placated with charm and agreeability.

Vincent said, 'Speaking of being busy, and knowing that I've got a meeting –' he glanced at an expensive-looking wristwatch – 'in less than ten minutes, was that the purpose of today's visit, Detective?'

Jimmy smiled, 'It wasn't, no. I wanted to ask you about Rae Diamond.'

'Oh?'

'Or, more precisely, his whereabouts.'

Vincent laughed, 'Sounds almost like you're looking for an alibi.'

Jimmy didn't laugh or smile.

Now Vincent said, 'Oh.' In an entirely different tone. And then, 'Whatever it is you think he's done, I can assure you it's highly unlikely.'

'All right . . .'

Vincent sighed, leaned forward over his desk. 'Between you and I, Rae had some . . . family trouble.'

'Family trouble. Like what?'

Vincent waved a hand in an almost apologetic fashion, 'I don't like to gossip, Detective.'

'This isn't gossip, Mr Vella.'

'Right, of course. There was a fight, between Rae and his brother.'

'Frankie Diamond?'

Vincent nodded, 'About a girl.'

'Roxy McCann?'

'Yes, that's the one.'

'She used to work for your dad.'

Vincent wrinkled his nose in distaste. 'She did, yes. Works for Faith now. In fact, as I recall, she started there whilst I was still at the helm. Nice girl.'

'So where is Rae now?'

'Well, that's the thing, Detective, and why I'm quite sure whatever you suspect him of isn't so. Rae has been staying with me at Farthing Park ever since the fight.'

Jimmy raised an eyebrow. 'Very generous of you to open up your home to him.'

Vincent smiled, 'I feel a sort of responsibility towards him.'

'Why's that, then?'

'My father treated him rather badly.'

'Not your fault though, was it?'

Vincent shrugged, 'No, but Rae and all the Diamonds helped out, didn't they.'

'With his capture?'

Vincent nodded.

'So you've been looking after him?'

Vincent laughed, 'I suppose so. Or my mother has, more to the point. Country air, home cooking.'

'And when did you yourself arrive back here, Mr Vella?'

Vincent paused but just for a split second. 'Yesterday. But don't take my word for any of it. Go and speak to my mother and wife. They've both been home.'

Jimmy smiled, 'I will do that.' He paused. 'And Rae?'

'He wasn't in a good way. I've left him there.'

'And your mother and wife don't mind?'

Vincent laughed. 'No, why would they? Even if they did, the place is big enough for them to avoid him if they wanted to.' He shrugs, 'My mother likes having people to look after.'

'I see.'

'Marvellous, and now, without wishing to be rude . . .'

Jimmy stood and they shook hands. 'Oh, one last thing.'

'Yes?' Vincent raised an eyebrow.

'Did you know Steffan Capel?'

Vincent tilted his head to one side. 'The physiotherapist involved in all that scandal a few years back?'

Jimmy nodded, 'That's the one.'

'I did, yes. He treated Mother from time to time. Frightful business that was.'

He looked like he was about to say more, but Jimmy cut him short and said, 'Don't worry, I'll see myself out.' As he was leaving, he asked the salesman, 'How much is that Jag?'

Just out of interest.

The price made his eyes water.

Some people had more money than sense.

Chapter Fifty-Six

Sunningdale Avenue

Sunningdale Avenue was certainly quieter since Frankie and Roxy had moved out. Beverly seemed to divvy up her time quite happily between her sister's new flat and the house. Shirley and Tyler were pretty much inseparable.

I watched them both baking biscuits, of all the bloody things. My mother barked out instructions to the little boy, fag dangling from her lip, ash dropping into the mix. I suppressed a laugh.

Shirley caught me and asked, 'What are you bloody smirking at?'

'You, the domestic goddess.'

Shirley blushed. 'Leave off.'

The doorbell rang and I stood, planting a kiss on my mother's cheek, 'It suits you, Mum.' And I meant it. It did.

Shirley rolled her eyes and went back to the biscuit mix, Tyler watching her with rapt focus.

I answered the door and was surprised to find Jimmy Rose standing there, and even more surprised to find how glad I was to see him. Though that dissipated quickly as I remembered he rarely had good news when he visited.

I hadn't seen him since I'd been at his flat pretty much accusing my own brother of murder. I hadn't seen him since he'd kissed me and I'd pulled away, walked out despite every fibre of my being wanting to stay put.

He smiled at me crookedly and I felt that stirring of attraction. 'All right, Faith.'

'Detective.'

There was a pause as we both looked at each other.

It was broken by Shirley clattering out of the kitchen with flour on her hands, asking, 'Who is it?' And then, 'Oh.'

'Hello, Mrs Diamond.'

She sighed, 'Detective.' And returned to the kitchen.

I told him, 'She's baking, would you believe, with Tyler.'

Jimmy smiled, 'Can we talk? Here?'

There was a clatter from the kitchen and peals of laughter.

I said, 'Let me grab my coat and we'll go for a walk, eh?'

We walked for a while until I found that we'd made it out of the suburban streets and into Kensington Park Gardens. There was a thick frost across the green and the pale sunlight twinkled off it. I knew that there would be something coming that I didn't want to hear or deal with. My mind went, of course, to Rae, who still hadn't surfaced after his fight with Frankie.

But last time I'd seen Jimmy, spoken to him, a policeman of all people, it hadn't been a small act of mindless violence that had had me worried. Those pictures were damning and Rae's reaction to them hadn't settled anything in my mind. He'd known who she was. What they implied.

As we walked along, crispy frost crunching beneath our feet, I found that my heart was racing, and I daren't ask Jimmy Rose anything. A large part of me didn't want to break this odd, unexpected moment that should have been awkward, but felt just fine.

Me and Jimmy Rose must have looked like a couple, walking through the white-frosted park. Bits of this place were beautiful, and I didn't mind the winters. When I was a little girl, I used to dread them, convinced each would be the one where the cold killed me or one of my siblings. But things had changed by the time Jimmy and I walked through Kensington Park Gardens arm in arm. My house was heated, the oven was always on, and there was food in the cupboards.

I waited for him to speak and when he didn't, I finally sighed and said, 'So. To what do I owe this honour?'

'Could I not just be popping in to say hello to a friend?'

I smiled at that, but it was bittersweet. I thought of him then, during the set-up of Marshall Vella. In interviews early on, he had taken time to calm me down, to tell me how he'd made it all a lot easier than it could have been. I'd always felt respected at the station, when he could have seen me as the enemy. My mum had always spoken of Cal Doyle with fondness; he had cut her breaks over the years, and, as a by-product, us too. Jimmy was cut from the same cloth. A good man. Better than any other men I knew, with the exception perhaps of Frankie. He'd brought Beverly in too, with thunder in his eyes.

But . . . we came from different worlds. Even though I'd moved away from the skulduggery that I'd grown up with, I still wasn't the kind of woman you'd put with a policeman. I shook my head as if to clear the thoughts that hung like cobwebs. Little puffs saying, *what if* . . .

I told him, 'We're not those kind of friends.' And found the words made me sad, even though they were true.

'I suppose not.' Then he said, 'All of the nude murders are linked by one thing.'

This is it, I thought. What he'd been leading up to. I said, 'Their occupation?' stating the obvious. Trying to delay any blows coming my way.

He smiled, 'Other than that?'

'Marshall Vella.'

Jimmy nodded. 'And he's in prison.'

Faith said, 'He is, and I came to you wondering about my brother.'

'You did.'

'You've questioned him?'

'No, no, not yet.'

'You're going to?'

He nodded, 'I am. He has an alibi though, at least for the last girl.'

I felt a swell of relief and then guilt for even considering him. But who could blame me? I still had nightmares about Rae stabbing Bass all those years ago. The few minutes before where the man had been in my bed, his hand sliding up my thigh. The fear I'd felt. The helplessness. I'd been so small and he was a huge man. I'd squeezed my eyes shut, thinking of the noises I'd heard coming from Shirley's room, the state of my mother some mornings. The weight of his hands, lightly tracing my body then, but knowing that they could curl into fists that were weapons. Not knowing which was worse, or which would do more damage, but understanding on a deep level that both would.

Then Rae. Dragging a man twice his size from me, fuelled by an insatiable rage and a need to protect me. His little sister.

Still now I'd wake thinking about various aspects of that night. Some things just stayed, like scars no one could see. Long holes, dug deep under the skin, once in place, never to be erased.

'Who gave him the alibi?' I asked.

'Vincent Vella.'

My relief wavered slightly at that. After Marshall had gone down, I'd thought on more than one occasion that Vincent had changed. He hadn't though, he'd just dropped some of his act. He'd always been the same, I just hadn't looked hard enough. It was easy to ignore flaws in someone who acted as your saviour.

I told Jimmy, 'Rae's been staying with him.'

Jimmy said, 'Yes, and Vincent himself has only just come back to London.'

Faith nodded, 'That's what I'd heard.'

'You know everything that goes on.'

'So do you.'

He laughed, 'It's kind of my job.'

I shrugged, 'It's part of mine, too.' When he didn't answer, I added, 'Diamonds is thriving, right?'

'Can't disagree with that.'

'The reason being, I know a lot. Who's doing what and why and where and, most importantly, how it might benefit me or my business.'

'You're very single-minded, Faith.'

'I've had to be.' My voice came out sounding sharper than I'd intended and I added, 'When I was little, all I wanted was to be safe.' I shrugged, 'What I learned growing up was money afforded you that to some degree.'

'You could have married a rich bloke.'

I snorted at that. 'The only rich blokes I've ever known are gangsters. Besides, why let someone else do for me what I can do for myself. That's the mistake women make. They don't know their own power.' He was staring at me so closely I blushed. 'What?'

'You remind me of someone.'

'Oh yeah?'

He nodded. 'My mum.'

I didn't know what to say to that – didn't know if it was a compliment or not and didn't want to ask.

But I didn't have to, it turned out, as he said, 'She was amazing.'

I looked away. However nice this chat might be, whatever complicated feelings I had about this man, he was looking for my brother.

Jimmy said, 'I'm going to drive out there, check with Vincent's mother and wife.'

I told him, 'I've met them.' Jimmy looked confused and I added, 'Vincent's wife anyway, not his mother.'

He said, 'Oh.' And I felt the spell burst around us. But this was our reality and you couldn't live forever in fantasy land. That got you nowhere fast. 'Really?'

'I went looking for Rae.'

'How was he?'

I sighed, 'Not good. In the midst of some sort of party.' I shuddered inwardly at the memory. 'They had some girls there, upmarket but clearly paid for. There was a politician there, too.'

'Do you remember his name?'

'Martin Parsons.'

Jimmy nodded, 'Interesting.'

I said, 'Do you know who he is?'

He nodded and asked, 'Do you know a Steffan Capel?'

I wrinkled my nose. 'The doctor pimp? Supplied top-notch arse for rich men, got that politician in shit, then killed himself a few years ago.'

Jimmy laughed, I supposed at my blunt summary. 'That's the one.'

'I didn't know him, but think he may have got a few girls from Marshall from time to time, via a third party.

If I recall rightly, Marshall wasn't overly keen on him. Called him a posh twat. He went on some demented rant about him one night at ours and I'd have forgotten all about it, but he was at Vella's a few times to see Vincent, and the name twigged. Plus, I do read the papers.'

He said, 'Vincent told me he was Nora's physiotherapist.'

I shrugged. 'Maybe he was.'

Jimmy said, 'I am starting to wonder which bits of Marshall's businesses he cherry-picked to keep on the quiet, though.'

I sighed, 'Me too.' Then I asked him, 'Has this got anything to do with my brother?'

'I don't think so. I don't know. It's just something I'm looking into. I can't say more.'

'Fair enough.'

We sat on a bench and there was that silence again, but this time it felt loaded. I was thinking about him. Our kiss. The first night we'd met. I wondered if he was doing the same.

He said, 'I heard Frankie and Roxy have moved out?'

I grinned and rolled my eyes. 'Love's young dream.'

'Must be nice.' And we paused, him looking down at me, my shoulder pressing into the top of his arm. His blue eyes, dark and deep. I wondered if he was going to kiss me again.

But a voice broke the silence. 'Hello, sir.'

We looked up at a young police officer in uniform. I stood abruptly. This was stupid. He was a copper, I was only just on the right side of the law, my family would

kill me, and there was a reason we were constantly interrupted. God saving me from my own stupidity.

I turned to Jimmy, 'I need to get going, Detective.'

The officer was still standing there, waiting for Jimmy's
attention, but Jimmy's eyes were on me. 'Are you sure?'

I nodded, 'I am.'

Chapter Fifty-Seven

Farthing Park, Kent

Rae Diamond wasn't there. According to Nora, a tall, handsome woman with an air of confidence, he'd left that morning.

She told Jimmy, 'He's headed back to work, I should imagine. I think the rest did him good.'

Jimmy smiled. Perched awkwardly on the edge of a Chesterfield. Odd settees that must cost a fortune but offered very little in the way of comfort. There was an entire tea set on the table between him and Nora Vella. Despite the fact he had declined a drink, she had been insistent, and he found himself holding a cup and saucer that felt too delicate in his rough hands. Eventually, he took a sip of tea and put the cup and saucer down on the table.

'How long was he here for, Mrs Vella?'

'Nora. Please.' She shuddered, 'My divorce is imminent, so I'll no longer be Nora Vella.'

'It must have been a tough few years for you Mrs . . . Nora.'

'With Marshall, you mean?'

Jimmy nodded.

She sighed and Jimmy thought there was something theatrical about it, as there was about her. 'My husband was a terrible man, Detective.' She looked at him, wide-eyed. 'I'm afraid I was young and impressionable when I met him.' She shrugged.

Jimmy knew full well that that was bullshit but kept up the ruse with, 'It must have been a terrible shock.'

She nodded, 'Awful, but my Vincent sorted everything out. Protecting me like he always did.'

'You're close?'

She nodded, 'Oh yes, very. Mummy and Daddy have passed and Vincent is all I have.' She added, 'All I've ever had, really.'

'Yours wasn't a happy marriage?'

'No, not at all. I mean he practically lived with that *tart* up in London.' She spat the word out.

'Shirley, Rae's mother?'

'Yes.'

'Yet you don't mind having him here in your house.'

She smiled, 'Not at all. He can't help who he was born to. My poor Vincent has Marshall as a father, but I wouldn't want him judged on that. He's a good man, as is Rae.'

'Who was here for how long?' he pressed.

She frowned, 'Oh, months.'

'When exactly?'

'July perhaps? He'd had a row with his brother.'

'And he hasn't left at all?'

'Not gone far. Not to my knowledge.' She beamed at him.

He asked, 'Vincent mentioned you used to see that sort-of famous physiotherapist?' He put the question to her as though he was embarrassed to even bring it up.

She was still smiling at him, but it was tighter, forced, or was he imagining it?

He said, 'Steffan Capel?'

'Yes, for my back, he worked wonders. Though I was obviously horrified with what happened.'

Jimmy said, 'Was he a good friend?'

And she looked at him blankly, blinking once. She reminded him of a china doll, with too-long eyelashes shutting on porcelain pale cheeks when you tilted her back. 'I just visited his office occasionally when I was in town, and obviously I haven't done so since he, well . . . terrible tragedy.' She waved a hand around, 'So, no not a good friend.'

'Vincent introduced you?'

'Vincent helps with whatever I need, Detective. He's a wonderful son.'

He said, 'He sounds it. You're very lucky.'

And Jimmy was rewarded with a real smile then as her painted lips pulled wide over her teeth.

'I'd like to speak to Mrs Vella now, Vincent's wife.'

Nora scowled then and he wondered if she might refuse, but eventually she said, 'I'll fetch her, but I warn you, she's not the best conversationalist.'

He was left sitting for minutes, wondering how far Nora had gone to find her daughter-in-law. How vast this house was and if you'd necessarily know who was in it and who wasn't.

A thin woman with delicate features came in and sat opposite him. 'I'm Hannah Vella. Nora says you'd like to speak to me?'

Jimmy nodded. He asked the same question about Rae, and Hannah said he'd certainly been staying, but she didn't see much of him so couldn't be sure of his movements.

Vincent paused. Thinking of what Faith had told him about the 'party' involving Rae, Martin Parsons, her husband and two women. Wondering how to put it delicately. Eventually, he settled on, 'Do you know Martin Parsons?'

And Hannah sort of guffawed. 'Old letch. I think my husband has been keeping him amused for the odd weekend.'

'Amused how?'

Hannah shrugged, 'Women, drink. The usual.'

'And you're comfortable with that?'

She smiled faintly and Jimmy thought it was one of the saddest expressions he'd ever seen. 'It really doesn't matter what I'm comfortable with, Detective.'

'Your husband . . . Does he . . .?'

Hannah frowned, then got the drift of what he was saying, 'Oh, I see. No, I don't think so. In fairness to Vince, he abhors the trade; his father's relationship with Shirley Diamond was a constant cause of pain for both him and his mother. You can understand why.'

Jimmy said, 'Yes.'

'He doesn't seem interested in that sort of thing at all.'

'Sex?'

She blushed but nodded.

'Without wishing to be rude, Mrs Vella, how would you describe your sexual relationship?'

She shrugged, looking away now. 'Infrequent to start with. Non-existent now.' She looked at him. 'And no children yet, sadly.'

'Were you in love when you got married?'

'I thought so.'

'Not now?'

'He tolerates me, and since we see so little of each other, it's not an issue.'

Jimmy thought on that. Living in this large, soulless house where you might not see another person for days. He suspected that Hannah Vella was very lonely.

'Did you know Steffan Capel?'

She nodded, 'Oh yes. He and Vincent were quite close, I think. Vincent was very upset about it all.'

That house was like a museum, Jimmy thought as he drove away. Nothing in it seemed to represent comfort or ease and Jimmy felt glad to be getting away from it. He was annoyed that he had missed Rae and couldn't help thinking that had been by design. He suspected Vincent had called him shortly after he'd been into the showroom.

Either way, it didn't matter. Jimmy still had nothing concrete to chase and Rae was alibied now. Whether Jimmy found that alibi one hundred per cent convincing was another question entirely and completely irrelevant if he couldn't prove it wasn't true.

What he did find interesting was the politician. After Dr Capel had met his untimely death, there had been a lot of unanswered questions at the Yard. Jimmy had always felt certain that that particular scandal reached further than it appeared to on the surface, and now two of the nudes were also linked to it. The fact that Capel knew Marshall, if not in person definitely by business, had treated Nora, and was 'quite close' to Vincent, was very interesting indeed.

Chapter Fifty-Eight

24 December 1964

Sunningdale Avenue

Rae had been back in London for a few weeks, but he hadn't been back to Sunningdale Avenue until today. Now he stood, looking at the house, assaulted by the hodgepodge of memories and feelings he always got when he was here. In this city, on this street, at this house.

He had hated living there. Hated the cold, the never having enough. Hated his mum for being so fucking ridiculous. But as he looked at his childhood home, he felt a bittersweet longing for her, for this place. It was Faith who had said to him he needed to get it over with. Go home, say hello and make peace. Especially at this time of year.

Faith had a thing about Christmas. Some idea in her mind about how lovely it could and should be. He didn't give a shit – it was just another day to him, and one where the pubs were inconveniently closed. But he cared about Faith.

He went to the front door and let himself in. It was quiet inside, but when he poked his head into the living room, he saw Roxy putting presents under the biggest, daftest Christmas tree he'd ever seen. Maybe coming home would be fun after all.

Roxy sensed someone behind her before she actually heard them. It could be anybody, of course; this was a busy house, people were in and out all the time. Loads of them had keys, herself included. She loved her flat with Frankie, was hoping it would be the first property of many that they had together. One day, she was sure, it would be filled with children. But she felt at home on Sunningdale Avenue. A part of something in a way she'd never known was possible.

As she turned to face him, though, she realised she'd had a bad feeling, had known who it was all along. Doing the job she'd done for Marshall had given her a sort of sixth sense when it came to danger. And Rae Diamond was the embodiment of all that was dangerous.

Roxy's hand shook, holding a small parcel. A bracelet that she'd picked out for Shirley. It was only costume jewellery, but it was pretty and had butterflies making up the chain links. She knew Shirley would love it. She slid down awkwardly and put it under the tree, now with Rae watching her each move with an unnerving intensity.

She tried to smile, but her lips didn't quite make it. All she could manage was, 'You're back, then.'

And he grinned, slow and relaxed. He was like a panther, lithe and agile. She had thought him terribly good-looking the first time he'd come to visit her, and she had, of course, refused payment, because all the girls knew that was what you did with Rae Diamond, the boss's right-hand man.

Despite his looks, though, she had never found him a comfortable person to be around and once he'd picked her out as 'his girl', she'd learned she had every reason to fear him. He was a maniac, without a single redeeming feature. Roxy loved Faith, looked up to her, and considered her the fountain of all knowledge. There was only one thing she was wrong about, and that was Rae.

'I *am* back, Roxy, and what a pleasant surprise to find you here.'

She swallowed. It was thick and gloopy and she pressed her hand to her mouth, lest she might scream.

He took two strides in and was across the room and at her side in seconds, 'You all right, Rox? You don't look so good.' And there was a familiar glint in his eye.

He put his arms out, one over each of her shoulders, and leaned down so close their faces were almost touching.

He asked, 'Home alone?'

'N-n-not exactly. I just popped in, with the presents.' She added, 'I don't live here anymore.'

He was still smiling, still engulfing her. 'No, I heard you and Frankie had set up home.'

Then she saw anger flash in his eyes and she was scared. Really scared.

He pressed his lips to her ear and she could feel his breath as he whispered, 'Isn't that lovely.'

Then she moved, ducking under one arm and pushing

past him, running blindly, but he was across the space faster than she could ever hope to be. He gripped her by the tops of her arms, pulled her into a close, claustrophobic bear hug, and lifted her off the floor. He carried her up the stairs like one might a small child, but there was no love in it. No tenderness. She was powerless.

He lay her down on a freshly made bed and told her 'For old times' sake.'

Chapter Fifty-Nine

25 December 1964

Sunningdale Avenue

I was wary of having everyone altogether. It would be the first time Rae had been back to Sunningdale Avenue and the first time he had been around Roxy and Frankie as an official couple. The morning had been fine. Beverly and Tyler opened an insane mountain of presents and all the adults had eaten the constant stream of food Shirley kept appearing from the kitchen with. As the clock inched nearer to one, though, I could feel my gut churning with nerves. I didn't know whether I was more worried that he would turn up or more worried that he wouldn't. But when the doorbell eventually rang, I nearly jumped out of my skin.

Rae came in and, I was pleased to note, seemed reasonably sober. In fact, within minutes, he was doling out gifts to everyone, cracking a few jokes with Shirley, and pouring whiskies out for him, Devlin and Frankie from the bottle he'd had in his bag.

I got up and poured myself one and said, 'Thanks for asking.'

Rae rolled his eyes. 'Whisky's a man's drink.'

I laughed at that, 'And business is a man's game, yet here I am.'

Devlin told Rae, 'You can't argue with that, man.'

So I joined the men sitting around, drinking and smoking, whilst Shirley and Roxy cleaned everything away. If I'd been my mum, I would have insisted everyone pitched in, but I doubted Shirley would ever change in her own house. Since I brought the most money in, I didn't feel too badly about sitting on my arse for one day of the year. Besides, and perhaps more importantly, I felt I needed to keep an eye on Frankie and Rae. So far so good, but it could all turn, of course.

Eventually, the conversation, revolving mostly around sport, started to bore me and I headed out to the kitchen, where my mum, Roxy and Beverly were sitting at the table. Tyler was drawing in chalk on a large piece of cardboard.

Shirley beamed at me and said, 'Look what Tyler drew.'

It looked like a blob, but I nodded and smiled because I reckoned that was the expectation.

As I slid in beside Roxy, who I'd not had a chance to speak to properly, I thought she looked very pale and I asked, 'You all right, mate?'

Shirley said, 'She's not feeling well. Been off colour all day, haven't you, love?'

Roxy nodded and she really didn't look right. Her eyes were dark-ringed and her skin was waxy. She said, 'Actually, I might go home soon. I'm really tired.'

I said, 'I'll drive you, yeah?'

Roxy shook her head, 'No need, I don't want to trouble you.'

'It's no trouble.'

Shirley said, 'You should stay here, Rox. I have said that.'

I could see the poor girl needed some rest and likely a bit of peace. 'No come on, I'll take you. I was gonna pop in and catch up on some paperwork at the club, anyway.'

Shirley looked up at that, incredulous. 'It's Christmas Day.'

I grinned, 'It's eight o'clock, Mum, the day has been and gone, and a roaring success it's been, too.'

Shirley smiled at that, placated.

It *had* been a good day. No dramas, and with Roxy going home, there was unlikely to be any further tension between the brothers, who seemed to have managed a truce. Whether it was an uneasy alliance or not, I couldn't be sure, but Rae had been on his best behaviour, swapping jokes with Frankie, laughing and drinking.

Still, I'd had enough of the lot of them for one day.

We'd said goodbye to everyone. Frankie agreed to stay at Sunningdale Avenue if he was worse for wear. He'd also offered to leave with Roxy, but she'd been adamant that he stayed put – all she wanted to do was sleep. Rae had even got up and kissed me and Roxy each on the cheek.

She was quiet in the car and when we pulled up, I said, 'Do you want me to stay with you, Rox?'

She shook her head, 'No, honestly, all I need to do is kip.'

'All right, mate.'

I waved at my friend as she went in and thought to myself that soon enough Roxy would be my sister-in-law. That made me happy.

I pulled up outside Diamonds, got out of the car and let myself in. It was dark, of course, and it was cold. I picked up the torch from behind the door and started to head up to my office. Then I stopped. It really was freezing in there, and eerie in the dark. Plus, I didn't really need to do anything as the place ran so smoothly. Our next big bash would be New Year's Eve and I'd already had some RSVPs from some pretty high-profile people. Diamonds was the place to be seen in 1964. It was sold out; we'd made a fortune on tickets alone.

I'd wanted to get away from my family, yes, but I realised that I'd also prefer some different company. I nipped back down the stairs and grabbed a bottle of bubbly from behind the bar.

Chapter Sixty

Jimmy Rose's flat, Acton

Jimmy almost didn't answer his door. For a horrifying
moment, he thought perhaps it was Merilyn. He'd been
on a few more dates with her, largely to avoid the disappointed look on her face when she dropped ridiculously
obvious hints and he tried to ignore them. But he'd
drawn the line when she had invited him to her family's
for Christmas lunch. He'd told her firmly but gently
that, actually, he couldn't see a future for them. She'd
pouted a bit, asked if there was anyone else, to which
he'd responded no. Then she had sort of sighed, smiled
and said she'd be waiting when he changed his mind.

Honestly, he'd been put off even more by that. She
was so . . . available. And so . . . nice. He knew logically
these should be plusses, but to him whatever that spark
was just wasn't there with Merilyn.

So he answered his door with slight trepidation and
was delighted, if not surprised, to find Faith Diamond
grinning and holding out a bottle of champagne.

'Merry Christmas, Detective.'

'Faith.'

'Are you going to invite me in, then?'

He did and she headed straight to the kitchen for glasses, then dropped her coat over his armchair, flopping down on the settee and popping the cork.

She said, 'I thought you might be out.' She nodded at the case files strewn across his coffee table, 'Looks like you haven't even taken a day off.'

He blushed and gathered everything up, including some horrifying images of the nude corpses in their various states of decomposition. 'Sorry.'

She laughed, 'No need to apologise. Not like you were expecting me. I figured you might be with your family.'

'I don't have any.'

She looked at him. 'Oh.'

He shrugged. 'My parents are dead. Dad in the war. Mum, well . . . cancer. Just before I came to London.'

He stood, awkward, feeling like he may as well have been naked for how exposed he felt. He dumped the files back on his desk in the corner of the room and took the still-fizzing bottle from her, pouring them both a glass, more for something to do than any real desire for a drink.

Faith stood and walked over to his fireplace, picking up the picture frame resting there. Lilly and James. Funny – he saw it every day, of course, but seeing them held in her hands, he felt something close to sad. Lilly would have liked Faith, he thought. She'd have described her as fiery. She reminded Jimmy of his mum. Something to do with a shared attitude.

She told him, 'I knew about your dad. That he'd passed.'

'Oh?'

She said, 'My mum told me.'

He frowned, 'Did she know him?'

'Yes. She told me when we were doing the whole Marshall capture. Said he came around and scared off Rae's dad more than once with Cal Doyle.'

Jimmy nodded, 'He sounded like that kind of man.'

'She was a kid then, really. Said he stuck up for her more than once. I was always glad someone had, even if it was Old Bill.'

He laughed at that and she grinned, but he had a lump in his throat. James Rose. The man he couldn't properly call to memory in any real way. A hero.

'Glad to hear he was a good man.'

She smiled and moved over to him, reaching up, wrapping her arms around his neck, 'Just like his son.'

And this time, it was Faith that kissed him.

Chapter Sixty-One

January 1965

Diamonds

The lights were low, the band were on stage singing the blues, and the atmosphere was relaxed and friendly. Frankie and Roxy had announced their engagement on New Year's Eve and I for one couldn't have been happier. Even the fact that Vincent and Rae were at the bar, holding court as though they owned the place, hadn't marred my happiness. They were firmly back in London and had made it clear to me that their business was now entirely separate from mine, which suited me just fine. Even if I did wonder exactly what they were up to. It should have been a relief that it was none of my business, but I can't say it was. I had an awful lot of bad feelings where my brother and Vincent were involved.

But feelings were just that, and from what I knew and what I could tell, they were dealing mainly in cars that were legitimate. They had mechanics out on the Heron Trading Estate and showrooms popping up all over the good bits of London.

I had my own stuff going on and not having to deal with Rae on a regular basis made that easier. I'd secured the lease to a new club in Mayfair and had started discussions with Devlin as to who would run what. My workforce would double, Frankie was to become my partner, and I had my eyes peeled for more suitable candidates.

It had been a funny few weeks. Waking up in a policeman's bed on Boxing Day was a strange thing and yet it had felt completely right. I'd told him in no uncertain terms that I wouldn't be owned by anyone, and he wasn't to get any ideas. He'd laughed at that, rolled over, lit us both cigarettes and asked me what I wanted out of life.

I'd told him about Diamonds, things he didn't know already, my plans for it, and I told him about the second club. He'd listened with interest and made a few good suggestions. I'd realised then that he wasn't a man who would be intimidated by my abilities and ambitions, as so many were. I suspected I had more money than him and certainly I planned to go on and be as rich as I possibly could. That idea, if anything, seemed to excite him.

Normally, I had short flings with younger men to avoid any complications. When I'd been out with men my own age, there was always the presumption that eventually I'd want to settle down or perhaps let them run my business while I pushed out a few kids. Fucking laughable, as if *that's* what I'd worked my arse off for.

But it was a new age. Poor kids like me could grow up and find their fortunes if they were clever enough and women could plan families, or not, as they so desired.

My way of life wouldn't be for everyone and I'd half accepted that I'd likely spend it without a significant other in any traditional sense. But Jimmy was different.

He wasn't here tonight, at Frankie and Roxy's engagement party, though he'd been invited by Frankie, who never forgot the good turn he'd done by Beverly, but he was out walking the streets. He'd quipped that it was a busy time of year in his line of work. And I supposed it was.

He was worried about the girls working. I liked the fact he cared. A lot of policemen, a lot of people, thought prostitutes were vermin. It made my blood boil. It was easy to look down on others when you had a roof over your head and food in the fridge.

I caught sight of Shirley at a table with Devlin, who, despite having the night off, was scanning the room. We'd shut off most of the club and invited a small, select list in for the evening.

Frankie came over, interrupting my train of thought.

I smiled at him. 'Looks like everyone's having a good time.'

He grinned and it was goofy and crooked. He leant over and put his arms around me, pulling me in for a hug. 'Thank you.'

I laughed, 'What's that for?'

He shrugged, 'Everything, sis. Look what you've done.'

'You'll be seeing over this place now.'

'And I'll do you proud.'

'And the family you're about to have.'

'Be different for my kids, Faith, won't it?'

'To the way it was for us?'

He nodded.

'Worlds apart, Frank. You'll make a great father.'

He said, 'Rae told me to call it off.'

I turned to him then, 'What the fuck.'

He held his hands up. 'Look, I know. But you know how he sees things; he has such a crooked way of viewing the world. I think he felt like he was helping me out.'

'What, don't marry a brass?'

He nodded, 'That was the gist of it, yeah.'

I shook my head, 'You'd think he of all people would understand. Shirley was surviving, just like any of us.'

Frankie shrugged, 'I think Rae had it harder than we did.'

I knew Frankie was right, but honestly.

I said, 'You love her, Frankie?'

'With all my heart.'

I turned to him and smiled, 'Then that's all you need, eh.' And I hoped it was true as I watched Rae, whose eyes never left Roxy. Roxy, who had spent a lot of the night sitting tucked behind Shirley and had been very quiet of late. I hoped that girl loved my brother as much as she should because I'd really hate to have to fall out with her.

Chapter Sixty-Two

11 January 1965

Acton

Noreen is sick to the back teeth of her layabout, idiot husband. Why she married the fool, she'll never know.

A voice whispers in her mind, 'Because you love him.' Which she quashes with another Cinzano and lemonade.

That, however, is the sad fact of it. She does love him, the fecking eejit that she is. And he'll be back before she knows it, she's sure, but tonight she is out and planning on enjoying herself as much as she can, whilst hopefully making a few bob while she does it.

The clubs are jam-packed and she is enjoying the vibrant nightlife starting to spring up around Shepherd's Bush. She and her pal Eleanor are out looking for a few nice fellas with a bit of a jolly, and so far it's working out all right. The drinks are flowing and though the men wouldn't have been her first choice, they also wouldn't have been her last.

On the whole, Noreen is an optimist and tries to look at the good in each situation. Her marriage, for example. He may be a bit of a shit, but she'd married for love, which is better than some do, and she's sure in many years to come, when they're old and doting, they'll look back on their fiery fights and laugh.

Hopefully with children and grandchildren by then, though they haven't been lucky so far.

She pushes the thought away and goes back to dancing. Eleanor comes and taps her on the shoulder, says they're leaving and, with no other offers, Noreen follows her friend and the two fellas out.

That's when she bumps into him. He has a trilby on, pulled low over his face and the others don't notice him at first, but she gives a little wave. When he beckons her over, she can't believe her luck and cheerfully says goodbye to her friend and the two – rather put-out-looking – gents.

She links arms with him feeling buoyed by his attention – he'd not given her a second glance before and God knew she'd tried to get his eye several times. He's a man with a definite wedge and if she plays her cards right, maybe she can make this a regular thing.

She is full of hope as she steps into his grey vehicle, blissfully unaware this night will be her last.

Chapter Sixty-Three

February 1965

Roxy McCann and Frankie Diamond's flat, Acton

I had forgotten that Shirley and Devlin were taking the kids out, to the zoo of all places. They were quite the little unit and I was just waiting for Shirley to announce Devlin was moving in for good. Bless them, they were such a joy to be around it was almost sickening. But she deserved it and so did he.

I'd had a busy couple of nights at work and the Mayfair club would soon be ready. Frankie was so far doing a stellar job at Diamonds and I had been after a cup of tea and a good old natter with Shirley. But since no one was in at Sunningdale Avenue, I decided to pop in and see my soon-to-be sister-in-law instead. Since Frankie had stepped in at the club, I'd hardly seen her and though I knew and understood that was what my friend wanted – now she was going to be married, she'd be leaving the club in a work capacity at least – I did miss having her around more.

I stopped at the florist below their block of flats and bought her a bunch of tulips, then headed up.

I was grinning and brandishing the flowers as Roxy's

small face peered around the door. To my horror, she looked like shit and she'd definitely been crying.

She stared at me blankly, tried to smile and instead burst into fresh tears.

I bustled the smaller woman in, closing the door, heading to the little galley kitchen and putting the kettle on. I told Roxy, 'Sit down.' And she did, slumping onto the lovely new settee, still sobbing her eyes out.

I used the time it took me to make two cups of sweet tea to compose myself. My mind was whirring, trying to think what on earth the matter could be. I was hoping against hope that Frankie hadn't been mistreating the girl. I couldn't see it. Not at all. But I knew I could be slightly blinkered when it came to my brothers.

I sat next to Roxy, plonking the mugs down on the little table and awkwardly patting her. I was never good with tears. Or any emotional displays really. Which didn't mean I didn't empathise; I just never knew how to react. 'Come on now.'

Roxy snivelled and wiped her face on her sleeve. Looking up at me from big saucer eyes. In that moment, she looked impossibly young and I felt my first tremor of real worry.

'Rox, what is it.'

She shook her head.

'Come on. You can tell me.'

She started crying again, but with less fervour this time.

I said, 'Are you missing work? I'm sure you could come back, it must be boring . . .' Frankie had told me they'd made the decision together that Roxy wanted to do the whole traditional wife bit, but maybe he'd pressured her.

Roxy shook her head, 'No. I mean, I loved working there, Faith, I'm not being ungrateful.'

'I know that.'

'But this . . .' she gestured around the room, 'being Mrs Frankie Diamond. It's all I've ever wanted.'

'And you will be soon. What's not to be happy about?'

'I'm pregnant.'

I took in the words and whilst, granted, it would have been nicer for everyone if they'd got the ceremony done first, it didn't strike me as being the end of the world.

'Frankie will be delighted.'

But Roxy was shaking her head again. 'No, no.' And the words come out strangled and tense.

I felt my innards deflate as the only possibility for such sadness occurred to me. 'It's not his?'

When Roxy didn't say anything, I knew I was right.

Roxy said, 'I don't know if it's his.'

The little bitch.

I was on my feet, and then so was Roxy.

I asked her, 'Who's is it then, Roxy?' with suppressed rage in my voice that she was savvy enough to pick up on.

She looked me in the eye and I was surprised to see not regret or shame, but a blazing-hot anger.

'It might be Rae's fucking baby. Do you think I'd willingly let him touch me?'

Chapter Sixty-Four

13 February 1965

He's kept this one a long time. Sometimes he does that. As though spending time in silent communion with them will . . . what? Absolve him. No, that isn't it. He isn't doing anything wrong. What the hell is there to absolve. He's like a cleaner. A cleaner of human waste. But usually these things, outings, moments, make him feel better.

This one hasn't exactly, and he wonders what the problem is. It has been a long time, he supposes, and that's intentional because he'd been getting sloppy. Overexcited.

He felt cheered by this one initially and certainly he'd kept her alive longer than he normally would. But it hardly seems enough. He needs more. And he starts running through possible candidates in his mind as he walks around familiar streets, greeting and being greeted by familiar faces.

They look at him with respect, admiration even. He wonders how they'd look at him if they knew, and a little snicker escapes his mouth. He puts a hand to his lips, trying to press it back in. Pretend it was a cough and nothing more. That is the dilemma. He wants to show off his work – of course he does, all good artists do. But he can never tell a soul.

335

Chapter Sixty-Five

February 1965

Acton

The investigation had become so big that it was unwieldy. There were too many moving parts and now another body – Noreen Moore. There were too many people coming forward with information that may or may not have been helpful. Plus, the usual barrage of nutcases wanting to be a part of something like this. They had so much to sift through, and everything had to be looked at. So far there had been too many tenuous links and too many dead ends. The manpower was immense and the press were, of course, having an absolute field day. The killer had been nicknamed Jack the Stripper. Poor taste, but certainly catchy. And these murders were not unlike Jack the Ripper's. Men hating women was a tale as old as time and he wondered when, or if, that would change.

Times were changing in a lot of ways. Women had taken on jobs during the First and Second World Wars. They'd tasted a kind of freedom previously out of reach and, unsurprisingly, they wanted more of it. Being female came with a set of problems Jimmy could never fully comprehend. He knew that, but he'd gained some insight from Lilly, from his job. Now contraception was changing, the economy was changing, and Jimmy thought these could only be good things. He hoped that in ten, twenty, thirty years, it would be even better. That women forced into street work would be a thing of the past.

It was dark and cold, but the streets were full. Women littered every corner and kerb crawlers drove alongside them brazenly. He watched the girls ply their trade, an eye on the men stopping for them. Some were familiar to Jimmy now. Some here night after night.

Jimmy did worry that a man cunning enough to kill eight times and leave little trace may have the good sense to stay away or at least stay out of the popular areas. Which was why he walked further away. Leaving the main streets behind.

The further out he walked, the more he was hit by the scale of the problem. The police talked about cleaning up the city, but so far hadn't managed it on any great scale. He found himself in less crowded, more residential streets now, heading towards the Thames. But the girls were still there, in smaller groups and alone. He was into the realm of the shyer customer, he supposed. He was worried, and he needed to speak to Rae Diamond, who no one had seen for a few days now and who he always seemed to have just missed. He'd gone gently with Rae, because of Faith he supposed, but now he didn't need to.

Faith had told him yesterday about a set of Polaroids she'd found and he'd taken them to the station. He'd had a hard time explaining to Cal why she hadn't come forward sooner and also why it was him explaining on her behalf, but she had refused to stay and make a statement at that point. They were the most damming piece of evidence they had. But Rae drove a blue car and, of course, had been alibied for at least two of the killings.

Something had changed Faith's mind about Rae, though. Made her give Jimmy those Polaroids. He had seen the pain it caused her, written all over her face, as she'd handed them in. But she wouldn't say what her reasoning was. Said she needed to discuss things with her family first. He was worried about her but had learned in this brief time that Faith wasn't a woman to be pushed. And if she said she'd deal with it, she would.

He looked up at the buildings he passed, so familiar to him now and inhabited by people he knew, with more pouring in all the time.

Then he saw a grey car parked up ahead, a woman leaning down. Petite.

And a tingly alarm sounded in his mind.

He stood still, taking in the scene for a moment. Things pinging around his brain like little fizzing fireworks. The men who'd seen a grey car drive away. Tina who saw poor Betty Preston step into what might have been a grey car. Flecks of grey paint found on the victims.

He headed over, keeping close to the wall and the shadows, the buildings hiding his approach to the vehicle from the other side. When he was close enough, he crossed the road quickly, leaning into the open window on the passenger side and coming face-to-face with Vincent Vella.

There was a beat where the two men stared at each other in surprise.

The girl said, 'I don't do doubles.'

Then Vincent smiled, that Cheshire cat grin. Wide and unafraid, though there was something in his eyes . . . A flash of fear? Covered quickly with a smooth, 'Detective.'

'What are you doing out here, Vincent?'

'Rather embarrassingly, looking for some company.'

Jimmy knew that Vincent didn't believe what he was saying any more than Jimmy did. He said, 'Get out of the car.'

And Vincent shook his head.

Jimmy clung to the door hard, 'Vincent, get out, we can sort it out, talk things through.'

Vincent paused, seeming to weigh it up, then moved his hand to the door handle.

Jimmy thought of all the things he wanted to ask, wanted to know, because he strongly suspected this might be his last chance.

Vincent got out, hands up and shrugged, 'I have a weakness for them, Detective. Not often, you understand.'

'This is your car?'

Vincent nodded.

'Hardly up to your usual standards?'

'It's a little run-around.'

Jimmy's eyes held Vincent's.

Vincent said, 'Look, I realise this isn't my finest hour, but in light of our shared history, perhaps you could overlook this, just this once.'

But Jimmy wasn't going to do that, and things were starting to click in his mind now. Steffan Capel. Vincent's obvious hatred of prostitutes, Shirley, in particular, and all of the victims looked just like her. The grey car.

'I took your dad down, you knew I had him on this, why do it to yourself? Why keep going?'

Vincent grinned then, a truly chilling sight. 'I don't know what you're getting at, Detective.'

Jimmy didn't move, not taking his eyes off Vincent. 'Do you know, I thought it would end there.'

Vincent laughed, but it was humourless. 'Come on now.'

'The victims, several of them, had grey flecks of paint on them. My guess is when we analyse the paint on your car, it'll be a match.'

Vincent's face fell slightly, 'There are hundreds, thousands, of grey cars in London.'

Jimmy shook his head, 'You were supplying girls to politicians, you took over bits of your dad's business.'

Vincent snorted, 'I made money, helped out other gents with various unusual preferences.'

'Arthur Stockwell?'

Vincent looked away.

Jimmy said, 'What did he have on you, eh?'

But things had already come together in Jimmy's head. The Polaroids at Stockwell's house, the business card belonging to Vincent.

Jimmy said, 'He had the pictures, Rae took them when we sent him there. That's why Rae had those Polaroids.'

Vincent wasn't smiling anymore.

Jimmy shook his head, 'I pinned them on your dad. You'd got away with it.'

Vincent shrugged, seeming to make a decision there and then, 'Turned out I couldn't stop.'

Jimmy took a step towards him, but Vincent lashed out at the last second with his foot, pushing the other man backwards, opening the car door, getting in and slamming it shut.

Jimmy was staggering up as Vincent started the engine, grinning.

'Goodbye, Detective.'

And he sped away.

Jimmy stood thunderstruck for a second, his heart hammering in his chest. The woman was across the road, glaring at Jimmy, and he shouted, 'You can stop looking at me like that, love. I just saved your life.'

Then he was running, back to the station.

Not Rae Diamond.

Everything was obvious now.

Everything led back to Marshall, then to Rae.

But the thing that linked it all was Vincent.

Vincent, who hated his father. His vices. His liaison with Shirley. This wasn't about Rae's hatred of his mother, which had crossed Jimmy's mind more than once, especially after Faith brought him the Polaroids. A man who was ready with his fists, who'd all but terrorised poor Roxy McCann and God knows how many other girls along the way.

Not Rae.

Vincent.

Smooth-tongued, respectable Vincent.

Not Rae's rage and anger. Jimmy should have known, because there was a quiet control in these crimes and that was something Rae had little of.

But Vincent . . . Vincent could play the long game and play it well. Look what he'd done to Marshall. How he'd levered things just so. Keeping Rae close, making him an ally, knowing surely he'd show up as a suspect for this. Arthur Stockwell, a beaten, bloody mess. Vincent's card in his flat: 'There are all kind of friendships, Detective.' He'd known about Vincent. He'd taken those photos, perhaps even been blackmailing him.

But Vincent couldn't control his own temper. He couldn't stop, even when it was in his own interest to do so. Even when he could have got away with it.

Chapter Sixty-Six

Diamonds

I sat at my desk. My hands wrapped around a large glass of whisky, my shoulders shaking. I had given Jimmy the Polaroids. I had told him that Rae was more than capable of killing those women, because he was. He was my brother. God knows, I loved him so much. But he was deranged. He took things and he ruined them, and he needed to be stopped.

I took a long glug of my drink. Diamonds was closed tonight, and I was there alone. I couldn't go home today. Couldn't face my family.

Frankie. Shirley. I cried, then. Heavy, heart-breaking sobs. I cried for the little boy that Rae was. For Frankie, who'd always lived in his shadow and had everything ruined by Rae. I cried for the terrible start he had. He hadn't stood a chance, had he? And I wondered then if evil ran in the blood. We didn't know if Rae and Frankie had the same father. But I knew that Roxy's baby might have that man as a grandfather.

What could I do? What should I do? It was so rare for me not to know. But I was lost in this. My heart was broken because I knew that Roxy was telling the truth.

I hoped that we'd make it different for Roxy's child, even if it was Rae's. Rae had been brought home into chaos. He'd borne the brunt of it all, much more so than me and Frankie ever had. He had an immunity to violence that was unnatural and a general disregard for other peoples' feelings — developed or innate, I didn't know. He *did* have feelings. Of that I was sure. But they weren't right. They were fuddled and twisted. Just like him.

I was crying so hard that I didn't hear the door open. But then Rae was standing in front of me. Disarmingly handsome, face screwed up in concern at my tears. 'I heard you wanted a word?'

Chapter Sixty-Seven

Roxy McCann and Frankie Diamond's flat, Acton

Roxy was crying as she told Frankie in a soft and quiet voice what had happened, and that the outcome of it might be growing inside her. She was bracing herself for something, but she didn't know what. For his rejection? His blame? Men could be strange and cruel like that, she knew.

She had been on the brink of happiness and hoped that it wasn't all about to come crashing down around her. Faith had said she wouldn't tell, so the option was there to keep it a secret. But the thing Roxy treasured most about her relationship with Frankie was the naked honesty of it. He accepted her, warts and all, as she did him. She wanted to be by his side for the rest of her life and she wanted to do it the right way. To make this fresh, bold start that she still wasn't convinced she deserved, and to build it on a strong and solid foundation.

She didn't look at him while she spoke, and he didn't interrupt her. When she was finished, there was a terrible silence. It was long and stretched out, filled with every single one of Roxy's fears. The main one being that his love for her would die with this awful truth. That their relationship was now polluted by Rae, just as he'd wanted. That he'd win.

Eventually, she felt Frankie above her and then he bent down and folded her into his arms. Pressing his face into her hair.

She pulled back, looked up, met his eyes and saw everything she needed to see. Then she cried all over again, but this time from relief. He held her until she was done, then he stood, picking up his keys from the coffee table, taking his coat down from the peg by the door.

She rushed after him. 'Where are you going, Frank?'

He stopped at the threshold of their little flat, smiled his crooked smile and told her, 'I'll be back. All right?'

And she nodded. Scared, because she didn't know what he would do. What fresh trouble this would cause. But he said he'd be back, and trust was what mattered, after all.

Chapter Sixty-Eight

Acton Police Station

Jimmy was like a madman. He took the narrow staircase two, three steps at a time, almost knocking over Merilyn and shouting, 'Where's Cal?'

'Upstairs.' Said with a frown. But never mind that. Not now.

He found his boss. Garbled out what had happened.

Cal made him repeat it more slowly, but he was already dialling the Kent police station because that was surely where he'd go, wasn't it? Jimmy had been out on his beat on foot. No way he could have chased a car. No way at all. Vincent had a head start.

Jimmy called out officers to go and look for the grey car and now he had a number plate to give them. Finally.

Too late though, he thought. Probably too late.

Then he slumped at his desk for ten seconds, twenty. Trying to catch his breath.

Cal got off the phone. 'They're headed to the house. They'll be there in less than five minutes, then they'll call.'

Jimmy nodded, 'Right.'

He dialled Diamonds. No answer.

He called Sunningdale Avenue and Shirley told him that Faith was at the club.

He half hollered at her, 'I called her there. There's no answer,' and Shirley picked up on the panic in his voice.

'What is it, Detective?'

'Nothing. Don't worry. I'll find her.'

Chapter Sixty-Nine

Farthing Park, Kent

Hannah Vella had never seen her mother-in-law flustered before, but she was in what could only be described as a panic. The phone had rung. Hannah hadn't bothered to move. It was never for her. Her parents had given up calling, since she had little to say other than she was fine. Everything was wonderful. Each time through gritted teeth, with tears in her eyes.

Last month, she'd gently broached the topic of their marriage, or lack thereof, with her husband. Suggested perhaps a separation might suit them both. These things were no longer unheard of and the thought of many lonely years here waiting in at Nora Vella's beck and call filled her with a dread so deep she knew she wouldn't make it through.

Vincent had stared at her blankly. Calmly. Then he'd walked over to her and put his hands around her throat. Pressing hard. At some point, she must have blacked out, and when she came to, she was half undressed, sore and absolutely horrified. She'd been in shock, she supposed. And had sat on her bedroom floor, teeth chattering, wondering how it had come to this and realising that her husband wasn't merely neglectful and inconsiderate – though he was definitely both of those things – he was quite mad.

Nora had come into the room, without knocking, and Hannah had tried desperately to cover herself. She had looked at her with disgust and knelt down beside her.

'Vincent told me that you threatened him.'

Hannah had looked at her blankly, still trying to take in what had happened. She had tried to speak, but her voice came out a jagged croak. It hurt when she swallowed. Nora could see the state of her. Could easily understand what had happened.

'You will not leave my son. Not ever. He chose to take a wife and I approved the marriage. How dare you attempt to humiliate him.'

As she spoke, spittle had flown from her perfectly painted lips and hit Hannah's face. She had resisted the urge to wipe it away.

'You are lucky to have him. Look at what I was married to. A slob who kept whores as his mistresses. He dragged my name through the mud. My family's name.' Her eyes had been wide and Hannah had tried to look away, only to have Nora grip her chin between two surprisingly firm fingers and lean into her in an almost tender fashion.

Then she'd spat in her face.

Since that awful night, Hannah had avoided her like the plague, but now Nora was rushing around in a frenzy. Moving a painting, which, it turned out, hid a safe. Her fingers scrabbled as she twisted the combination and the door sprang open. Nora grabbed items – just what, Hannah wasn't sure. She put everything into a bag and headed for the front door, brushing past her daughter-in-law with no acknowledgement whatsoever.

Ten minutes later, the police showed up and Hannah started to think perhaps her living nightmare had come to an end, after all.

Chapter Seventy

Diamonds

I didn't pause. Didn't stop to think. I was out of my chair and flying at him, my brother, fists pounding into him. Arms flailing, fingers like claws, digging for purchase. He stared at me open-mouthed, until he'd had enough and gripped me in his big arms. Tight. A bear hug with a terrible undertone. I had never felt scared of him, never felt weaker, but my heart tremored then.

I said, 'You raped Roxy.'

And he pushed me forwards. I landed hard on my knees, the pain jarring its way into my hips, but I ignored it and quickly righted myself, leaning on the desk for support. Every emotion was heightened, everything inside of me hurting, pained.

'Fucking raped her? How can you rape a fucking whore. She was mine before she was his.'

I looked at him incredulously. 'She's a person, not fucking property.'

He sneered then, 'Of course she's property. *My* bloody property, Faith.'

I shook my head. Astonished at his thinking. That

mine was so different. I told him, 'That's how Bass felt about Mum.'

But Rae just shrugged, and I saw him then. Really, truly saw him, for the first time.

He hated our mother, and Shirley knew it, God help her. I had calmed her down about it many a time before. Told Shirley over and over again that he loved her, deep down. My mother would smile sadly every time and tell me the same thing she always did. *He's my son. I love him, but he's never felt the same about me, Faith.* I would deny it vehemently, believing even myself. Such was the depth of my delusion when it came to my big brother.

I looked at him standing there, unremorseful, and saw the reality of him. The bare-faced contempt.

I half whispered, 'Bass thought he owned me, too.'

And Rae's face softened at that, his head shaking. He took a step towards me, 'And that was wrong, Faith. You were a good girl, an innocent child.' He added, 'You're nothing like Mum, or Roxy.'

'Or the dead women littering the streets of London?'

He shrugged and I knew that he didn't care one iota for those women; the ones he saw as little more than cheap costume jewellery. 'Nothing like them.'

'Because I don't charge, Rae?' He flinched at that and I understood that he didn't love me like I loved him. He wasn't capable. Something vital was missing. It was about possession, not love. Ownership. *His* little sister. I goaded him then, realising that his image of me was important to him, that women fell into one of two camps.

I said, 'I sleep with who I want, whenever I want, Rae. Did you not know?'

He took a step closer, head shaking, 'Shut up, Faith, I don't need to hear it.'

I raised an eyebrow. 'No? I'm sleeping with that policeman right now. Jimmy Rose. The man who put you away.'

And he lunged then, his hands rolled into fists. I reached out to the desk, hands sliding around the first thing I touched. I grasped the letter opener, running on instinct alone, and let out a ferocious scream as I plunged it deep into my brother's neck.

Chapter Seventy-One

Sunningdale Avenue

Shirley put down the phone and felt a shudder run through her body. Then a pain in her chest so acute it pushed the breath from her.

Devlin was beside her, taking her by the elbow. 'Who's that?'

'The detective . . . Rose. Jimmy.'

'What did he want?'

'To find Faith.'

'Thought he was after Rae?'

She looked at him and as he said her son's name, her insides crumpled. Her children. The cause of all her pain and all her joy. If anything happened to Faith . . .

Shirley felt the familiar swell of grief that often accompanied thoughts of her first-born. For that baby in her arms, brought home to a cruel man, shunted painfully from her tiny, not fully grown body, into a world that wasn't equipped for him. To take care of him. She'd wanted to do her best. She'd loved him. Despite all that she got wrong, she had loved that baby with all her heart. With a fierceness she hadn't known was possible.

She sank down, her face pale, silent tears streaming down her cheeks.

Devlin stared at her, amazed. She was tough as nails, Shirley. Despite her diminutive size, she was hardened. He'd never seen her cry like this.

He knelt down. 'Shirley?'

Eventually, she looked up, wiped her eyes and told him, 'Come on.'

He didn't ask where they were going until they were in his worn-out little car.

Chapter Seventy-Two

Diamonds

Jimmy arrived at Diamonds just as Frankie pulled up. The large young man got out of his car, his face set in a grim expression, and Jimmy watched him go over to the door.

Jimmy ran over and Frankie looked at him curiously and said, 'Faith never leaves it unlocked.' His set of keys dangling from his hand.

Then there was a terrible sound. A wail so long and so awful, it sounded like it might not even be human.

Jimmy said, 'Faith.'

Then he and Frankie were running up the stairs, tripping over their own feet.

Jimmy pushed the door open and found her standing there, hand out, grasping something that glinted in the light. Dripping with blood.

Rae was on the floor, a terrible choking sound coming from him. Jimmy went to him immediately. Tried to stem the bleeding. Tried to save his life.

Frankie knelt next to his brother and smiled down at him in a way that could have been loving. But he leaned close to his ear, his voice a whisper, and Jimmy heard him say, 'We'll raise our child, Rae, and they'll never even know your name.'

Rae looked at his younger brother and Jimmy could feel the hatred, the animosity, even as the blood surged from him.

His final move was to reach out a hand towards Frankie, pushing Jimmy and his feeble attempts away, and grasping for his younger brother's throat. Violent until the end.

Chapter Seventy-Three

March 1965

Acton Cemetery

People had turned out from far and wide for Rae Diamond's funeral. The man wasn't popular, but he'd known a lot of people.

Jimmy watched the mourners come in and thought the guest list served as a kind of 'London's most wanted' list. There would be no arrests made here today, though. The investigation into Rae's death remained open and plenty speculated over who might have done it. The general consensus was that Vincent had killed him before he'd done a runner, though that just fed into the larger conversation of what the man was running from.

Jimmy knew, Cal knew. The ranks at Scotland Yard knew. They had everyone involved come in and give evidence on the down-low. Faith. Hannah Vella. Tina Munroe, who said he looked a match all right. Vincent had been seen many times with Steffan Capel. A lot of the girls he'd been involved with had said it was universally known that Vincent could get out of hand. He had strangled one girl Steffan introduced him to until she'd passed out, and then paid her handsomely to keep quiet.

Arthur Stockwell, the paedophile who'd been happy to pay for a night with Beverly McCann, admitted he had seen Vincent that night on the banks of the Thames. Had taken the photos and tried to blackmail him. It had gone on until Rae showed up, at Faith's direction, and had used the opportunity to relay a message from his boss, take back the photos and scare the man into silence. So Rae had known and seemingly hadn't cared. Any lingering remorse Jimmy felt about Rae's death, and his part in covering up what had really happened, cleared while listening to people open up about him.

The problem for the police was that Vincent Vella was long gone. He had money and connections and means. Chances were that they could look for years and never find him. They released images of Vincent and Nora Vella nationwide, saying he was wanted in connection with the crime. The papers frenzied over it for a while, then other stories came up, life went on. And eventually everyone would forget about the eight dead women.

Jimmy wouldn't, though. He knew their names, the names of their children and the sad stories of their lives. Vincent wasn't behind bars, but he had at least been evicted from his life and the streets of London would be safer without him.

The thing niggling at him, though, that woke him up in the night, was Vincent's confession to Jimmy that he himself had thought he could stop and found he couldn't. The detective guessed it was akin to an addiction. A sick addiction.

He'd have to settle for cleaning him out of London for now. But one day, he hoped their paths crossed again, and if they did, he'd take him down.

One way or another.

Chapter Seventy-Four

Acton Cemetery

The day was intense and pressured. I stood between Shirley and Frankie. Devlin behind us at a reasonable distance. I shook hands and took people's condolences with muttered thanks. But I sat through the service dry-eyed. I hadn't shed a single tear since the day he died, and I had started to wonder if I might never cry again. It was as though all of the emotion within me had sunk away on the office floor along with Rae's blood.

I'd always known I had the ability to kill. After Bass, I knew that next time, if there was one, I would stick up for myself. If I could have overpowered Marshall and killed him, I would have. It was only right.

I wanted to think that's what I had been doing as Rae lunged at me. But I wasn't sure. I was frightened, but not like I had been back then. Rae would never seriously hurt me, I knew that, even on that day.

I hadn't been scared so much as hurt and those two feelings seemed almost one and the same.

I'd always tried to see the best in him. Fought his corner when no one else would.

Loved him.

People had suffered needlessly because of it. I'd turned a blind eye to plenty over the years and I was no fool in any respect, except when it came to Rae. Until Roxy opened my eyes.

At the end of the service, we watched him being lowered into the ground. Shirley stepped forward and threw the first hand of dirt in over her son. Her first-born. The eldest of the Diamond children. Shirley knew there was more to this than her remaining children were telling her and, for now, she'd let it be.

Everyone filed away, slowly. Shirley, Devlin, Frankie and Roxy stood waiting for me. But I saw Jimmy Rose by a tree on the other side of the cemetery and I told my family to go on.

He came to me and stood by my side. Not speaking. Looking down at the newly filled-in grave that held the coffin that held my brother.

Eventually, I told him, 'He wasn't always bad.'

And Jimmy didn't speak because there was nothing to say.

The truth was, it didn't matter. Bad and good were funny things. Right and wrong was a funny thing. But I knew there was such a thing as evil and I thought Jimmy did, too. He'd seen it in those women, bare and tortured. Seen it daily in his job as I had throughout my life. In the faces of the men who battered their wives, the gangland bosses who bought and sold women like cattle. Who killed each other without a second's thought.

I'd seen it in my brother, Rae Diamond.

Born or bred was a moot point. Frankie and I had the same start Rae did, and we weren't like him.

So many thoughts about all of these things buzzed around my mind, eroding any sorrow.

Eventually, Jimmy said, 'Come on, I'll drive you.'

And I let the big detective put an arm around my shoulders and I leant into him. Feeling the strength of my love for him and knowing that with my family around me and him by my side, there were brighter days ahead.

Chapter Seventy-Five

March 1966

Rio de Janeiro

Brasil Jornal

15 March 1966

A prostitute has been found strangled and left outside
in an alley in Vila Mimosa. She was naked and her
underwear had been stuffed into her mouth. Local
police have no suspects but are warning sex workers
to be extra vigilant and ask members of the public to
come forward with information which may relate to the
case . . .

Credits

Niki Mackay and Orion Fiction would like to thank everyone at Orion who worked on the publication of *Loaded* in the UK.

Editorial
Lucy Frederick

Copy editor
Jade Craddock

Proof reader
Clare Wallis

Contracts
Anne Goddard
Paul Bulos
Jake Alderson

Design
Debbie Holmes
Joanna Ridley
Nick May

Production
Ruth Sharvell

Editorial Management
Charlie Panayiotou
Jane Hughes
Alice Davis

Finance
Jasdip Nandra
Afeera Ahmed
Elizabeth Beaumont
Sue Baker

Audio
Paul Stark
Amber Bates

Operations
Jo Jacobs
Sharon Willis
Lisa Pryde
Lucy Brem

Publicity

Ellen Turner

Rights

Susan Howe

Krystyna Kujawinska

Jessica Purdue

Richard King

Louise Henderson

Sales

Jen Wilson

Esther Waters

Victoria Laws

Rachael Hum

Ellie Kyrke-Smith

Frances Doyle

Georgina Cutler

Don't miss P.I. Madison Attallee's heart-racing cases:

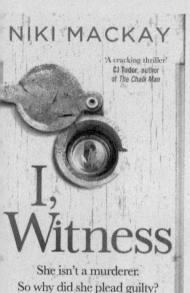

NIKI MACKAY

'A cracking thriller'
CJ Tudor, author
of *The Chalk Man*

I, Witness

She isn't a murderer.
So why did she plead guilty?

They say I'm a murderer.
Six years ago, Kate Reynolds was found holding
the body of her best friend.

I plead guilty.
Kate has been in prison ever since, but now her
sentence is up.

But the truth is, I didn't do it.
There's only one person who can help: Private
Investigator Madison Attallee, the first officer on
the scene all those years ago.

But there's someone out there who doesn't want
Kate digging up the past. Someone who is willing
to keep the truth buried at any cost.

Last night I betrayed my husband.

This morning my daughter disappeared.

husband may have forgiven my first mistake.
But he will never forget this.

And so I have to find her.

Before it's too late. For all of us.

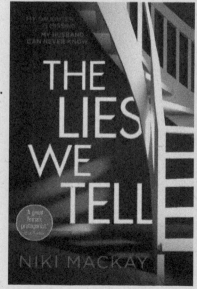

**Both available in paperback,
audio and eBook now!**

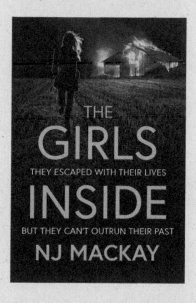